THE
DARK
WILD

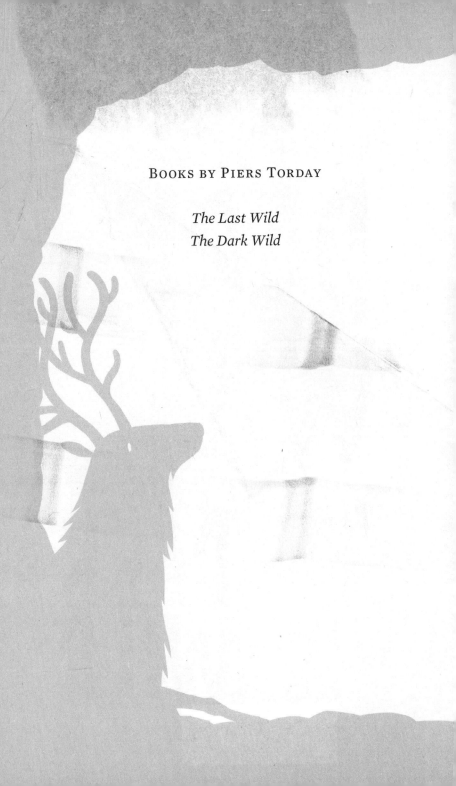

BOOKS BY PIERS TORDAY

The Last Wild
The Dark Wild

THE
DARK
WILD

PIERS TORDAY

VIKING
An Imprint of Penguin Group (USA)

VIKING
Published by the Penguin Group
Penguin Group (USA) LLC
375 Hudson Street
New York, New York 10014

USA * Canada * UK * Ireland * Australia
New Zealand * India * South Africa * China

penguin.com

A Penguin Random House Company

First published in the United Kingdom by Quercus, 2014

First published in the United States of America by Viking,
an imprint of Penguin Group (USA) LLC, 2015

Text copyright © 2015 by Piers Torday
Map and spot art by Thomas Flintham

LIBRARY OF CONGRESS CATALOGING-IN-PUBLICATION DATA IS AVAILABLE
ISBN: 978-0-670-01555-9

Printed in the USA

1   3   5   7   9   10   8   6   4   2

Designed by Eileen Savage
Set in Mercury Text

o o o o o

For Will, who always
has to read everything first

THE
DARK
WILD

Thus nature's human link and endless thrall,
Proud man, still seems the enemy of all.

    —"Summer Evening," John Clare (1835)

FIRST, A HELICOPTER

In the shadow of our apple tree, looking out across a river at a city full of glass and whispers, I take my dad's hand and watch our enemy fly toward us.

The black dot of an enemy, which is getting closer all the time, leaving Premium far behind as it slices over the water, the blades whirring *whup-whup* in the air above. The sun is setting beyond the dark towers, and the sky has gone the colour tangerines used to be, the last rays of orange light bouncing off the flying dot.

The dot that is now no longer a dot, but a large flying metal machine.

A helicopter. A purple helicopter with a large "F" painted on the side. And that's all you need to know for now.

(Although I should tell you where we are as well.)

The apple tree we stand under is in Dad's garden, behind our house in the Culdee Sack. No one's been out here for six years, and everything is overgrown and tangled. Dad grips my hand tight, which is his way of telling me not to worry. Like that's an easy thing to do when there's nowhere to run.

On my other side is a girl holding a large toad in her arms. The girl from the deserted house in the north, who cured me when I was ill, who saved my life once already. She turns her tousled head up at the sky, twigs trapped in her hair, shivering in her T-shirt.

Polly. My best-ever friend.

And standing behind us, my other friends, the ones I can talk to. The great stag, his ears trembling. A wolf-cub, his side still all bandaged up, and a harvest mouse on his back doing her special Dance of the Flying Metal Machine. (It involves a *lot* of spinning.)

Last but never least, on my scarf, the General of all the cockroaches, his massive orange shell shining like it has just been polished, his antennae flicking like crazy.

All around us, in the dusk, are nearly a hundred other animals of all kinds. An otter, polecats, pine martens, rabbits, and a very jumpy red squirrel. Birds in the trees, bees on the bushes, and—under our feet in the grass—too many bugs and insects to count.

"Hide them," says Dad, not taking his gaze off the helicopter.

I look at him for a moment, not understanding.

He turns to me and Polly, eyes blazing. "If you want your animals to stay alive, hide them now. Go!"

And we do, me yelling orders to my wild as they dive under bushes, disappear behind trees, some even burrowing into the soil of the flower beds, Polly grabbing armfuls of fallen branches to cover them. Even the brave General leaps off my scarf and into my shirt pocket, folding his antennae away out of sight.

None of the animals says anything. They're too used to running, too used to making themselves invisible, and all we can hear is *WHUP-WHUP—*

Now there's no time to even think anymore, we just have to hope they can't be seen in the dusk, camouflaged behind overgrown plants and creepers. The last to find a hiding place is the red squirrel, running round and round in a panic, until at the final moment he shoots under a withered rose bush.

Then twigs and leaves are swept up into the air, swirling around us, clouds of grit choking my throat and making it hard to breathe.

Cold spotlights beam down, blinding us. The rush of air forces us back. It flattens a circle in the grass, and Dad is ducking, pulling Polly and me out of the way.

The helicopter sways lower and lower, and I can just hear the wolf-cub growling at the back of his throat. We can no longer smell the garden or the river, only oily fuel, the hot rotors making my eyes water as they grind past each other. The rivets in each panel look close enough to touch now . . .

I am a Wildness, a leader of animals. I wait, facing up to the light and the roar and the wind.

The helicopter lands. Slowly the spinning blades judder to a halt.

Polly clutches my hand.

For a moment the dark helicopter is silent, and then—

A door is dragged open on rails. Folding steps tumble down onto our grass. In the dusk behind us, Polly's toad gives a little croak.

We peer into the shadows of the cabin, shrinking back as men thunder down the steps and into our garden. Cullers, clanking in helmets, padded uniforms, and boots. Without a word, they raise their long dart guns and point them. At Dad. At Polly. And at me.

Nervously glancing at one another, we raise our arms in the air.

Then, in the darkness of the night, comes another man. A small man in a grey suit, skipping down from the helicopter light and fast.

A man whose picture I have seen once before, in the Doctor's room at Spectrum Hall.

The man looks down at his feet and rubs his hands together for a moment. He adjusts his cuffs and smoothes his fine hair down over his head. Then, his eyes hidden behind a pair of shiny glasses, he clears his throat and smiles. "I'm sorry to drop in unannounced like this, Professor Jaynes," he says to Dad, who doesn't say anything.

In fact, I think Dad is shaking. I've never seen Dad shake before, but his hands are definitely trembling. It only makes me want not to shake at all. Which, it turns out, is much harder than it sounds.

The man turns to me instead. He takes off his glasses

and pulls out a handkerchief to rub away a grease spot. "Do you know who I am?" he asks.

I nod.

He smiles again and puts his glasses back on. "Good. Do you know what I do?"

Where to begin. Spreading viruses that kill the world's animals so you can make us all eat your fake replacement food, culling the creatures who survived, lying to everyone that humans could get the virus when they couldn't, locking my dad up just because he invented a cure . . .

"You may think differently," says Selwyn Stone, his voice all quiet and controlled, like a wire that could snap at any moment, only it won't because it's made of steel, "but what I do is keep order. I make difficult, unpleasant decisions on behalf of everyone. I prevent starvation, I keep the money going round and round, and I protect every single one of us from a hostile planet." Mr. Stone clasps his hands in front of him like a priest. "The only thing I ask from you in return is a little bit of help." Then he steps forward, his polished shoes sinking into the grass. Polly and I shrink back.

"For example," he continues, "I might ask you not to waste time designing a cure for a virus that we are eradicating from the face of this earth. Or I might ask you not to illegally bring infected animals right into the centre of our capital city. Things like that."

I'm shaking now too, my legs wobbling, and there's nothing I can do to stop it. Polly has gone super-quiet, as if she hardly even dares to breathe.

In the night sky, the moon is full and high behind us, showing the shadows of the skull under the man's skin. Mr. Stone sticks a hand into his jacket pocket and pulls out a small object.

A pistol version of the cullers' dart rifle.

"And if you were still protecting those animals, I would expect you to tell me. Is that so very much to ask?"

No one move a muscle, I order the creatures behind us in the dark.

Stone turns toward me with the pistol. I swallow hard, hoping he couldn't tell I was talking to them. "So. Kester. Tell me. Are you concealing any animals in this garden?"

"No," I say. It's the only word I can say out loud to other people.

He nods, and places his free hand on my shoulder. His voice is friendly. "I understand that you might not want to tell me. I know you've been through so much. You probably think you've been very brave—escaping from Spectrum Hall, rescuing your young friend here after we took her parents in, finding all those animals and bringing them all this way, setting your father free . . . I know I'd be exhausted!"

He smiles like it's a joke, except no one laughs.

"But don't worry, because you don't need to tell me straightaway. There's no rush. We can just wait. Because even the best-trained animals in the world can't stay still forever."

I want to punch his stupid smiling face and tell him that they're not trained, they're wild animals, and it's just that we *understand* one another, something he will never ever be able to do—but I don't, and instead, we wait.

Mr. Stone's one hand lying on my shoulder, no heavier than a leaf, another holding a gun. Polly next to me, trying not to cry, only sniffing a bit. Dad a bit farther along, his head bowed.

We wait . . .

The cullers with their guns raised around us in a circle of helmeted silhouettes looking like giant plastic soldiers.

We wait . . .

The helicopter, the big metal bird that dropped onto our lawn, just sitting there dull and lifeless. Beyond it, the towers of the city, casting their long shadows over us all. Reflected on the river, I see the moonlit sky above filling with clouds faster than I can count them.

Still there is silence in the garden.

We wait . . .

And then—with a squeal of panic, the red squirrel streaks out from under the rose bush, quivering with fear.

What's happening? he yells at me. *Are we—*

His voice falters as he sees the cullers and Mr. Stone. He freezes on the spot with terror.

Run— I start, but it's too late.

Without taking his eyes off me, Mr. Stone points his gun and fires. A dart speeds through the air, and the squirrel falls with no sound but the thump of his body hitting the ground. The cullers move forward and bundle him into a net, clambering back into the helicopter.

The lights fire up, and the blades begin to whirl round again.

Dad lowers his arms slowly. Mr. Stone puts his gun back in his pocket. "We can come back for the rest later," he says calmly. "And we will."

He moves, as if he is about to walk back to the helicopter, and then stops. My heart nearly stops too.

"Oh, I nearly forgot," he says. "There is another option. I might be persuaded to let you keep your animals. On one condition."

The helicopter's big light turns onto the garden, like a giant eye searching something out. It hovers over Dad, who buries his face in his hands. It seeks out the stag behind the tree and the wolf-cub in the bush. It blinds me for a moment, making me turn away, feeling the General burrow as deep into my pocket as he can.

Then it moves on. To the girl next to me, her hair beginning to blow around her as the blades whirl faster and faster, ready for takeoff. Like her hair is burning in the light.

Mr. Stone walks over to Polly. He reaches into his jacket once more, and this time I prepare to go for him. I don't care how rich and powerful he is, or how many armed cullers are in his stupid helicopter. If he touches one hair on her head—

And he pulls out some flowers. Like a magic trick.

A big bouquet of black flowers, which he forces into Polly's hands, raising his voice for the first time to be heard over the machine. "Polly Goodacre. Your parents have told me everything. If you really want to save the animals, give it to me. Give me what you have."

He waits for a moment, but she just stares at him. "Give me what you have," he repeats. "You have forty-eight hours—or I will return, and I *will* kill all of these animals."

Then without another word he turns and climbs back into the helicopter, slamming the door shut behind him. The craft's engines shudder and roar as it begins to accelerate up into the velvet sky, the white belly lifting farther and farther away, the spotlights fading to a dull orange glow, until—as if it had never even meant to come near us—the Facto bird is swooping out across the river and back upstream.

Which is when, clutching her black flowers tight—

My best friend begins to cry.

PART 1

POLLY'S SECRET

My story begins again with me waking early in my bed, then tossing and turning, unable to get back to sleep.

And if you think that sounds like fun, you should see my bedroom. It's just as I left it six years ago. My duvet has some cartoon on it, and the bookshelves are full of stuffed animals that I would never play with now. (I have real ones for that.)

In other words—*nothing* in here is for a kid of my age.

(Days away from being thirteen—and even skinnier than I was.)

The room is at the top of our house, which is all white and modern, at the end of the Culdee Sack in the part of Premium where hardly anyone lives anymore. If you went outside you would see lots of other houses, with electric gates and cameras, but there wouldn't be any people living there. They all live in the glass towers on the other side now. And there definitely wouldn't be any animals like the ones in our garden.

All of which means it's dead quiet. In fact, the only noise you can hear right now is a slow, vibrating hum, which could be a tank rolling down the street. But it's just Dad snoring in the room next door.

Farther down the corridor is Polly. She's sleeping on a camp bed Dad made up for her in Mum's old study. At least, I *think* she's sleeping. After last night . . .

Who knows what she's doing after last night. After the helicopter left, she dropped the flowers on the lawn and ran to her room. She wouldn't talk to me or answer any of Dad's questions.

It doesn't matter. I don't care what Selwyn Stone said. I'm not going to let anything happen to my wild.

Not after what we've been through together.

I brought the animals all the way from their home at the Ring of Trees—far away in the north of the Island—to the city. I brought them here for a cure, which Dad invented, which Polly and I helped him make. We were chased by wolves, shot at by cullers, half drowned, and nearly burnt alive. We saved the animals and rescued Dad. I sent a flock of pigeons back to the Ring with supplies of the cure for the animals who couldn't come with us.

Along the way Polly saved my life. Twice.

I first got to know her at her house, Wind's Edge, right on the farthest edge of the Zone. I broke in looking for help, because I thought I had the red-eye virus. She pointed a gun in my face and called me "Kidnapper." And then, in the dirtiest kitchen I'd ever seen, she made me a cup of herbal-medicine tea for my fever.

She made me feel less scared of things.

Although if you think not being scared of things makes you braver, you'd be wrong. Everything we did that everyone calls being brave didn't feel like being brave at the time. It felt like the only thing to do, and I can't imagine myself doing anything like that again. Not now, when I'm lying here in my room full of toys and piles of comics on every surface.

"Can't or won't?" Mum used to say. I don't know. Reaching for the green watch she gave me, just repaired by Dad, I press the side button and squint at the brightly glowing screen.

It's getting-up time.

But after what happened last night, I don't want to get up. I feel a knot in my stomach and turn over for the hundredth time to stare at the wall, wishing it all had been a bad dream. The helicopter, the men inside—the squirrel I couldn't save from them. And the flowers they left behind.

They being Facto.

Factorium, the biggest company in the world. The company that made all the food until the red-eye virus killed nearly all the animals, and then tried to cull all the survivors to "stop the virus spreading to humans." But they lied about that. They lied too about there being no cure. When Dad first developed one they locked him up, sent me away, and destroyed all his work.

All so that Mr. Stone could get rich making us eat his disgusting fake Formul-A food, which only ever tastes of prawn-cocktail crisps.

He is not a man who makes threats for fun.

I'm not surprised he's cross with us. We broke every law in the land bringing diseased animals into the city, which is meant to be an infection-free zone. We defeated his chief culler, Captain Skuldiss, in a battle on the street right outside my window.

Skuldiss.

When we were first captured by Captain Skuldiss, Facto's head culler, he told us that Polly's parents had been arrested for trying to get formula (what everyone normally calls it) in the northern city of Mons. Perhaps she is just trying to be brave for them, like she was for me.

But I'm tired of us all having to be brave.

We were just starting to be a family again back at home: everyone making breakfast together, Dad working down-stairs in his pyjamas, Polly and me looking after the animals in our garden.

This is my home and they are my family. And no one is ever going to take them away from me.

Suddenly there is so much to be scared of that I don't want to think anymore. I pull the duvet over my head and sink down underneath it.

Just as I finally start to doze off again, my door swings open, and the duvet is dragged onto the floor. Polly is standing there, arms folded and head cocked, her fierce eyes studying me. She doesn't look scared or tired, and she definitely isn't crying.

In fact, she looks at the room like it said something to annoy her. She flicks on the light, sweeps the comics from my bedside table, and puts in their place a vase holding one of the flowers Stone gave her last night.

There is a croak, and I look down to see the toad staring up at me from her feet.

"Come on, Kidnapper," Polly says, rubbing her hands together. "The Professor wants to see us. In his lab."

As if nothing had happened.

I blink in the light, confused—

"It wasn't an invitation," she says, disappearing back out of the door with a toss of her hair, the toad hopping quickly after. "It was an order."

Downstairs in Dad's lab, under its glass roof, I can hear the chatter of the city from across the river, the water lapping at the edge of the lawn. The lab is full of the black flowers that Selwyn Stone gave to Polly. They are laid out in rows across every surface. On the white worktops Dad has dissected their leaves, their stems, their heads—and in true Dad-style, everything has gone everywhere. There are leaves stuck to the soles of our feet, and just from touching my face, my hand comes away with a petal on it, like a slick of black paint.

I look at Polly, who picks up her toad and places him carefully on Dad's chair. She goes to the plants piled high next to a large microscope, turning over the thin flowers in her hands. She's gone very pale.

I don't get it. They're only *flowers*.

If Dad notices, he doesn't show it. Instead he leans against the big window wall of the lab, folding his arms.

"So . . . you're the expert . . . what can you tell me about Mr. Stone's gift?"

"I don't know what he meant, Professor; I don't have anything that belongs to him. You have to believe me."

Dad nods his head. "I'm not talking about that. Just tell me what you know about the, you know . . . flowers."

Polly knows her plants. Her parents were natural historians; they taught her everything she knows. Still white as a bone, she pulls herself together, staring hard at the flowers.

"Well . . . they're irises. These are special black ones, I think, only they're not really black if you look close up, just a very deep purple."

The colour of everything Facto, from vans to helicopters.

Dad waves his hand like he's swatting away a fly. As if it was a signal, the butterflies and bees covering the bushes outside begin to hover near the windows as we talk.

"Yes, yes, I know they *look* like iris chrysographes, but of course they, you know . . . can't be, can they? You're not thinking hard enough."

She rubs her brow, confused, and looks at me, as if perhaps this is some game of Dad's that I know and she doesn't. And then at the flowers again, peering at the purple-black velvet petals.

"Because they're—" she starts, but Dad interrupts her.

"No! Nothing to do with the flowers themselves. It's the flowers that are the problem, though."

A thought begins to rumble into my head. It's like a riddle, but . . . Dad must see me concentrating. "You should know this too."

I look at the flowers around us, their scent nearly choking us, it's so strong. I look at the animals outside, the bees buzzing round the glass, the only ones left alive in the world that we know of—

Polly beats me to it. "There can't be any flowers, Professor. We didn't see any on our way here, not through the whole Quarantine Zone. Because . . ."

There aren't any insects left to pollinate them!

"There aren't any insects left to pollinate them!"

We both say the same thing at the same time in our different voices. The toad croaks with excitement, leaping about at Polly's feet. At all the noise, the rest of the wild also start to move up from the lawn, noses, ears, and whiskers crowding in at the open lab doors.

"Exactly," Dad says, beaming. "The only, you know . . . things left that could spread enough pollen for this many flowers are"—he waves his hand at the insects outside the lab window—"buzzing about in our garden. Whoever grew these knows something we don't."

But Polly isn't smiling. She's frowning hard again, looking at the irises. Taking a couple, she places them under Dad's microscope and peers through the lens at the petals—and the leaves, and the stalks. Again and again.

I'm just about to give up and go and find someone (or something) more interesting to talk to outside when she lifts her head. "There's something else strange, though, isn't there, Professor?"

This time Dad isn't smiling. "Your friend is a very clever girl," he says to me. He looks at her. "Go on."

Polly holds out a sheaf of irises to me. "Look at them, Kidnapper."

I do. They just look like plants to me, a bit wilted now, but a load of plants. There's nothing special about them, they're just . . . all the same.

Our eyes meet. "You see, don't you?" she says. "They're all the same. And I mean *exactly* the same. They're identical. Every single one."

"Yes! Not just the way they look," says Dad. "I ran some tests last night. They're identical on the inside as well as out."

Which means Facto just . . . made these flowers? I say. *In the same way they make fake food for us to eat?*

He holds his palms up, speaking to me alone in the animal voice that we share. (Which is what freaks me out the most, as he still hasn't explained why.) *Perhaps.*

And so giving them to Polly means what?

I don't really, er, know, dear boy . . . This is all very new, you see.

I take a deep breath, trying to control myself at his vagueness. *She must have some idea what they mean. Ask her again.*

He puts his hand on my shoulder. *Kester,* he says. I brush him away. *She's your friend—*

No! I want to know. I turn to face her, grabbing a handful of flowers off the table. *Ask Polly what they mean. She must have some idea.*

Dad looks at my friend, pale and trembling, and scratches his head. There's a pause—and then before he can say anything to her, the wild are pouring into the lab, crowding round us and butting in.

Yes, why did that metal bird come and take the squirrel? says the wolf-cub, his paws scattering a pile of Dad's paperwork across the floor. *Did I scare it off? I know I am the best at scaring off giant metal birds ever.*

Are we safe here? That's what I'd like to know, says the mouse, shaking her tail from side to side over a computer keyboard in a Dance of Typical Mouse Anxiety About the Future.

Yes! says a skinny rabbit, up on his back legs. *Are we safe yet? We want to know! The metal bird took our squirrel. That ain't right . . . I just want to be safe.*

Then suddenly all the animals are shouting and yelling, the rabbit worrying if they're safe again, if we shouldn't find somewhere to hide from a machine that brings flowers, and the stag telling them to be quiet, and the toad croaking when—

SHUSH, all of you! bellows Dad. The rabbit dives under a desk, his ears twitching with fear. *I know you all have many questions you want answers to.* He picks up one of the identical irises off the worktop and holds it up. *Questions . . . that I want answers to as well.*

He takes us all in with a sweep of his bushy-eyed gaze and turns to Polly, translating for the animals as he goes along.

"The man who gave you these flowers is very powerful and very dangerous. He wants us to be scared; he wants us to be confused. So we need to be one step ahead of him."

Polly looks down at her feet. "How do we do that, Professor?"

Even though it's a sunny day outside, it feels as if a cold wind has just blown through the room. Every animal that I rescued, that I brought hundreds of miles to be here, turns its head and wide eyes up to my friend, waiting to hear that they will be safe. Dad stretches out a wilting flower toward her.

"I've told you what I know about these. You've spotted that they're all identical. These are your animals too. You brought them here as much as Kes did." He lowers his voice, softer, sounding a lot less like Professor Jaynes and a whole lot more like a dad. "Polly. You need to tell us the truth."

She steps back. "No . . ."

He shakes his head gently. "You've got to tell us before they make their next move. It's up to you to save these animals now. Tell us what you have."

For a moment Polly just stares at my dad. Then she drops the irises all over the floor, leaning on the worktop to steady herself.

I put my hand on her arm. I don't want her to worry. I'm sure she'll work it out. She always does.

Then Dad is bustling over too. "Oh dear . . . I didn't mean to, you know . . . You don't have to tell us straightaway. Take your time and all that . . . Look, why don't you do something useful, take your mind off things, eh? It's time to give your pals their medicine."

He picks up a tray full of glass vials and thrusts it into her hands. Vials of purple Laura II—the prototype cure for the virus that we helped my dad make, named after my mum. The animals seem to be getting better, but Dad wants to keep on administering small daily doses for a while to be absolutely sure.

Polly gazes down at the tray for a moment, and then I

take her hand and lead her out through the glass lab doors and into the garden, the wild trotting behind us.

They are used to the ritual now, and line up in a row as Polly and I pass along with the tray.

We start with the small animals like rabbits and polecats, who still wriggle and jump as we try to put a few drops of the cure in their mouths. By contrast, the stag takes his medicine obediently, his mouth open and ready. The toad leaps around from flowerpot to bush, Polly running after him till she is exhausted. But he takes it in the end.

Then we test the animals' blood, for things like their sugar levels. You get a microscopic pinprick of blood with a super-thin needle and drop it on a strip of really tiny dots called "microdots," and a handheld meter measures the strip and the blood-sugar level straightaway.

The only unhappy animal is the wolf-cub. His side is still bandaged after being shot by Captain Skuldiss, and he needs a different special drug to help the wound heal. So after the cure and blood test I also have a small bottle of painkilling pills for him.

He doesn't like swallowing them. *I only take these because you are the Wildness,* he growls.

I know, I say, tipping three chalky tablets into his mouth. *You are the best at taking pills in the world!*

To my surprise he doesn't reply but crunches the pills up and slinks off—as if I said something to upset him. I was only talking to him in the way he likes to speak.

The cure always makes the wild sleepy, and as they

drift off afterward to doze in the shade, Polly flops down behind me on the concrete steps to the lab. She sighs, chin in her hands, the toad for once sitting still at her feet.

I slowly put down the tray of discarded vials and sit next to her. I put my hand out, on top of hers—but she snatches it away.

"I don't want to talk about it right now."

My face suggests that we, and my animals, don't have the option to anyway.

She nods, picking at one of the long creepers trailing over the steps before beginning to twist it round and round in her hands for a while. When she speaks again, it's in a voice so small I only just notice—the voice I haven't heard her use since we lost her cat, Sidney.

"Kester . . . do you have any secrets?"

I wish I did. Not that I can think of.

"You and the animals—there's nothing that you all know but I don't know, is there?"

Well . . . the animals have their secrets. They have their dreams, which are stories about their animal ancestors, passed down from beast to beast over the generations. I learnt from the pigeons that the dream they tell one another the most is the one about my gift. I know it begins at the First Fold, the first ever sheepfold that we passed on our journey down here.

But I am not allowed to hear it, as they consider dreams sacred and for animals only.

All I know is that it foretold everything that happened

since I met the wild. The stag knew things were going to happen before they did. It made me feel safe even when we were in terrible danger, knowing that everything was happening for a reason. But he only tells me what the dream says once it has happened.

So it's not really *my* secret.

"No."

Polly picks up the creeper again, threading it over and over till I think I'm going to scream. Then she just says it straight out.

"Would you mind if I did?"

We both stare at each other for moment, as a long cloud passes overhead, casting a shadow across the whole garden. Then Polly shoves the creeper in her pocket. "It doesn't matter. Pretend I didn't say that."

She's not getting away that easy. I put a hand on her shoulder.

"OK," she says with a sigh, pulling the creeper out of her pocket. It seems to be getting longer and longer, strands twisted together. "You have to understand that there were things I couldn't tell you until I could trust you—"

Until she could trust me? The girl I saved from going over a waterfall?

"I'm sorry, but Mum and Dad made me promise not to tell anyone. *Anyone.*"

That's not good enough. We've been through too much together. I kick at the ground between her feet until she waves the creeper in the air, like a flag of surrender.

Then she's fierce, leaning forward and looking around her all the time.

"All right! But you must promise not to tell your dad. I don't want to get in trouble. It's not my fault, you see."

That's going to be really difficult.

"Swear!"

She sticks her hand out. I place mine over it. "Swear on the Professor's life that you won't tell him," she says. "Even if you can't speak out loud, I'll know if you're lying."

I swear inside. Our eyes meet for a moment over our bound hands. I feel red-faced and jerk my hand away.

"OK, OK." Polly looks around again. Then she takes a deep breath and begins to tell her secret. "You thought you and your animals were the first ever to take on Facto. But you weren't." She glances away at the animals lying all over the lawn. "There was already a rebellion against them." This isn't news. We'd met outsiders on our journey who hated Facto. "And my mum and dad are leading it. Or at least they were . . ."

That makes me sit up.

Polly holds her palm up as if to silence me.

"Why do you think I had a gun when you found me? What do you think Skuldiss was really looking for at Wind's Edge? Not just one sick cat, that's for sure."

Suddenly my mind is jumping back into the past, trying to piece together parts of a puzzle I've only just discovered. Sidney was Polly's cat, who had the virus. I thought Polly was coming with us to the city to find her a cure, but when we jumped in a river to escape Captain Skuldiss, she was swept over a waterfall. I rescued Polly, but I couldn't save Sidney.

But Polly didn't go back home after that. She stayed with us.

"They started when Facto made the countryside a quarantine zone. Mum and Dad didn't see why they should leave their home when no people had actually caught the red-eye. They thought Facto wanted to put the countryside out of action so everyone would have to eat their disgusting formula. So they decided to stay and fight."

I still don't see what any of this has got to do with flowers.

"They formed a whole network with the others who stayed. Why do you think I went with Ma so quickly by the river? She didn't force me. She was one of them."

Ma was a farmer we met who'd lost everything to Facto and the virus. We thought she was on our side at first, but she only wanted to feed my wild to her starving workers.

"Facto called us all outsiders, like we were the losers, the ones left with no formula to eat and no nice cities of glass towers to live in. But it's not the name we called ourselves."

Polly twists the creeper over and over in her hands again, threading it tighter and tighter.

"We had a secret name—so secret we weren't even allowed to say it to each other, in case anyone was spying on us."

She stretches the creeper taut between her hands and won't look at me.

"The name was secret because Facto didn't know what we had." Polly has wound the creeper into what looks like a noose. "Mum called it our secret weapon. It wasn't a gun or a bomb. Mum said it was more powerful against people like Selwyn Stone than things like that."

She pulls the noose tight, making a fat knot in the creeper.

"Hope. We had something that gave us hope, Mum said. It could change everything. We could defeat Facto and start again with it. Just the thought of it made me feel safe and happy. Until I got those flowers last night."

The cogs click into place in my head—

"I swear to you on my life. They asked me to look after it, and so far I have. It's the one small thing they gave me that I did manage to bring safely from home." Sidney flickers briefly into my mind. "But you have to believe me—I still don't even know what it is. They said I would be in danger if I knew anything more than . . . the name."

Brought it with her? Confused, I half expect Polly to take a concealed test tube out of her pocket or show me a hidden locket hanging round her neck. But instead she just tightens another creeper knot and gazes down the garden at the dull white glow of the afternoon sky on the river.

"But as soon as I saw those flowers, I realized he must know our secret. Because . . ." She cups her hand over my ear and whispers in it, *"Because the name was Iris."*

We sit still on the steps. I feel like a ticking time bomb, without knowing what's making me tick. The clouds press down on everything, making it feel hot and sticky.

I look at Polly, with her bare knees—still covered in bruises and scratches from our journey—drawn up under her chin. I have to know more.

But to my surprise she leaps up, winding the creeper round and round her hand. "I'm sorry, Kidnapper, I shouldn't have told you. I don't want to put you all in any more danger than I have already. It's just that . . . I promised Mum and Dad, you see."

Her eyes flick to the wild still dozing at the bottom of the garden, and back to me. "I promised them, swore on their lives, that whatever happened . . . I wouldn't let Facto get the Iris."

Then she turns and runs back into the house. I race after her, just in time to hear Polly pounding up the stairs and slamming her door shut.

My thoughts are spinning, and now I'm starving too. I head into the kitchen for some breakfast. The bright red kitchen, which was like a bomb site when we first came back, has been swept, cleaned, tidied, and polished, just like when Mum was around.

I grab a bowl of formula from the counter.

(Although Polly being Polly, it's not just formula. Somehow, in the mess of rotten flowers and weeds our garden had become while Dad was locked up, she found stuff to eat. Wizened berries that still just have flavour when blitzed in our blender and a handful of shrivelled herb leaves both make our meal taste not quite as chemical as normal.)

Slumped at the kitchen table, I click my fingers at our ultrascreen, which takes up the whole of the opposite wall, washing away my muddled thoughts with a wave of amplified noise.

A tanned man in a suit stares out at me from a bright TV studio, his name hovering just below the knot of his shiny tie. *Coby Cott*. Pictures and words whirl behind his head like a tornado.

MORE WEIRD WEATHER—
AMSGUARD COMPLETED—
BABY LEARNS TO ROLLER-SKATE

When I click on the second headline, a new picture swerves into view.

Coby Cott is now outside, with a huge bridge of concrete and metal behind him, rising up from the river.

"The world's greatest civil-engineering project ever undertaken is nearing completion, Factorium officials revealed today," he is saying. "The Amsguard, nine concrete pillars and nine steel gates rising forty metres high at the mouth of the River Ams, will protect the Island from another storm surge, if the world's ocean should rise again . . ."

Polly couldn't believe her eyes when she first saw the ultrascreen. "We never . . ." She even had to touch it to make sure it was real. "In the countryside . . . after the quarantine came . . . we were cut off. Everything is so much further ahead in the city."

Perhaps—at least, when it comes to screens and the Amsguard.

I swipe Coby Cott away. I've got enough to worry about already without thinking about the Amsguard or roller-skating babies.

I feel hot and bothered and mad at so many different people I don't know where to start. I'm mad at Polly for not telling me the truth before, and she's still only told me half of what she knows about this stupid Iris. I'm mad at her mum and dad for making her lie with their promise. I'm so mad at Selwyn Stone—for starting all of this in the first place. For taking the red squirrel and so many other animals.

Most of all, and this is the worst part—

I feel mad at myself, and I don't know why.

But there's no one here I can say any of this to. So instead I just turn to go and rinse my bowl out at the sink beneath the window.

Please, I say to myself, I've done so much. Why can't everything stay normal for a bit?

Just then, I hear a whisper.

Whispering from the drain.

At first I think it's just the noise of the water, gurgling away down the plughole. But water noise doesn't rise or fall, or get right inside your head—not like the animals' voices do. There's more than one voice, and I can't make the words out at first, only that they're harsh and jagged and spiky, not anything like any animal talking or singing that I've ever heard.

It can't be my wild. They're still out back dozing in our garden.

Hello? I say, thinking perhaps the General might be playing a trick on me, hidden somewhere. But he isn't.

I look up out of the window, to see if the noise is coming from there. And on the other side of our quiet and otherwise empty street, I see the strangest thing.

An animal where there shouldn't be one in an animal-free city. The only animals we know are alive are the ones in the garden behind me, and the ones at the Ring of Trees waiting for our pigeons with the cure. But there is one standing right across the road.

I have only half a memory of these creatures from before the virus came. A neighbour had one as a pet that used to jump on me and lick my face. But I don't know the names for all the different kinds.

It's a dog.

This one is massive, white and strong-looking, with a tiny tail, a big-snouted face, and pointed ears. I can't see if his eyes are red or pink from here. As I'm trying to get a closer look through the window, he turns slowly, and stares at me.

The whispering grows louder and louder in my head. Loud enough so I hear what the voices are saying. Coming from somewhere far away, no more than a distant murmur, each word stabs into my head like a needle.

The earth! say the whispers. *The earth will rise!*

Louder and louder the whispers go, chanting in my head.

Then the dog slowly begins to open his mouth. And the shock makes me drop the bowl in the sink with a clatter, because it's so horrible—

Inside his mouth, where there should be teeth, there are none—just ugly pink ridges. Where there should be a tongue, there's only a raw little pink stump.

A dog without a bite.

For a moment I catch sight of my face, reflected in the window—my ginger curls in need of a good cut, my green eyes staring as if they are trying to tell me something I don't want to know.

When I look outside again, the dog has gone, and the whispering has stopped. There is no sign that I ever saw or heard anything in the first place.

But what do you think it all might mean?

For the rest of the day I lay on my bed, trying to get the whispering and Polly's story out of my mind. But now I can hear her getting ready for bed—running taps, closing drawers—and have to go get some air.

Air and advice from those friends I still trust.

It's night again and I'm back outside, only now hidden from the house by a cluster of tall glossy bushes. There's a corridor between them and the high walls, the coolest, shadiest part of the garden—in fact, so cool and shady tonight that I've got my favourite striped scarf wrapped back around my neck.

I don't understand why it was so hot this afternoon and so cold tonight. The news on the ultrascreen was right. The weather has gone weird. The clouds of earlier have completely disappeared, leaving the big silver moon to shine down on us.

It doesn't matter. I always feel safe here. This is where I used to hide from Mum and Dad when we played in the garden. But I won't ever be playing here again. Because lined up along the bottom of the wall are rows of shallow grassy mounds.

The members of the wild who fell at the Culdee Sack. A brave hare, one of the otters, the hedgehog, three rabbits, and a woodpecker. Who would shoot a woodpecker?

The way animals see it, they have gone for the Long Sleep. And this strip of damp lawn is now officially a Garden of the Dead. The other members of the wild are too scared to enter it alone, which makes it a perfect place for me to meet the stag, mouse, General, and wolf-cub when we want to talk in private.

We overcame our fears of such places a long time ago.

The bushes block out so much of the light from the city across the water that I can only occasionally make out the gleam of the stag's horns. He paws at the ground with his hoof as he listens to me.

Stag, I say, *the black flowers that man brought yesterday. Do they mean anything to animals that I don't know about?*

Yes! bristles the General, to everyone's surprise. *Yes, they do.*

A meaning unknown to me, in that case, says the stag. *Would you care to tell us more, Cockroach?*

Of course. They mean that we should declare war on the entire human race immediately! I shall lead my valiant troops aboard that flying machine and bring it down, while you shall both gallop ahead with the Wildness and destroy this Iris—

The wolf-cub's eyes catch a glimpse of light through the leaves. *I like this idea! I shall find all the irises in the world and rip them to shreds. I am the best at eating flowers ever!*

This is not helpful! snaps the stag. *The black flowers are not our concern. Even if you do want to eat them, Wolf-Cub.*

But I am not a cub anymore, mutters the wolf-cub, scratching at his bandage. *I am a brave hero who nearly died. And I am nearly full grown too.*

Very well. I shall lead the charge alone! declares the General, jumping with excitement at our feet.

The stag is right. This is not helpful. I look at him again.

Have you told me absolutely everything? he says, his gaze boring right through me.

It's impossible not to tell the truth when he looks at me like this. So, feeling embarrassed, I tell them about the voice I heard in the Forest of the Dead, toward the end of our long journey here. The voice that told me I did not speak for all animals, that there was another wild that would come into plain sight when I was least expecting it.

There is a stony silence from all the animals.

Why did you not tell us of this before, Wildness? asks the stag eventually.

*But nothing happened . . . * I start, trailing off as they all continue just to stare at me.

Then there is a voice from the stag's back—a voice that has not yet spoken. The mouse, her black eyes shining brightly, her tail flicking. She does not sound her normal cheery self.

But something did happen, didn't it, my dear?

She rubs her whiskers with her paws. And I tell them all about the dog with no bite, the whispers I heard from the drain.

The earth will rise? she repeats.

I nod. She leaps off the stag's back onto the grass beneath our feet. We all take a step back, clearing a circle for her.

That sounds like an old call I once heard, she says. *It is a dark old call all right.*

Nonsense! says the General. *There are no such things as dark calls. They are just tales for scaring young ones.*

The mouse grinds her teeth at him. *There are dark calls, if you don't mind, and we have heard them in our tunnels, Cockroach, even if you have chosen to ignore them. You ignore a dark call at your peril.*

But I'm not listening to her anymore. None of us is. We're listening to the sounds of squealing tyres, smashes against wood, shouts and screams—

Someone, a lot of someones, are breaking into our house.

And we're running, all of us—

There's a girl standing in our hall.

And it's not Polly.

The door hangs busted open behind her, the chain dangling loose, the glass panel shattered all over the floor. There are shouts from the street, the sounds of bikes wheeling and revving. Their headlights cross and fill the doorway with a glow that fringes the stranger's hair like a halo.

Hair is piled in curls above a lollipop sticking out of her mouth. A formypop, the synthetic pink sweets made by Facto for children. You only ever got one at Spectrum Hall if you tattled on another kid. They stink of nail varnish— and I can smell this one from here.

Formypop Girl does not look happy. In her hands she is holding a long blue prod. A prod with a rubber handle and two sharp prongs on the end, like a giant fork.

Dad leans over the banisters in his striped pyjamas, his

hair in its normal tangle. "What is the meaning of this—oh, what do you call it—intrusion?"

The girl glances up at him and just shrugs. Then she looks at the stag, who has galloped straight in up the steps from the garden. His nostrils are flaring, his horns lowered, but she just takes out her formypop and jabs it in his direction.

"What is you?" she asks.

The stag looks at me, confused, and I shrug back at the girl.

"What you doing with that dirty animal? You trying to get us all infected?" Her head jerks over her shoulder. "Eric, get rid."

A large boy in a grey hoody squeezes through the doorway behind her. As he clomps across the floor in heavy boots, he tries to take a series of swipes at the stag, who thrusts back with his horns, sending the boy stumbling back and crashing onto the floor at the girl's feet.

The girl sighs and looks down at him. But she doesn't move. "Where the Iris?"

I look blank. She does seem very young to be working for Facto, though, I have to admit.

"Don't play games with me, boy, I not in the mood. Where she?"

"N-no—" I stammer my one word out.

"No not good enough." She squeezes the blue rod, and it shudders into life. A pale electric light sparks between the two prongs. She points the rod at the stag and repeats her question as he rears back on his hind legs at the fizzing electric charge, his horns touching the ceiling, casting jagged shadows in the glow of the lights streaming in from the Culdee Sack.

Formypop steps forward.

"I going to ask you one more time. Where the girl with the Iris?"

"No—"

"Stop saying no! We saw the helicopter. We watch you come into the city. We know she must be here. So I need to start hearing some yeses, understand?"

The intruder jabs the rod at the stag, making it spark again and again. Without meaning to, I glance upstairs again, toward the spare room at the end of the landing.

"Thank you," says the girl, and turns off her electric prod. She yells over her shoulder. "Found her! Come!"

"That's it, I've had enough. I'm coming down," mutters Dad, but it's too late.

The bikes outside go quiet as another kid pushes in from the street to join Formypop and her chubby mate. They all glare at me like the bullies from Spectrum Hall. Everyone is dressed in the same way as the girl: ragbag clothes that are covered in dust and grime. Perhaps Selwyn Stone is using the kids in his own schools to do his dirty work now.

Fat Eric, up on his feet again, is followed by a boy with a purple Mohawk wearing a grubby sweatshirt that reads 123.

We all stare at one another for a moment—and then they

are pushing and forcing their way past us, up the stairs, knocking Dad over as he tries to come down—

"No!" I yell after them, and leap on the stag. He careens round in the hall, his hoofs gouging pale half-moons out of the floorboards. Then we are clattering up the stairs past the kids, who scream as we press them against the wall. As the stag thumps muddy hoofprints across the landing, he catches the ceiling lamp with his horns so it swings and nearly knocks me off before we skid to a halt outside Polly's room.

And there is Formypop, standing in the doorway, her prod lowered.

Dad lumbers up behind us, dusting himself off. "What is the meaning of this absolutely outrageous—" he starts, but stops as soon as he can see what we all can.

A candle stands alone on a stool by the bed, flickering shadows over the low windowsill and the pots of garden cuttings lined along it. One single iris in a vase lies knocked over in a puddle of water, the thin blue curtain billowing over it like a sail, through the open window. Somehow I don't think it's the Iris everyone is looking for.

The glass roof outside, covering Dad's lab, is smooth and steeply angled—you would slide straight off if you tried to walk on it. She can't have left that way.

"Where she hiding?" says the girl, thrusting her electric prod under my chin.

I shake my head fast, frightened.

"Now look here, young . . . I don't know your name, but

you can't just, you know . . ." says Dad, waving his big hands about.

"My name is Aida True, and you can shush your noise, old man," says the girl. In a single movement, she swings the prod across, tapping him lightly on the hand. It looks like nothing, but there's a flash of blue light and Dad cries out, falling back onto the bed clutching his hand.

Dad! I shout in my head.

Aida True sticks the prod under my chin again. "You know where the Iris is?"

I don't even know what it is, never mind where it is.

The girl sighs. When she speaks next, it's as if she isn't just talking to me, or Dad, but to the whole room. "You have to understand, we need the Iris. Why you think Facto come here in that big shiny helicopter? Because right now, the Iris—it the most valuable thing in the world. Course they want it." She strokes the stag's flank with the prod, and he shivers. "We all want it. Even this crazy horse with horns wants it."

"But why, though?" mumbles Dad from the bed, rubbing his hand.

Aida's eyes narrow. "I told you already. It the most valuable thing in the world. That good enough for you?" She turns to her gang. "So what you waiting for? A magic trick? Find her! Find the Iris! Now!"

Eric and 123 push past me and the stag, brandishing torches and prods, opening drawers, and emptying cupboards. Polly isn't hiding in them or under the bed, nor do they find anything that they think could be the Iris. Then 123 crouches down, the torch held between his teeth, fiddling with something below the windowsill.

Something tied to the radiator.

He jerks a line in through the window that whips and knocks over more plants with its thick knots.

A rope—wound together from garden creepers.

Polly's gone.

Then the girl and her gang are too. As quickly as they blew in, they blow out again.

She pushes past me, Dad, and the stag in the bedroom doorway, the others tumbling after her, back down the stairs and out through the splintered door frame.

I look at the empty room for a moment—Polly's plants. The irises. Aida True seemed to know what the Iris—whatever it is—was and want it just as bad as Mr. Stone. Whoever her gang were, they also knew Polly was here.

And now they've gone to get her.

Not waiting for the stag this time, I'm racing after them, yelling, "No!" at the top of my voice.

But I'm too late.

Outside, in our Culdee Sack—the street that ends in a curve of smart houses, gates, with a small circle of grass in the centre—the girl is already on her bike, alongside the rest of her gang.

In the neon glow of the streetlights, I can see their machines gleaming silver with a tiny engine on the back wheel. A single, massive headlamp sits between the bars on each one, like a silver eye. As the others rev their engines, waiting, she twists the handlebars toward her. A line of green light shoots round the frame, pulsing, and the machine begins to vibrate.

Aida turns to look at me. Her eyes burn fierce with light nearly as bright as the bike glowing and shimmering beneath her. Her cheeks glow with anger. But for a moment our eyes lock—and she is just another skinny kid like me. Is that something else I see in her expression? Is that...?

I hurtle down the drive and lunge for her hand—

But the engine growls, her wheels are spinning on the cracked tarmac, and just as I reach out, they are gone. Any chance of finding Polly or the Iris disappears up the street in a glowing cloud of silver.

They have left something behind, though—in my hand. A grubby fingerless glove.

One of Aida's gloves. It came off when I lunged for her and she swatted me away.

What use is a glove? I turn it over, peering at it in the orange streetlight, hoping to find some clue. But there is no Iris to be seen in the pattern, nothing that tells me where Polly or the gang might have gone.

I stand like this for who knows how long, staring at the glove in my hand. Only the smallest rustle from behind makes me turn around.

At first, in the dark, I don't see them all. Just gleams of eyes and claws in the open door, or a strange-shaped shadow on the roof. They are all there, though.

Dad, with my wild.

Pine martens leap along the roof, otters perch on the windowsill, and rabbits sit bolt upright on our front steps. Dad stands watching from the doorway next to the stag, whose horns are silhouetted by the hall light, while the mouse dances sadly between his feet. And sitting alone, in the middle of the drive, watching me with that look of his, is Polly's toad.

They don't say anything. They just watch.

I squeeze the glove tight and close my eyes for a moment. I know what has to happen now.

For a few special days, I had it all back. The smell of the garden, the feel of my bed, Dad looking over my shoulder—but now everything has gone. The helicopter's blades have blown everything apart. My best-ever friend is a secret rebel, now on the run from Facto and a bike gang, with apparently the most valuable thing in the world.

Whatever that is.

I turn to my wild. *I'm sorry . . .*

But the stag stops me before I can say any more. *What are you most sorry for? Finding us a cure or saving us from the men who wanted to kill us?*

Everything. I wanted to save everyone but just seem to have made things worse.

But I don't want to leave you all—

I will keep this wild safe until you return. Have no fear of that.

Dad steps forward, a shaggy silhouette. *You don't, you know, have to go, Kes. I'm sure your friend can look after herself...*

In a city she's never been to? With both Facto and an armed gang after her?

He raises his hands. *I'm sorry. You're doing the right thing. Find your friend. Find this Iris whatchamacallit. Just make sure you do before Mr. Stone returns here.*

But what if he shouldn't have the Iris either?

He gives me a big hug and I feel safe again for a moment. *Let's cross that bridge, eh? The stag and I will protect the wild here for now. And I'm sure you'll be back here in no time—we can make a plan to outwit Facto then."

He pats me on both shoulders at once, which is what he always does when he's expecting me to believe complete rubbish like that. It makes no difference, though.

I guess that Polly ran away because she wanted to keep the Iris safe from Facto, as she promised her parents. But now—she could be anywhere, in a city she doesn't know.

She's my friend. I brought her here. She's lost her cat, her parents. She didn't know any of this would happen.

It's just—I don't want to leave everyone again. It's too soon.

Then there is a jaw biting on my hand so softly that I only just notice it. Wolf-Cub's amber eyes gaze up at me, his ears laid flat back. *I will come with you, Wildness. You will not be alone. *You probably can't even smell where the strange she-child on her metal horse has gone, but I can follow her track easily!*

There's no way I'm going to find Polly and her Iris before a gang on electric bikes do. But perhaps if I can find them . . . *How?*

By her false paw.

He sniffs the little glove eagerly all over. *And I can see in the dark better than anyone.*

I hang my head for a moment. I don't want this. I want to stay. But . . . I take a look at my new family one last time. I glance back at our house, the black windows glinting with reflected eyes, and, taking one last gasp of the air floating over from the garden, say good-bye to my wild.

Do exactly as Dad says. We have made enough cure to see you through for the next few days at least. I meet the toad's stare. *I will be back as soon as we have found Polly, I promise. And I will find her.*

Then, flinging my arms around Dad first, and then the stag's warm neck, squeezing him tight, I turn and head down the drive, where the wolf-cub is waiting.

And where exactly do you think you're going, soldier? chirps a voice from my shoulder. The General's shell looks a very angry orange in the streetlight.

It might be very dangerous, General—

Exactly what I'm hoping!

But what if the stag needs you?

He is big and wise enough to look after himself.

I feel stung. *Are you saying I'm not?*

There is a long pause.

Well—I sigh—*at least try to keep out of sight.*

So he crawls into my pocket as I follow the wolf-cub out of the drive and up the deserted street of the Culdee Sack. Up ahead, I can hear the angry buzz of a helicopter somewhere in the city.

As Wolf-Cub sniffs the ground more and more, every paving stone and lamppost and weed, he begins to stride faster and faster. And then, as the streetlights grow farther and farther apart, we find ourselves walking into the unlit shadows of the city that I don't know anymore. The cub begins to pick up speed, and I'm following behind with the General, as fast as I can, as we run into the dark.

Hold on, Polly, I say, clutching the glove tight. We're coming.

As I run after the wolf-cub, the night sky slowly turns pale grey over our heads. But the light is still dim, filtered through even more clouds than there were yesterday, as if they're breeding.

Cameras perch like eagles on the corners of buildings. The wolf-cub and I dart under trees and press ourselves along walls to avoid their scan.

I have to pause for breath on the bridge over the Ams that leads back into the centre of Premium, as curls of fog drift up off the water, hiding us from view. For a moment I stand and lean on the stone wall, gasping for air. Farther up the river, I can just make out four black chimneys poking up above the mist.

The Four Towers of Facto, where the helicopter came from. Every now and then we can hear the far-off whirr of another one, hidden by clouds. I try not to think about

Polly and where she might be, but it's hard. Is she still on these streets, cold and shivering somewhere? Has she gone to some secret hiding place her parents told her about?

I know if she was here she would tell me to stop worrying, that she's fine, but somehow . . . I turn to look behind us instead, where the heavy river flows past our lawn and out to the sea. On the distant horizon, where water meets water, there is a row of nine giant white blurs, low clouds that shimmer into concrete and steel as the sun comes up over them.

The Amsguard is completed.

We must not delay, Wildness! mutters the wolf-cub, nipping at my hand. *The scent will only hold for so long.*

I blank towers and the Amsguard from my mind, turning away to follow the cub into our city's Central District. He pays no attention to the glass skyscrapers or huge shop windows, but keeps his snout hovering just above the ground, weaving in and out of the road.

He is no longer running as fast as he was, but I am dripping with sweat trying to keep up.

Barely half a moon away from the battlefield and already the mighty warrior grows soft and fat, says the General, lounging between the wolf-cub's ears.

And you will be soft and squashed under my paw if you do not watch it, Cockroach! snaps the cub. Although he is beginning to look less like a cub by the day. I don't want to admit it, but he's changing. He's grown bigger, even since the injury. He sounds less like a cub too, snapping at us all more than he used to.

My father will be avenged, he said, after he left his pack to follow us from the Ring of Trees. I know one day he will have to leave us again to join his fellow Guardians, his fearsome mother—I shiver and pull my coat in tight.

Nothing feels like it used to. It feels strange to be with the wolf-cub and the General but not the stag or the rest of my wild. I keep telling myself that they will be safe, and that I will return to them soon, but the more I do, the less I believe it.

As we follow the trail, Premium comes to life around us. The sunset curfew must have ended. Lorries and cars fill the potholed roads, puffing smoke into the air. The farther we head away from home, the more entangled the city seems. The broad streets of the centre narrow into sooty lanes, twisting and crossing over one another, like the roots of a massive weed.

I do not like this city of yours, the wolf-cub moans, his tongue hanging out. *It is too hot and there are no fish-paths anywhere to cool our faces in.*

If there were ever any fish-paths here, they've been covered with tarmac and now—as we emerge blinking from the shade of an alley—railway tracks. We race above them along the top of an embankment.

Far down below, a cargo train, the giant yellow "F" for Facto plastered across every car, thunders along the track toward a huge glass-roofed station up ahead. I know what will be on board. Everyone here lives on formula, but it's made in the factories of Mons, the northern city, and delivered here by rail.

We plough straight to the land beyond the station.

The land lies under the swooping white concrete ramp we took to enter Premium just over a week ago. The traffic roars along the road so fast the pillars beneath hum with the vibration. We are both knackered, the cub limping in the shade of the underpass, his bandage beginning to peel off his side. Only a week ago he was lying on Dad's operating table.

We stop for a moment by an old billboard fastened to a pillar. I lean against it, flicking sweat off my forehead. The billboard is covered with curling paper sheets, pictures of missing cats and dogs beneath phone numbers.

When the virus first came to the city, followed by the cullers trying to eradicate it, people didn't know where all their pets had gone. We know now why all the animals disappeared from the city—it wasn't just the virus. Facto's own cullers did their job all too well.

But the wolf-cub is pawing me again. *There is no time to lose, Wildness, if you want to find that she-child. There are many other scents here . . . I have not hunted like this before.* He hangs his head. *I am losing the trail.*

Still heaving for breath, I bend over, resting my hands on my thighs. *I thought you were the best ever at hunting?*

He looks away, his ears standing up straight. *I don't talk like that anymore,* he mutters.

Like how?

Like a stupid cub, he snarls, and perhaps it is my imagination, but it sounds like he is trying to make his voice sound deeper than it is. *I faced death and lived, Wildness. I am a wolf now. Just like my father. One day I will rejoin my pack, and then you shall see.*

He does not lower his back or flatten his ears like he normally does, but stands tall, not looking away.

I am the one who blinks first. *OK. Lead on, Wolf-Cub.*

He bounds ahead in silence, and I stagger after him, trying not to notice the prickles of crossness across my own neck. I can talk to him how I like. I am his Wildness, aren't I? I command *all* creatures; that's what he said.

But as we head into the dazzling light beyond, those thoughts fade away into the midday shadows behind us.

Because spread out ahead of us is a whole new city—on the edge of the other one. Not the city of glass skyscrapers, smart houses, and shop windows behind us, but one of shacks, caravans, and tents.

The whole place stinks—a hot, rotten, sweet smell that makes me gag.

Something smells very delicious indeed, says the General, who is now poking out of my shirt pocket and tasting the aroma.

Half the world flooded. The other half dried up. The

rest of the world came to our Island and our four cities. It looks like we ran out of room.

The campsite city is linked together by overflowing washing lines and kept apart by fences of corrugated iron. There is rubbish everywhere, lining the dusty track ahead in piles of plastic bags as high as hedges. And people. More people than rubbish, but only just.

People in flip-flops dragging carts behind them piled high with junk, half-naked children ducking in and out between their legs. Some have green bins strapped to their backs, stopping every now and then to pick something up from the ground.

The noise is deafening. Yelling at the people from every side are men in fluorescent vests, trying to sell what looks like salvaged trash. Pots and pans, shoes, plastic bottles—who knows what you can buy here?

The biggest queue is for a man with a giant plastic keg that has only the word PINK spray-painted down the side. Staying out of sight in the shadows, I take a closer look at him—bald and unshaven, with a battered clock face dangling round his neck on a chain. Every time someone with a bucket on their head comes up he grins at them, and a gold tooth catches the sun. He checks the clock hanging round his neck, the customer drops the bucket and presses a few notes into his hand, and he fills their bucket with the liquid in the keg, something that steams and burns my nostrils even from here.

But before I can see more, the wolf-cub has just dived

straight into the crowd. I plunge in after him, and nobody pays any attention. It's as if they're sleepwalking as we wind and bump between them.

How much longer they won't notice is a different matter. As I squeeze between two people dragging a cart behind them, piled high with rusting washing machines tied down with ropes, the bright light disappears into shadow.

I look up.

In the centre of the camp a mountain rises from the forest of dusty heads and flimsy roofs surrounding it. A mountain of rubbish.

One scarred with the empty caves of dead fridges, wires trailing out like creepers. Chair legs stick up like broken trees among barbed-wire bushes. Here and there, white puffs of gas rise from the mess. The mountain is dotted with climbers, spread all over the slopes with their green bins.

It's as we're staring, lost in wondering where so much rubbish came from, that I hear the voice.

"Wolf."

Not an animal voice, a human voice.

I turn around. The man with the clock round his neck. His sharp eyes, in between checking his clock and counting his money, have spotted us. He points at us, his smile glinting.

The women filling their buckets put them down. "Wolf!" they say. And as if the word is being carried along on the breeze, it passes from mouth to mouth—to the men selling sunglasses, the half-naked children, the families trailing luggage behind them in the dust.

And the slow-moving band of drifters comes to a halt, a hundred eyes staring at us. Hungry, hollow eyes. Then, drawing in like a sea rolling onto the shore, a crowd of pointed fingers and raised weapons. Sticks, lengths of pipe, broken umbrellas. I never realized piles of rubbish could be so dangerous.

"Wolf! Wolf!"

The wolf in question raises his hackles and growls, but he could take out one or two at most before he fell under a barrage of sticks and piping. We press ourselves against the mountain of rubbish, leaning against a filthy old sofa, the springs bouncing out.

The General is on my head. *Ha! Call that an army!* he sneers at the angry faces taking step after step toward us, till I can smell the sweat, see the hunger carved into their faces. *My cockroach legions would scatter them in an instant.*

But his cockroach legions are not here now.

I stand in front of the cub, arms outspread. "No!" I say.

The crowd just comes closer, sandals scuffling in the dust. A thin arm swings out with a metal pole, and as I swerve out of the way, the wolf-cub pulls back, tight against the sofa. We have no more room to run.

The wolf-cub crouches, ready to leap—

Clockface raises the length of wood in his hand, a rusty nail sticking out the front—

Then, with a click, both he and the whole angry mob disappear from view. The dirty old sofa swings back, like a door opening. As it does, we fall back with it, out of the sunlight, away from the crowd—and into the mountain of rubbish.

PART 2
WASTE TOWN

As the sofa swings shut behind us, the wolf-cub and I pick ourselves up off a floor of uneven planks. We seem to be in some kind of tunnel, lit only by the faint glow of old traffic lights slung along the sides at intervals.

The General tramps about in my hair, his antennae quivering. *It's a good thing I manoeuvred us into position by a secret door,* he mutters, *or that could have ended rather badly.*

But something tells me it hasn't ended. In fact, it's only just beginning. Because following the line of traffic lights down, I can see a fierce glow at the end of the tunnel.

We are inside a mountain of rubbish, right at the edge of the city. My dad and my wild feel very far away. The hungry mob outside still feels very near. I have no idea what we're going to find at the end of that tunnel—but none of that matters. I am here for my best friend and the Iris.

I have to find her—and it—before Stone comes back for my wild.

We edge down the planks, toward the glow. It's shining out from clouds of lightbulbs and fluorescent strips dangling on wires from a ceiling far above, filling the space with light.

They appear to be hanging from a huge dome hollowed out right inside the rubbish mountain. You would have no idea it existed from the outside. The ceiling looks like it's made out of old mattresses and car doors, the walls stretched tight with tarpaulin, only just holding all the rubbish in.

A tower of scaffolding poles and rough planks stands in the centre of this dome, black rubber coils draped over the top like the creepers in our garden. But these creepers are connected to row after row of glowing electric silver bikes on the ground, pulsing away. Enough bikes for an army, never mind a gang.

The wolf-cub is at my side, panting like an old steam train after running all this way. The cockroach leaps from my hair onto the cub's back, his antennae quivering with excitement as he sniffs the rubbish around and above us. The smell is not as bad as you would imagine, but it's enough to make me cough and my eyes water.

I never thought such a paradise existed, the General says to himself in wonder.

Crouching low, in case I'm spotted, I follow the wolf-cub through the rows of bikes toward the tower. He sniffs each machine suspiciously as we pass. *The trail grows stronger,* he says. I feel the fingerless glove, scrunched tight in my pocket.

At the foot of the tower, he leaps onto one of the low scaffolding platforms, and I follow him up, scrambling from level to level like we're in a video game.

Each level is loaded with different things—salvaged computers, wires sticking out of their open backs, or music players and headphones slung over iron bars. There is a platform with a mound of handbags threatening to topple over at any moment, next to boxes of jewelled necklaces and watches.

Piles and piles of expensive stuff. And I bet it's not meant to be here.

As we reach the next to last level, stacked full of fridges still in their wrapping, I motion to the wolf-cub to stop. Standing on one of the fridges, I peer cautiously over the top.

The domed space echoes with noise coming from dozens of kids sitting on recycled car seats and deckchairs, gazing up at screens in front of them, each one speaking into a headset. Overlooking the gang from the other end is an ultrascreen four times the size of ours at home, filled with pictures that change every second.

In one corner of the screen, Coby Cott mouths silently in front of pictures of the Amsguard. The rest of the display shows CCTV pictures of the crowd outside, still waving their bars and planks, looking for the wolf they just missed.

Then the white ramp road. The bridge and the Culdee Sack we just came from.

It's like these kids can see through Facto's cameras. They must have seen us enter the city, the battle of the Culdee Sack . . . Everything. No wonder they didn't miss a helicopter landing in our garden.

"That's right, not much we don't see," says a voice. Two booted feet appear right in front of me. A bare hand reaches down. "You got something that belongs to me, I think."

By my side the cub crouches low and silent, which means he is not in a mood to be messed with. *Why don't you let me take her now, Wildness?* he growls. *This child will be no match for me.*

For once, Wolf-Cub, I think you're right.

He needs no more encouragement and bounds over the platform, jumping straight onto the girl, pinning her down with his claws.

But Aida just sighs. I see the same look on her face as when she saw the stag. More like disgust than fear. "What you setting this stinking thing on me for? You crazy? Call him off now."

"No," I say in the firmest voice I can manage. She's the one living in a rubbish heap. Nobody's going anywhere until I get some answers. About Polly. About the Iris. And who those crazies are outside.

Wolf-Cub sniffs her face. He could tear it off in an instant, but she only yells up from the floor, "You better get him under control, you understand? We not frightened of animals, not like them Facto idiots. But we got rules too, you'll see. And rule number one—you our prisoner now."

Her gaze flicks behind us for a second. Turning round, I see Eric and 123 pointing electric prods right at my head.

And that, I'm afraid, says the General, *is what they call a pincer movement. Trust me, I should know.*

For a moment I look at the two boys, then back at Aida and at the wolf-cub crouched over her. Then, with a sigh, I call him off, and they lower their prods.

The she-child was not afraid of me, he mumbles, retreating back to me with his tail between his legs.

She was terrified—didn't you see her face? Your father would be very proud, I'm sure.

You really think so? he asks eagerly.

"If that overgrown mutt," says Aida, dusting herself off, "is the best you can do, you have a lot to learn."

For once I'm grateful that animals have only limited understanding of other humans. The girl looks at us for a moment. "Still, you tried. Many others wouldn't. Come along!" Aida reaches out her glove-free hand and hoists me up onto the platform. She's stronger than she looks. "Welcome to Waste Mountain." Pointing at the kids on their screens and headsets, she goes on. "And we the Waste Mountain Gang, you get me?"

Kind of.

The girl jabs me in the chest. "What you think we do?"

I don't know, apart from break into people's houses with electric prods, kidnap them, steal music players and jewellery . . .

"The gang," she announces. "We all kids like you, understand. Kids with no home. Kids with no mum and dad." I know what that can feel like. "Kids Facto would like to put in one of their schools. You know what I mean."

Schools like Spectrum Hall. Full of kids like Justine, who I now remember was there for being in a gang. A gang of thieves who got around everywhere on bikes, nicking not just tins of food but anything else they could get their hands on.

"Thieves, hackers, bikers—we got them all. Before Facto did. First we stole food when we was all hungry. Then we stole . . . well, lots of stuff. And now we all working together to keep us fed."

I think of the starving mob outside. Aida looks at my clothes, caked in dust, my face covered in scratches from our close shave outside. Reaching out, she moves to touch my grazed cheek, and then thinks better of it.

"You know that man outside with the clock who tried to eat you and your trained pooch?" she says.

I nod but feel the cub bristle by my side. He may not understand the exact words, but he knows when he's being talked about. Pictures of us being attacked by the mob flicker onto the ultrascreen. Aida points at the man with the gold tooth.

"He sells pink. Cheap formula. Not made by Facto, but

by crooks like him—from recycled rubbish they find on the tip out there. Sometimes it OK, and not kill you"—I think of the women holding their breath, the acrid liquid filling their buckets from the keg—"but never have pink that gone off. Every batch got a four-hour time limit—it's unstable, you understand? It deadly. It burn, dissolve your mouth, your teeth. Everything."

The man checking his clock—so he didn't kill people. If he could help it.

"Real formula, it running out. There's not enough for everybody. Unless you live in one of them glass towers. So we steal it for them. We trying to do good, you see?"

But I'm not listening to her anymore. All I can see are the latest pictures on the ultrascreen. Grainy nighttime shots of another girl, the girl I thought we were going to rescue. The girl I thought this gang would find.

My best friend, climbing into a helicopter surrounded by cullers.

Parp! Parp!

Under the dome of rubbish, a bike horn blaring out of nowhere sends the wolf-cub's tail up with alarm, as he stares down the room toward a lopsided canvas shack beneath the ultrascreen, fronted by patchwork curtains.

Standing in between the curtains is a boy in a floppy sun hat, fastened under his chin with string. He's clutching an old-fashioned cycle horn, which he points at me.

Parp!

"So, the famous Kester Jaynes. Well, well, as I live and breathe. This is a treat and no mistake! Eh?" he says.

Parp!

I flinch, but not just at the noise. How does he know my name? Not only that, but he doesn't even sound like a boy. The other children step back as he rolls toward us with a bowlegged walk. He's dressed like one of the kids here, in a dirty T-shirt and baggy shorts, but although his face looks smooth, his hands are wrinkled and spotted. A big smile creases his smooth cheeks as he gets closer and shakes my hand up and down like he's my best friend. His face looks young, but his eyes and teeth look worn and old. He glances up at the grainy pictures of Polly on the screen. "We just missed her. Awful bad luck!"

Parp! Parp!

He leans over and pinches my cheek. It's meant to be friendly, I think, but it really hurts. "That look on your face! Quite right too—I'm completely forgetting myself. How very remiss of me." The man-boy sticks out a damp hand. "You can call me Littleman—everyone else does. Because as you can see, I am!"

He laughs, shaking his floppy sun hat and small white shoulders. When I don't laugh back, he stops abruptly. "Very well," he says. "I suppose you came here looking for her."

No, I think, I just wanted to get me and my wolf-cub half killed by a starving mob in a rubbish dump for a laugh.

Littleman screws up his eyes and peers at me. "Jolly good—that makes two of us. And because I'm awful nice, I'll show you why. We've been watching you both right from the moment you entered the city, you see. My associates"— he gestures to the kids who broke into our house—"are very skilled on their clever computers at finding out little things like names, addresses—even your shoe size, I shouldn't wonder. So do stop me if I start banging on about things you already know . . ." Littleman clicks his fingers at the screen, and the pictures of Polly dissolve to show a photo of a man and a woman. The woman looks familiar, but I know I've never seen her before. They're standing in front of a house, a house that—it's Wind's Edge.

They're standing in front of Polly's house.

"Simon and Jane Goodacre. Your young friend's parents." He blows the horn twice in my face and grins. "Did you know they were nature historians, for example?"

Yes, Polly had explained why their house was full of so many dried flowers pressed between old books, bones and shells laid out in glass cases. They had taught Polly everything she knew about plants, so they could all survive in the Zone after the animals and crops disappeared.

"Tremendous collectors too, as you no doubt discovered. Unstoppable, they were. Every leaf of every plant in their garden, every fossil they ever found on a beach, even—bless their cottons—every animal bone they found. Believe you me, six years ago there were a lot of those!"

Parp. Parp.

He must see the way my face falls. Polly and I saw enough of those in the Forest of the Dead—not something I want to be reminded of.

"Forgive me—I'm getting ahead of myself. You must be wondering why I know so much about these plant and bone collectors up in the north."

Littleman mops his brow with a big spotted handkerchief.

"Your chum Polly probably didn't like to say—because it's all very 'Top Secret.'" He makes little inverted commas with his spotted hands. "But they ran a sort of club. A club of all those outsiders in the Zone who don't have a nice glass tower to live in. A club working very hard to get rid of the nasty Mr. Stone."

His brow is shining and glistening with sweat. A drop rolls down his nose, and he licks it off.

I turn away. I know all this. Polly did like to say. She trusted me, in the end. But Littleman grabs me by the shoulder. "Aha! But let me tell you what you don't know. That we had a friend in their secret club. A friend named Ma."

Parp! Parp! Parp!

No wonder she made friends with Polly so quickly.

Seeing my face at this news makes him laugh. He's fizzing with energy, skipping in circles around us, waving his horn. Whenever he comes close enough, I can smell stale prawn-cocktail crisps on his breath.

"Ma told us all about a secret weapon that these collectors were preparing. A weapon known as the Iris Capsule. A weapon that someone we both know had in her safekeeping."

Capsule? That's the first time I've heard that word. Perhaps a capsule small enough for Polly to keep on her at all times without me knowing.

He clicks his greasy fingers, and the grainy pictures of Polly being led aboard the helicopter are back on the screen. We both gaze at them for a moment. "There's just one problem. That's all we know about it. The Goodacres were so secretive that we don't know exactly what the Iris is."

Littleman wipes his hands on his shorts again.

"But my interest was purely commercial. I'm a collector too, you see. The Goodacres collected plants and bones. I mainly collect what others call junk and find a use for it. Like these."

He points to the prod dangling from Aida's waist. "When all the cows died, farmers didn't need these anymore. We found crates of them, gathering dust in warehouses, didn't we, my sweet?" Aida raises an eyebrow. "Well, I say found, but . . ." He smirks and dances behind Aida and the others, sticking his head out between them. "Not just inanimate junk either! Aida was one of the first to join my collection, weren't you, my lovely?"

Aida glares at him. "You said we needed the Iris because it could change the world back to the way it was. Without Facto or Selwyn Stone." She spits his name out like it's burning her mouth.

Parp!

"Only for the right price, my dear—only ever for the right price. And now that Mr. Stone seems to have got his fingers on our only clue to its whereabouts, I'm not sure that's a price worth paying."

"But that's not true. You know we could—"

He throws his hands up in pretend shock. "Aida, my sweet, I didn't know you had been put in charge of us all. When did this momentous event take place?" Then he is suddenly leaning right in, digging into her shoulder with his long nails and spitting in her ear. *"Never, apparently. So listen. They have the girl and no doubt the Iris to boot. We're too late. You of all people must know that."*

The whole room is listening now; the chatter has died down, pale faces twisting round on their seats. I can feel their eyes boring into us.

Aida tries to lift his hand off her shoulder, but he tightens his grip, making her wince. He raises his voice so everyone can hear. "You're mine. You're all mine. I found you. I took you all in"—he sweeps his arm around at the platform of computers and kids—"when you had nowhere else to go. Your parents couldn't feed you anymore. It was here or Spectrum Hall."

Aida puts her hand on Littleman's arm as if to calm him down, but he flings her off and carries on, gesturing at the ceiling of old mattresses and wire mesh.

"I provide board and lodging of the highest quality. I keep you all safe by not picking battles we can never win. I gave you your chance with the girl, and you blew it." He glances at me. "So thank you for coming by, my dear, but you and your travelling zoo are no longer required."

I look at the rest of the room, screen-washed faces staring through me as if I'd already gone. I look at the other gang members who broke into our house, but they gaze at their feet. Eric examines his knuckles as if he's never seen them before.

The General whispers in my ear. *Wildness, I do not get*

a good feeling from this man or these children. We should return to our wild. Besides, that dark call you heard, the stag said it was in the dream, that we should—

His voice fades away in my head as I turn to look at Aida. She's staring straight at me. Her gaze—it's like a beam cutting through the murk and glare of the rubbish dome. A beam that hits me dead in the chest, smashing everything else—Littleman, his gang, the animals' dream—far away into the shadows.

I've only seen an expression like that once before. On the face of another girl, in a messy kitchen far, far away. An expression that means only one thing.

Help me.

Polly's gone. And with her the Iris, which she promised her parents she wouldn't let Stone get. I only hope it means he won't be coming back for the wild now. But Aida seemed to think there might be a way of getting Polly and the Iris back.

I've helped the animals enough. Maybe it's time to help some humans.

The others are still looking at the floor. Now is the moment. *Wolf-Cub?*￼ I say. *Do you want to prove how brave you are again?*

Always, Wildness, he replies. Not taking his eyes off the old-young man, he crouches low, growling and baring his teeth.

But with a glint in his eye, Littleman just chuckles. "Oh, it's like that, is it? Well, two can play at that game." He sticks two fingers in his mouth and whistles. The wolf-cub stiffens, ears pricking.

Parp! Parp!

And there, standing in the patchwork doorway, staring at us, is the animal I saw on our street.

The dog with no bite.

The big white dog stands proud on his massive paws in the doorway to the shack. Seeing him clearly for the first time, I realize he is even more ugly than before. His eyes are tiny black dots above a long snout, purple gums sticking out over rolls of flesh like they're swollen and too big for his mouth. He pants heavily in the heat.

Hello, dog, I say. *We mean you no harm.*

But nothing comes back in reply—not a word, not a thought. Just silence between us.

The first animal I have not been able to talk to.

The wolf-cub, hackles raised, also challenges the dog, meeting his stare dead-on.

Dog! Answer your ancestor. What are you doing here?

The air is empty. It is like talking to a void. The dog just eyes us and pads over to Littleman. Aida gives the dog a strange look as he lumbers past her. Not fear exactly, more like sadness. The dog sits at his owner's feet, staring up at the images on the ultrascreen with a fixed gaze.

"Now, my dear," says Littleman to me, in his friend voice again, grabbing the white dog by the scruff of his neck. It looks really painful, but the dog doesn't resist. "I'd like you to meet Dagger, our house guard dog." He squeezes Dagger. "Say hello to our guests, there's a good boy."

And the dog opens his jaws wide, just as he did outside our house. It wasn't a dream. He was there. The inside of his mouth looks exactly the same as it did then. No teeth, just raw sockets and a red stump of a tongue.

"Do you see now why I call him Dagger? That's his dagger, right there!"

Littleman points to the stump, which does now—close up—look like a short dagger. Not a very frightening one, though.

Who did this to you, dog—tell your ancestor, and he will rip out their tongue!

The wolf-cub is readying for a fight, and I place my hand on the back of his head to steady him. But the dog just stares at us and closes his mouth.

The man slaps Dagger's flank and stands up again. "He was nothing but junk, tossed onto the street, like these kids. I rescued him from his nasty former owners. I protected him from the virus. I saved him from the cullers. And how did the brute repay me at first? He ran away."

Littleman has skipped away from the dog, who stands

facing the wolf-cub head-on. He whispers in my ear, with his prawn-cocktail breath, "So do you know what I did, dear? I fed him some bad pink. And I'll do the same to you and your pal here if you don't watch it."

He squeezes my neck tight, as if I were the dog. I think of the man outside with the clock around his neck, the acrid smell, what Aida told me it did. Then Littleman spins around, twirling his hand in the air.

"So set your little friend on him or me, please—be my guest. Although Dagger's never lost a fight yet, I have to tell you. Of course . . . house rules *do* apply." He rattles around in the pocket of his baggy shorts. "After I'd punished Dagger, he never disobeyed me again—did you?" He kicks the dog with his foot. "So I felt it only fair to give him back what I'd taken away. On my terms, of course."

His hand comes out of his pocket, and I catch a flash of steel. Then, quickly, he forces something into the dog's mouth. He stands back, and the dog chews for a moment before opening his jaws once more. Jaws that are now filled with false teeth. Razor-sharp steel ones.

Dagger hunches forward, gnashing them together, and the cub recoils. *Wildness, I want to be brave like a full-grown, but . . . I have never fought with a creature like this before.*

"Still want to play?" asks Littleman, grinning.

Which is when the alarm goes off: a howling siren, followed by the old traffic lights on the walls flashing like crazy. Now it is the white dog's turn to recoil, withdrawing from the pulsing lights back into the shadows.

The ultrascreen is suddenly full of maps whizzing across and a network of grids that I don't understand.

Aida steps forward. "You see!" she says triumphantly to Littleman. "It's a Code 8. You said we might get the girl and the Iris back for the right price." She jabs her finger at the screen. "Now we got our chance."

We all look at one another, waiting for Littleman to respond.

A sly grin creeps over his face. "Indeed you do, my dear." He squeezes his horn a couple of times and says to me, almost apologetically, "A Code 8 is my young associate's somewhat military term for a formula delivery. Of the most substantial nature."

The thundering trains we passed on the way here. A whole train full of precious formula.

"Exactly," says Aida. "You said it yourself, formula is running out. If we took a Code 8, we could ransom it in return for the girl and the Iris . . ."

The old-young man furrows his brow. "But what if you don't succeed? What if he doesn't agree?"

Now it's her turn to laugh at him. "You stress too much, old man." A slyness creeps into her face. "You wanted the Iris, remember? A prize of immense value, you said. A weapon that could destroy Facto once and for all, you said. Wouldn't we all want that?"

There's a cheer from the watching kids.

Littleman is backing away, cringing. "I know I *said* that, but when it was easy to get, a matter of just kidnapping a little girl . . . Now I fear . . . the price might be too high."

"Trust me," says Aida. "We'll get you your prize after all. He gonna help us too."

She points at me.

No way. I'm not robbing a formula train . . .

But Littleman places his long-nailed hand on her shoulder and gives it a squeeze. "Very well," he says. "Go. And take him. If he really wants his friend back, make him work for it." He smiles at me. "Everything for the right price, my dear."

"No!" I stand in front of the cub, while Dagger peers at him through my legs, growling.

The old-young man in his sun hat and T-shirt shrugs, turning back to his shack. "Fine. Then you will probably never see her again. People who go to the Four Towers tend to . . . disappear."

I run after him, pull his shoulder, but he whips round and grabs my wrist in a grip that is super-strong for someone who looks so old. "If you want to see your friend again, this is the only way," he hisses. "Or do you have a better offer?"

I worry whether Littleman having the Iris is any better than Stone—but as if she is right by my side, I can hear Polly saying, "Come *on*, Kidnapper, there isn't time for that now!"

Our eyes lock, then Littleman squeezes my wrist hard before letting my arm fall. He turns around and sounds his horn one last time before disappearing behind the patchwork curtain into his plastic shack.

I crouch down and stroke the wolf-cub's head. *Listen— you were very worthy of your father just now. Can you be a good full-grown wolf and hold off attacking this dog until we have completed this mission?*

Speak for yourself, cub, but I may be unable to restrain myself, pipes up the General, who has somehow made his way into the fur between the cub's ears.

I'm serious, General! If what they say is right, this is our best chance of getting Polly back.

Hmm. I still have grave misgivings about this operation, he grumbles.

If that silent descendent of mine comes near me with his metal teeth, I shall destroy him, warns the wolf-cub. *I have the sharpest teeth in my pack.*

I don't reply but pat the cub on his flank and stand up. Aida is waiting to give me a large empty rucksack. Eric and 123 line up behind me to also collect a bag from her, although they are putting things in theirs. A crowbar made from an old car bumper. Binoculars made out of bottle ends and tin cans. An ancient computer held together with string and tape. Things I'm clearly not going to be given.

It reminds me so much of Polly stocking her rucksack at

Wind's Edge before our adventure started, and suddenly I have to turn away from them all, hoping no one can see the brightness in my eyes.

But there is a voice behind my shoulder. Softer than she's ever spoken to me. "Listen," says Aida. "Just to be clear—I don't like you. I mean, I *really* don't like you. I don't like your nice house or your stupid scarf. This thing you've got going on with animals, it's weird. And I never met this Polly, but just the idea of her bugs me big-time."

I turn around to face her. She's really got the knack of making someone feel better about things. I thought she wanted my help.

Her gaze doesn't falter for a moment. "But I respect you. You came after us. No one ever comes after us. You stood up to me; you even stood up to the boss. So just you remember—I respect you."

I'll bear it in mind. I try to push past to follow the others down to the bikes, but her gloved hand stops me square in the chest. "I ain't finished yet," she says. "That doesn't mean you can get any fancy ideas. You know nothing about me, you understand? You know nothing about where I come from or who I am. So don't ever pretend that you do."

Then she turns, and I'm hurrying after her back down to the silver bikes, which glow into life like the fluorescent creatures once found at the bottom of the ocean.

I know what she just said should freak me out, but somehow it's OK. At least I know where I stand.

No, what freaks me out is what Dagger does just before we prepare to leave. He twists his massive head, his black eyes bulging, metal teeth gleaming, to give me a look.

A look that I have never seen any animal give me.

One I hope I never see again.

The convoy of four bikes slips up the tunnel out of the mountain, through the crowds and rubbish beyond. Glancing back, I see the sofa swing shut behind us. The Waste Mountain looks as massive and closed up as before. There are still rubbish pickers dotted about on its slopes, with helmet lamps, like the twinkling faraway lights of a distant city. Waste Town doesn't seem to care about the curfew.

As we speed past Clockface snoring fast asleep under his keg of pink, we spray him with dust. Aida leads us out under the white road, Dagger bounding along without even breaking a sweat, the wolf-cub just behind, slowed by his wound.

The night air is thick and dry, burning the back of my throat. Premium spreads out before us, living and glowing. The moon in the sky above is a little less full than it was but still bathes us in cool blue light as Aida guides us away from the lit main roads, down side streets, shooting across pavements, bumping off kerbs, now through wasteland, then straight down the middle of a dried-up ditch before heading back onto the road.

Faster and faster we go, trying to outrun the twitching cameras on every corner.

The bikes slow as we reach the edge of the city, the no-man's-land where I had to leave the stag when we first arrived back here. At a wire fence, Aida dismounts and slides her machine through a cutout hole. We follow and wheel ours in silence behind her, down a slope of grey chippings and onto a bridge, above the railway line we passed before.

We lean our bikes against the bridge. The rails beneath are silent and lifeless. About half a mile ahead they are swallowed by the open black mouth of a tunnel. We're much farther out than the railway line I passed before.

Far off in the distance, I can hear the steady buzz of a helicopter. I think of Polly being hustled into one, and where she might be now, whether she's wondering why I'm taking so long to come and get her.

Aida sees me looking up at the sky and sneers. "That nothing to worry about. Just a Facto patrol, checking the curfew. It miles away, tough man. Now let me check that."

She grabs my wrist and studies my watch before leaning over the bridge. She raises the big pair of home-made binoculars from her rucksack, now hanging round her neck, to focus on the tunnel ahead. Dagger is panting at her feet, his short tail wagging as he presses his paws up against the bridge wall, trying to peer over. Wolf-Cub keeps his distance, crouching next to me and giving the dog suspicious glances.

We are just some kids on a bridge overlooking a railway in the middle of the night. That doesn't stop my chest from suddenly feeling tight and my mouth going dry. In the distance there is a very faint rumble. It might just be the wind, but somehow I don't think so.

None of the others speaks. Eric is hidden by the shadows of the wire fence just above; 123 is at the end of the bridge, sitting low beneath the wall, both keeping lookout, prods at the ready.

Perhaps the General was right. I'm really starting to wonder if this is a good idea. Aida must see the doubt in my face. "Hey. The trains are unmanned, controlled by computer from Four Towers. We stop them, no one gets hurt, and we got a big ransom for your friend. There is nothing to worry about."

But how do you stop a moving train? More to the point, how do four children, a dog, and a wolf-cub stop a moving train?

A smile curls up on Aida's face. "Of course, when I say *we* stop it, I mean you. You got the most to get out of this—you take the biggest risk."

I stare at her.

"Come on," she says. "We don't have long. We gotta be real quick, you understand, unless you want to join your friend in them towers rather than get her out." Aida flicks on a torch, making Dagger flinch at the brightness, before shining it down onto the tracks. All I can see are the lines and joins of a railway line, straight and then forking apart, one line leading off into a siding with buffers at the end.

"Points," she explains with a grin. "We change the points just before the train arrives and"—she claps her hands together—"it runs into that side track there rather than reaching the city. Which is where you come in."

"No," I say, without even thinking. Wolf-Cub rises to his feet.

But her eyes don't even flicker. "What—you thought I brought you along for decoration?" Aida lifts the electric prod dangling from her waist and points it in turn at every member of the gang before aiming it head-on at . . . the wolf-cub. "We've all done it," she says. At her feet, Dagger bares his razor teeth with a growl.

I am not scared for you, Wildness, says the wolf-cub. His eyes tell a different story as he huddles down behind the wall.

The rumbling is growing louder and nearer. It's definitely not wind.

Aida is prodding me. "You need to hurry." She aims her torch back at the line, at a rough metal lever sticking up from between the rails. "All you do is pull that. And then run."

I look again down at the track. The rumbling is turning into a very definite approaching roar.

"Go now," says Aida. "Go!"

I slip-slide down the gravel on the side of the embankment, sending clouds of dust up into the air, until I come tumbling onto the track. I crouch and touch one of the rails. It's still warm.

Polly, I say to myself, this had better work. The Iris had better be worth it. And then I think of her sitting on the lab steps, her bruised knees hugged in tight, staring down at the river and worrying about her parents.

I look back to the bridge. Aida is watching me, Dagger next to her. "That's the manual points override. Just pull it toward you," she hisses. "Pull it right down, flat to the ground. Then get back here."

I stand frozen for a moment, almost unable to believe I'm actually about to do this. Then I grab the heavy iron switch lever in both hands and try to pull it toward me.

It's either broken or rusted up, but it won't move.

I try again, pulling as hard as I can.

Nothing.

Bracing my trainers against the tracks, I bend right over the lever, trying to force it down with my body weight.

It moves a tiny bit—then stops.

I look up at the bridge, but Aida just waves at me. "What you waiting for? Pull it all the way down! Hurry."

The rails my feet are resting on begin to vibrate and

hum with noise. Sweat running down my sides, I try one more time. I push and pull that lever until the skin on my hands starts to come away.

Looking up to wipe my forehead with my sleeve, I notice two lights I hadn't seen before. They are far off in the black tunnel ahead, but heading toward me, like twin suns.

I try pushing the lever back to the starting position, to see if I can maybe loosen it that way, but now it won't move in either direction at all. It's jammed.

I look back at the bridge to see Dagger staring at me again, his heavy paws resting on the wall. He opens his mouth, almost like he's smiling.

The twin suns begin to rise up out of the tunnel, and with them a noise, as the formula train clanks and roars into view, rocking its way down the tracks toward me.

Sorry, Polly, this isn't going to work. I'm getting out of here.

Except I'm stuck. I go to move and get jerked back.

Shining my watch, I can see what by.

My scarf. Aida was right. It is stupid. Because somehow when I bent over the points switch, pressing down with all my weight, both dangling ends got trapped in between the lever and its rusted pivot. I try to pull them free, but they're trapped tight.

The formula train is now thundering down the track, the headlamps glowing in my face as I scrabble to unravel the scarf from around my neck, fumbling—

Jerking the scarf free with a rip, I fall flat on my back—

The bullet head of the train, its black windscreen, the scream of the wheels bearing down on me—

And then they are there. Out of nowhere, scrambling and skittering along the rails.

Squirrels.

Grey squirrels, their fur turned silver by the moonlight. Hundreds of them, streaming out of the tunnel, bounding along the ground, ahead of the train. They swarm onto the lever, their pairs of tiny claws dragging it down to the ground. With a scream that sounds like they are ripping open the rail itself, I can hear the points slide open.

Squirrels. But I didn't call them. They just appeared.

Shuddering, the train veers onto the side track at full speed. This sends a wave right through its whole jointed body, which convulses, sending the cars tumbling over as if they were made of cardboard boxes rather than iron. As the train rolls, its engine gives an angry moan. The rusting wheels skid off the tracks, scraping the containers behind them along the embankment.

The greatest noise you ever heard. It feels like every piece of metal on earth has rained down from the skies like hail, bouncing off the walls, tunnel, and tracks.

I am flat on the ground, burying my head under my arms, as a rusting shard shoots straight over me, slicing open the embankment wall above and showering me with brick dust.

And then, after the banging has drawn to a close and the clouds of reddish-black dust have risen and settled . . . a strange silence.

Aida and the others scramble down the slope on their bikes, the dog and wolf-cub careering behind them. As the squirrels see them approach, they chatter quickly to one another and melt back into the shadows before the children even notice that they were there.

Wait! I yell, but they're gone.

For a moment Dagger looks after their disappearing tails as if he is going to follow them, but then he turns his back on them and picks his way over the wreckage toward the first car. It is lying completely at the wrong angle— the wheels facing in different directions. He sniffs at the upended corner, his tail wagging like crazy, jumping from side to side with excitement.

"You found something, boy?" Aida calls to the dog. "He got a real nose for formula," she says to me proudly.

No wonder, after being force-fed the fake stuff. And no sweat, by the way, I wish I could add. I'm fine. That was no bother *at all*.

Aida and Eric hurry after Dagger and haul each other up over the wheels, each of which is about their size, onto the sloping side of the car, and begin trying to slide open the massive doors. After pulling and grunting, they decide to take just one door between them as we watch.

"OK, get ready," warns Aida. "If any of them formula

kegs have bust, there's gonna be a lot of pink dust. You hear me? A *lot*."

Sleeves over mouths, they strain and pull until the door judders open with a roar.

"What the . . . ?" says Aida.

Because, as I can now see, there is no formula in this train. There is, instead, an unexpected, living cargo.

Wolves.

In the slanting light from the crashed train, I can see that their greyish-brown fur now hangs loose over their bones like a coat that's too big, and the teeth in their long snouts look more yellow and rotten than when I saw them last. The pads on their feet have shrunken in, exposing longer but blunter claws. Tongues swollen, eyes bloodshot—not infected, perhaps, but covered in too much dirt to tell—these six creatures have changed so much from when I first met them.

But there is no mistaking who, or what, they are.

Guardians. The beasts appointed by my wild to keep them safe in their sanctuary at the Ring of Trees. When we first met, they blamed humans for the virus and tried to kill me. The stag intervened and saved my life but killed the wolf-cub's father in the process.

The cub who then ran away from his pack to follow me

and save the wild. The cub now desperate to rejoin them as a full-grown wolf.

For a moment we are all looking at one another. Wolves staring at children, a lone dog at a pack, and a mother at her cub. Mother Wolf is not the largest of them, but I will never forget those eyes that stared after us as we left the Ring, with her mate and leader lying bloodied at the bottom of a gully behind her.

At first no one says anything. There is only the hiss and steam of the buckled train engine, the steady panting of the wolves, and the drip of oil leaking onto the tracks.

Then, with a snarl, the cub's mother bounds out of the carriage and onto the tracks. She lands with a wobble, but she stays upright and shakes her fur. Aida instantly raises her prod, as do the others, but the mother ignores them.

I touch Aida's hand, and she whips round. "You think I scared of these things?"

I don't, but I think I might be able to handle them better. She sighs. "You got a way with them too? Then ask them what happened to our food."

I wish it was that simple. But she lowers her prod and signals to the others to do the same.

The new leader of the wolf pack doesn't head for the children. Or the dog, who is watching everything with his blank stare. Or even me. The cub told me she is sworn to kill both me and the stag, as revenge for her mate's death. I stand back, feeling her dirty fur brush past me, as she instead stalks toward her son.

Wolf-Cub snarls and cowers at the same time. He is nearly large enough to match her strength now, but he was shot a week ago, and she looks like she has not eaten for days.

Standing over her son, she looks down her nose at him. It's only as the stray headlamps of the derailed train, shining through us at a disjointed angle, catch her eyes that I see the sadness in them. Bending down, she licks and nuzzles him. She nudges his bandage softly, investigating it, pulling it off.

The cub begins to relax. *Mother . . .*

At this her eyes harden, and she straightens up. *It's strange,* she says. *You look like my son. You smell like my son. And yet here you are running with humans and a sworn enemy of your pack. So you can't be my son. Not anymore.*

And she opens her jaws and grabs him by the scruff of his neck, almost hauling him clean off the ground, shaking and shaking him, pulling at him till blood starts to spill down his coat—

Stop! I can't take this any longer. *Leave him alone. It's not him you want. If you want to avenge his father—take on someone your own size.*

The minute the words are out of my head, I wish I hadn't said them. Mother drops the cub, who collapses in a whimpering heap on the ground. She stalks toward me, and now the other five tumble out of the carriage behind her, the children raising their prods but taking ten paces back. Only the dog refuses to move.

The fur on Mother's face is two colours: black around her eyes, white around her muzzle. In the darkness it is almost like looking at a pair of amber eyes floating above a white cloud.

Oh, I'm sorry, human. Is this wolf-cub your son now? There must be so much he can learn from you that he never could from me, she says in her husky voice. *Shall you teach him to walk on two legs and wear cloth?* She glances at the carnage of the train wreck behind her. *I see you are already introducing him to the kind of destruction that only your kind can achieve.*

I don't think now is a good time to try to explain that it was squirrels who stopped the train, not me.

From behind her there is a whimper from the crumpled black heap of fur lying on the ground. *Please, Mother, I never meant to hurt you, I swear—*

You know, Cub, Mother says coolly, without even looking back at him, *the weaker you sound, the easier it is for me to despise you. A fatal flaw, just like your father. It was his pride that got him killed, and your downfall will be your cowardice.*

She takes another step toward me, and I can smell her breath, no longer rich and meaty as before, but dry and stale as dust.

"You have this under control, yeah?" says Aida next to me, not taking her eyes off Mother for a moment, or lowering her prod. "You're telling them not to attack us? This is no time for life stories, understand? Facto will be sending a patrol right now."

I turn back to Mother. *He is no coward. He got hit by a firestick trying to save my life.*

She curls her lip. *I'm not interested in your stories. All I know is he left his pack, betraying his oath to the Guardians.*

Your cub helped us save your wild. He risked his own life. For the wild you were meant to protect.

Save? Her voice echoes around the steep stone walls of the cutting with disbelief. *They could not be saved. The berry-eye had done its worst. There was no wild left to be saved.*

So you decided to save yourselves.

I'm really hoping she's wrong or lying. I think about the pigeons, flying north with the cure, through the middle of the Zone, under storm clouds and over cullers. With no way of telling if they even made it out of the city or not. But if Mother is lying, she doesn't even blink.

We left the wild and tried to find the human land you had gone to. We found a place of glass tall-homes, but it was too near to be the one you spoke of. Glass tall-homes hidden in a valley of rock.

Mons, mountain city of the north. Where Polly's parents were captured by Facto and where formula is made before being sent in all directions on trains like the one behind us.

We found no wild, though, and no wolf-cub. There was

no food for us in your glass place, only this sand, the colour of salmon. Formula is transported as a dry powder and mixed with water for eating—the only "cooking" the grey dinner ladies at Spectrum Hall ever did. *It tasted of nothing good, but we ate it. And then the metal box it was in started to move.*

In the distance, a siren gives a solo whoop, which could be for us, could be nothing. There's another sound too, very quiet at first, but I know straightaway what it is. Whispering, from the drains and grates sunk into the rails around us.

The whispering I heard in the drain.

The whispering I heard when I first saw Dagger.

I shake my head as if to clear it, like the buzzing of a fly, but the noise stays steady in my head. And I can see that the wolves and the dog have heard it too. They look at one another.

Aida hisses under her breath to me. "Whatever you saying, there's nothing for us here. Come." She points her prod at the upturned carriage, where Eric and 123 have found nothing but formula crates chewed apart, pouches clawed open and licked clean by the wolves. Barely a crumb left to fill up three huge, empty rucksacks.

I turn back to the animals in front of me.

So you came here looking for food?

Mother's tail lowers, but only by a fraction. *I think you know perfectly well why we came here.*

I look at Mother Wolf and her pack, their eyes full of

hunger and hate. Wolf-Cub has pulled himself to his feet, his tail hanging so low behind him. *Wildness, please—if she will not listen to me, please tell my mother what I have done, how brave I was.*

His own mother still does not look at him even as he says this.

Aida turns back up the slope toward the bridge. "Come! This is a bust, we done. Leave these mangy beasts. The cullers will sort them out, you'll see."

Mother talks straight over her, to me. *We hid on these metal boxes and travelled here because we heard a dark call come to us in the night.* She is not looking at me now, though. *A dark call we intend to answer.*

And then she snarls before running off down the track into the tunnel, followed by her pack—without even a second glance at her cub. To my amazement, they are followed by Dagger, bounding after the six wolves as fast as he can.

The children stop their bikes for a moment, Aida turning and yelling. "Dagger! Come here now, boy, you hear?"

Wolf-Cub howls after them. *Mother, come back, don't leave me . . .* But he doesn't move, almost clinging to my side.

The whispering grows louder and louder in my head.

Can you not hear it, Wolf-Cub? I ask him.

Don't listen, he says miserably. *No good will come of answering a dark call.*

I know. They all warned me. Yet I can't help it. That

white dog appeared immediately after Polly told me about the Iris. That was when the whispering started. Now these wolves have ruined the one chance we had of getting Polly and her secret back.

Polly always told me not to be frightened. She was the first to follow a lead—following Ma to her farm, telling me to be brave in the Forest of the Dead.

I turn back to look at the Waste Mountain Gang standing in a knot of bikes at the bottom of the slope. Aida puts her hands on her hips. "Don't you even think about it, animal-boy," she starts. "Not even for a second."

But I can't help it.

The whispering in the tunnel draws me on.

I will never be allowed to forget that I have a gift. I can hear things others can't.

I am a Wildness, and I hear the darkness calling me.

Ignoring his shouts of protest, the wailing of the wolf-cub, I charge at Eric and his bike, knocking them both over. Weighed down with his rucksack, he is too slow to stop me from grabbing the handlebars—and I set off along the tracks in pursuit of the wolves and the white dog.

I cycle as fast as the bike will go up the track, my ripped scarf blowing around me as the machine swerves over the rails and bumps along the concrete sleepers in between. It needs charging, and the engine keeps spluttering.

I keep twisting round, looking back, half expecting to see the rest of the gang in pursuit or my wolf-cub chasing after me.

But they aren't. I know they will be returning to Waste Town with a story about me running away. And somehow I don't think the cub wants to go anywhere near his mother again for a while. I just have to hope he can look after himself and his oversized insect passenger until I return.

I have to find out the connection between this white dog and everything that has happened, the meaning of these whispers that brought a pack of wolves here from the Ring of Trees.

Our one plan to get Polly and the Iris failed because of them.

I have to know why.

As the tracks run on into this valley of stone-brick walls, the lights of the city fade away. The only sense of being outside at all comes from the strip of purple sky I can still see hovering above the orange glow of the city at night, crisscrossed by pylons and overhead wires. The mouth of the black tunnel ahead looms up to swallow me, just as it has the dog and wolves.

As I ride inside, the rasping bike echoes against the damp walls, and the beam from the big silver lamp catches speed signs and giant fans clogged with dust. Then, just occasionally, far ahead—the glimpse of a bounding dark tail.

The overhead wires hum in the air, and my head is filled with the sound of wolves calling out to one another as they spread across the tracks in front. Talking seems to sap their energy, though, and soon Mother's short commands fade to heavy pants and snarls. I am following the skitters of their claws on the polished tracks.

I have to keep focused on the chase ahead.

I pedal on in silence. There is no cockroach in my pocket to point out how slowly I am cycling, no wolf running by my side to boast that we have nearly caught them. I begin to wonder if the stag would have let me just ride after the wolves like this, whether Polly would actually be cheering me on.

It doesn't matter. None of them are here. I am completely alone, only the sound of my own breath and a spinning electric bike chain for company. But with every spin of the wheels, the strangest thing is I start to worry less about what I should be doing for my wild, and Polly.

It sounds weird, but the more alone I am, the more free I feel.

Only the dark call beckons me on.

I am alone, I say to myself. For the first time in a long time.

Or are you just running away? says a voice from the top of my head. *Running farther and farther away from your wild, it seems to me.*

Oh. It turns out there is a cockroach after all.

General, however strange he might be, that dog has done nothing to deserve being torn apart by a pack of hungry wolves. His fake teeth might help him to put up a good fight when he is caught, but I don't want any more animals to die. Isn't that what a Wildness is meant to do?

Of course. You must do as you judge to be right, he sighs, fluttering down onto the handlebars.

I don't understand this weather—last night in the Garden of the Dead it was freezing cold, and now it is boiling hot inside a tunnel. It makes no sense at all. My neck is damp with sweat, and I can hear the engine starting to fade, my legs, arms, and back aching as I try to catch up with the wolves.

Plus I'm starving.

The formula I had at home feels a very long time ago

now . . . I can almost hear my own stomach grumbling with hunger in the silence.

Then it hits me—the silence.

I stop the bike for a moment, and with a groan the big eye of the headlight and the green frame light power down completely. I hold my breath.

The wolves' pants and clashes with the tracks have faded into nothing. Nothing, apart from—

Whispering. The voices I heard from the kitchen sink are all around. Chanting more clearly now in this empty tunnel—the same dark call the mouse heard long ago.

I can't turn back now. I jump straight onto the bike and press the button. The engine splutters for a second and then fades back into nothing. I press the button again and again, but nothing happens.

Nothing for it but to pedal on, overriding the engine. Now in total blackness, following the ridge of the tracks as my guide. I only hope that another formula delivery isn't due soon. The tunnel seems to stretch on forever, blackness ahead of me, blackness behind.

All the while, the whispering grows louder and louder, as if it is rising out of the ground itself. The chants start to pierce and stab in my head, as if I'm being attacked.

I have to get out of this tunnel.

Sweat runs down my forehead and into my eyes.

The whispering grows louder and louder, and I can no longer think, and begin to feel dizzy.

The handlebars grow slippery with sweat, and the bike

swerves as it bounces into a rail, and then I judder off the tracks onto the chippings, and the wheels bump along as I try to find the rail again to guide me.

My foot sticks out in the dark, trying to feel for the metal, but the lines seem to be widening, drifting apart, and the bike is bouncing along the space in between the tracks when I hit the concrete block—

A spare sleeper, just chucked to the side—

The front wheel hits it hard with a bump, and the back of the bike tips up, sending me flying over the handlebars.

I thrust my arms out in front of my face, bracing for the fall, the cut and bump of sharp chippings against my head and hands . . .

But they never come.

I'm falling—

And falling.

Wherever I am, it's cold.

Deep bone cold, like the sun has never reached here, unlike the steaming city above. There is not one ray of light, not one shaft or crack to tell me whether it is still early morning or the next night.

The whispering that led me here seems to have faded back into the ground.

Although my head hurts—a large bump is swelling on the front of my head, too painful to touch—the rest of me seems still together. Both my arms move up and down, and I can stretch my legs out, wiggle my toes, and twist my neck from side to side. There is spongy soil beneath me, firm enough to have knocked me out but nothing worse.

General, are you OK? I say, remembering my passenger.

There is no reply.

General?

Feeling around with my hands over the ground, I find

no sign of a cockroach or an oily chain or spinning wheel or anything that might be a bike. I hope for a moment that perhaps at least the headlight has come loose with me, but all I can feel with my hands are clumps of gritty earth.

Which is when I remember my watch. I feel for the button and press it, showing the time with a luminous glow. It's six in the morning, but you wouldn't know it from the blackness down here.

I try to stand up, and can. I wave my hands around till I hit something. A metal panel. Aiming the watch light, I can see the panel forms one side of a shaft that slopes up and away from me. Toward the surface and open air, I bet—a maintenance shaft for the train track, or some kind of drain.

I try to scramble up, but the sides are too smooth to get a grip, and time after time I slither back into the pit with a bump.

I unstrap my watch and shine it around to see if there is anything I'm missing. Maybe a ledge, the rungs of a ladder, or even a hole in the ground. But there's nothing. Only tightly packed walls of concrete blocks stretching far above my head on four sides, at the bottom of a slippery metal shaft. I'm trapped in a concrete box with no way out.

I swing my watch light around one more time, just to be sure I haven't missed a crack or a hole, when—

What was that?

Am I imagining it?

No. I'm not. There they are, in the corner. Two white dots of reflected light.

Eyes.

Dagger? I say.

There's no reply apart from a scratch in a corner of the box, like something moved. I whirl round with the watch, but there's only more concrete, silent and still in the pale beam.

Then there are more scratches behind me. I whip round again and just spot a blurred shadow slipping out of sight, on the fringe of the watch's beam.

Surprised, I drop the watch.

Now I'm blind again, sinking to my knees and fumbling around on the ground to find my one light source. My hands hunt in the dark for the plastic strap and find nothing but soil, gravel, and—fur.

Greasy fur over a warm body that pulses and squirms away from my touch.

I jerk my hand and fall back on the floor—

Then the fur grows legs, running over and around me. A tail whisks, teeth chatter.

Silence.

I can't see anything without my watch. But I know there is another creature in this pit with me somewhere—watching, waiting.

Hello? I say, my hands held up to cover my face.

Whatever is there doesn't speak, but it's not Dagger; it was too small to be a dog—and certainly not a wolf. But those legs and tail did not belong to a mouse.

There's a snuffle in the corner, more chattering of teeth.

I sit up now, straining to see in the gloom. And there are those eyes again, staring back from the corner of the concrete box directly opposite me.

The eyes of a very big rat.

I come in peace, Rat, I begin. *I'm sorry if I—*

I'm interrupted by a very big, drawn-out sigh, followed by a very miserable voice. *Yes, yes, off you go.*

The voice is so flat it sounds like it's bumping along the ground toward me. *You're just like all the rest. You're sorry, but you have to go. If I had a piece of grain for every time I'd heard that—*

No, you don't understand . . .

What is there to understand? says the voice, with another long sigh. *What's the point? Off you go, follow the others, have a nice life, thanks for dropping in. I'll just get back to being on my own. It's all I deserve, really.*

Then there's a snuffling, and I can hear the rat start to scratch and poke around the box, his long tail frisking over the uneven ground. As he does, he half sings to himself, almost as if he thinks he can't be heard.

> *I'm a lonely rat, as lonely as can be.*
> *Old and fat, don't mind me!*
> *Don't take a second glance, don't say another word.*
> *Why should you stay, that would be absurd!*
> *I'm a lonely rat, as lonely as can be . . .*

But Rat, I'm not going anywhere. And leaning my head back against the cool stone wall of our prison, I add, *I'm really not.*

Promises, promises, says the rat, muffled, like he has his back to me. *And just so you know—the longer you do stay, the more miserable I am bound to be when you leave. So there really is no point in prolonging the inevitable disappointment, is there?*

But I can't leave! I'm trapped!

Yes, yes, I suppose we're all trapped, ponders the rat. *Trapped in our thoughts, no way out of the misery.*

I can imagine my mum rolling her eyes and saying, "Give me strength."

No—I'm actually trapped, Rat, in this hole with you.

There's a patter of feet, and I can feel the rat draw near, a blast of stale breath. He leaps up to nip my ear, and I cry out in pain, jerking away. *What did you do that for?*

To see if you were real. I've never met a human who can talk properly before.

And are you satisfied?

The rat gives a groan that is so long and ghostly it could be wind blowing down the shaft. *I'm never satisfied, human. And you chattering on like any old rat is a bit off-putting, if you don't mind my saying. But at least you haven't disappeared immediately, not like the others.*

A prickle of fear and excitement runs across the back of my neck.

What others? I say.

They didn't talk to me, of course. Why would they? I'm just a fat old rat who nobody cares about anymore.

He edges a bit closer. I put my hand out and feel that, in fact, the rat is anything but fat. He's long and skinny, nothing but loose fur, poking ribs, and claws.

An old, fat rat, he repeats in a voice nearly as young as mine, *left here to rot till the flesh falls off my bones.*

Rat, I say, as cool as can be, ignoring the sound of my heart thudding in my chest. *These others—*

Barging straight in, the rat continues, as if he hasn't heard me. *Not even a how-do-you-do—just ran straight past me as if I wasn't here, when they know perfectly well—*

Please! I don't even bother to hide the frustration in my voice this time. *Rat, this is really important. You have to listen to me.*

There's another unhappy wail from the darkness, like a rattle of wind chimes.

But of course, I should know better by now. There's always something more important than a useless fat old rat to think about. It's all right for them lot—places to go, animals to see . . .

I spell out my words as clearly as I can. *Them lot, those rude others who . . . ignored you. Were they . . . ? Did you see a white dog following some wolves?*

And then, to my surprise, the miserable rat begins to snicker. He begins to chortle, chattering his fangs. I can feel him shaking softly from side to side. He's laughing. I've made the most miserable rat in the world laugh.

Oh splendid, he splutters. *That is good, I must say, really quite priceless. Oh dearie me, you poor fool, you're even more of a lost cause than me. That does make me feel a bit better.* He scampers onto my chest. *Did you actually think the dog was* following *the wolves?*

I can feel his whiskers brush my chin. His claws clamp into my belly, pressing me down. He doesn't seem so young anymore.

Yes, the dog chased after the wolves down the railway track, following them into the tunnel . . .

The rat laughs. A ratty laugh, honking all over my face. *Oh dearie me, I really do take it all back. You are the most entertaining visitor I've had in moons.*

He leans right in, and even in the gloom I can see the sharp flash of his bared incisors as he hisses straight into my head. *But he wasn't following them, you foolish visitor from above. He was guiding them.*

A feeling of dread tightens round my heart. *Where? To what?*

Why—to his lair, of course.

PART 3
UNDEREARTH

I push the rat onto the floor of our underground prison with a *flump.*

What do you mean? What's this really about?

The rat is less miserable now, darting around me in the dark, pricking his claws into the soil with each word. It's like the more stupid I seem, the happier he is. *Ah, well, that's for me to know and you to guess, isn't it?*

With that he scuttles back off into a corner. I can see I'm going to have to try a different tactic.

On all fours, feeling my way toward the sound of his grinding teeth, my fingers find my watch and I shine it once more in the rat's face. The two orbs of his eyes reflect the light back with a ghostly glow, and his sluggish body recoils from the flash. He covers his face with his short front paws. *Put that away! Why are you trying to look at me?*

I'm just trying to look around and find out what's actually going on down here.

There's no point in that, he says. *Nothing worth looking at here, I can assure you. Hasn't been for years.*

I try to argue and tell him to stop being so stupid, but he won't back down. *You will discover that in the Underearth, looking is not nearly as important as listening.*

What's the—

Shh. Please. Not so much talking, I'm simply not used to it. If you want to find out more about your friends, try listening for once.

If he had any idea how many times I've had to do that... But I keep quiet, crouch with him in the corner and listen.

Wait, he orders.

Then, with his sharp little paws, the rat scratches and nips at three blocks right in one corner of the concrete wall. The surrounding mortar comes away like dust. From its place comes a soft breeze from below, wafting through the fresh cracks in the wall.

And with the breeze comes something else. I can hear it again.

The whispering I heard from the drain, that I heard in the tunnel, leading me on. Except now it sounds more like humming and chanting.

Animals chanting, in some echoing chamber below. Thousands of animals, so many voices of all kinds. Sometimes it is just humming, and sometimes there are words:

The earth will rise!

Leaning in hard against the wall to hear more, I topple

forward and land on a jumble of hard edges as the blocks fall out of place under my weight. Picking myself up, cool air blowing fast in my face now, the chanting all around us, I shine the watch toward the sound and see a tunnel, dimly lit by a bluish glow rising from its depths, that seems to pulse with the chanting.

I start to head toward it, only to find the rat has scooted ahead and is rearing up, his fangs and claws raised at me.

Halt! No one shall pass!

But I told you, I'm following that dog—

No one shall go to the Underearth past this sentry without permission. He pauses, clutching a claw to his head. *And please turn that light machine off—I've got a sore eye. If only you knew how I struggle with my eyes down here. It's a curse, it really is.*

The chanting rises and falls behind him.

We have heard dark calls in our tunnels, the mouse had said. *Dark calls don't exist, they're only tales to scare the young ones,* said the General.

This sounds very real to me.

I'm sorry, Rat, I have to go down there. I'm a Wildness. I can just see him shake his head from side to side.

Not down here, you're not.

I flash my watch again and see that the rat has curled up in front of the bricks, blocking the entrance to the tunnel, while he inspects his claws.

Yet the call of the Underearth, the song of these tunnels,

is drawing me on, whether I like it or not. So I try another approach, shuffling back from the tunnel toward the shaft I fell down.

Right. In that case, I'm going!

It will be very hard to leave the way you came in, the rat says, still coiled up, although not sounding quite as smug as before. *The only way out is through this secret tunnel behind me.*

For a moment Polly's face swims into view in my mind. Polly, just as trapped as me, in the Four Towers. Right now I couldn't be further from helping her escape. But the rat's right. I'm also trapped. I can't get out the way I came in. And no one knows I'm here.

Which is when I have an idea.

That's what you think. How do you know I can't sum-mon help on this human light machine? I could be out of here anytime I wanted.

Before I know it, the rat is throwing himself at my feet, wailing, *Please don't go, human who fell from above! Please don't leave me here all alone! Not another one!*

I stand up.

Only if you promise to take me to this . . . Underearth.

The rat starts to sob. For the first time, I almost begin to feel sorry for him. Almost.

But I can't . . . If only you knew . . . I'm such a disgrace to my wild, you see. They all hate me . . . I'm forbidden.

What do you mean, forbidden?

They . . . They exiled me here, to guard the entrance to their lair.

I crouch down. The Guardians drove the stag and me out of his wild as well. They exiled their own wolf-cub. I know how this rat feels. I stroke his ratty head.

Who exiled you? Why?

He sounds his saddest and most ashamed. *I . . . I didn't agree with their plans. So they banished me.*

Who? What plans? I shine the watch bright in his eyes, grabbing his jaw. *What plans, Rat? You have to tell me!*

He twists away, out of my grip, his face drooping with sadness. *But I can't. They will kill me.*

We pause, the breeze and sounds from below blowing around us and in our heads. *Rat . . . if I promise not to leave you here, will you show me what lies down that tunnel?*

What? The rat is still sobbing to himself.

If I promise not to leave you, like the others—will you show me this . . . Underearth?

He is wiping his face, as if there are tears to dry away. *You promise? Not to leave me?*

I feel heavy as I say it, but I don't know why—I am sure my wild will welcome this rat as one of their own, once we have escaped from this dungeon. *I promise.*

The rat is scampering round and round in circles of excitement. *You really promise? You aren't lying like all the others?*

I give you my word. As a Wildness.

Then let me be your guide, new friend!

Without another word, he turns about, his tail waggling in my face as he slinks over the blocks into the tunnel entrance. I slowly start to follow on my hands and knees, crouching low as we crawl together toward the breeze, all thoughts of my friends and the Iris fading away as the blue light and music lead us on, deeper and deeper into the earth.

Right after leaving the concrete box, the ground begins to slope sharply down. I don't know what I'm going to find down here. I just hope the others will forgive me for following these chants and whispers instead of doing what I said I would. All I know is everything started to go wrong the moment that dog appeared.

And I need to find out why.

The rat scampers along so fast on his paws that I struggle to keep up on my hands and knees.

Try and stay close, my new friend for life! he urges, before adding to himself, *Oh dearie me, I know I'm going to regret this. I always make bad decisions.*

I keep on crawling in silence, trying to ignore the pain in my shoulders, the cuts on my hands and elbows, the powdered stone choking my throat. A few moments later, the rat twists back to eyeball me—

But you aren't ever going to leave me, though, are you, new friend? Not ever? Promise?

I nod as best I can in the narrow tunnel. I thought it might be warm and damp down here, but the farther we go, the colder it gets. As we wind our way farther below the earth, I flash my watch at the walls of the twisting passage to get an idea of where we're going.

And to try to remember the way back.

At first the walls are rock, changing in colour from the pale grey of our prison to a midnight blue, then changing again to compressed banks of sandy clay, webbed with hairline fractures and an earthy ceiling that showers us with soil if I so much as brush it with my head.

Careful, new friend for life! says the rat. *I'm afraid it'll be me who has to repair this walk-under if you damage it . . . Although as my friend for life, you will be here to help, of course . . . It'll still be many thousands of moons of work, believe you me.*

Rat, I start, *when I said I would never leave you, I didn't exactly mean that I would—*

Shh, new friend! No time for chatter now—we have the rest of eternity for that. And besides, the closer we get, the more likely they are to hear us . . .

I try not to worry about what the rat has said and keep on crawling in silence, all the time flashing the watch at the sides of the tunnel. I can see what he means by how long it would take to mend them. There's so much stuff stuck in the clay walls, perhaps holding them together or propping them up. Fragments of what look like glass blocks or the ends of girders. A builder's yellow helmet, brightly coloured coils of cable with sheaves of copper wire exploding out the ends. Squashed drink cans, plastic bottles, phone handsets, and sunglasses.

The last great human age before this one, new friend, says the rat, as he sees me flashing the watch at them.

Then the tunnel dips steeply, and I nearly bump my head on a black wooden beam stretching out across the path. Beyond, we find tin tankards wedged in the soil, bricks and shattered china plates, and hundreds of tarnished coins scattered everywhere like pebbles.

And now the human age before that, he says.

The music and singing from below grow louder, and the rhythm is like the beating of a drum—a drum that my heart now beats to. Even in the chill air, sweat begins to bead and roll down my forehead into my eyes.

The black beams in the clay eventually give way to carved lumps of stone, broken arches, fragments of red pottery, and ugly faces that loom out of the dark into my watch light.

And the human age before that, says the rat, as if it is the most normal thing in the world. His voice starts to echo as the now muddy tunnel opens up into a bigger space, and I find myself crawling through a trickle of water, then sliding after him on my bum down a smooth rock into a cave. But the water is not the strangest thing about the cave—the strangest thing is the colour.

The walls here are white, reflecting and spreading my watch light so I can see them clearly. They're chalk. Everything feels lighter and airier. Water runs down the chalk slabs and out of the cracks, streaming everywhere, splashing and rippling over a plain of slippery stones. Like a river that once was, now reduced to a trickle.

Do try and be a bit quieter, new friend, hisses the rat. *We have nearly arrived.*

Where?

He just tuts, waddling off over the underground river-bed and into the shadows beyond. Shining my watch after him, I see that there now seem to be about seven different chalky tunnels that we could go down. I only just catch his tail flicking round the corner of the hole straight ahead. At least, I think it was the one straight ahead—they are all so close together.

I hurry after him, half crouched, half running down the hole, the noise now so intense it's hard to think straight—

Stop! whispers the rat.

I skid to a halt as I nearly fall straight over him. With my watch I can see he is peering over a rock edge.

Please keep out of sight, whatever you do, he says, and I shuffle closer on my belly. I turn my watch light on again, but he nips me fiercely in the hand. *Are you trying to get us killed? We have plenty of time for that, new and dear friend.*

Following his beady gaze, I can see I don't need the watch light. We are perched high up on a precipice, looking down into a huge cave that seems to stretch on for miles underground. Arching above, a great domed ceiling pin-pricked with a million tiny holes, down through which beam a million rays of cold early daylight.

The sun must be coming up over our garden at the Culdee Sack. Creeping through the gaps of the Waste Mountain dome. Maybe even sliding through a crack at the Four Towers.

They all feel very human and very far away from here.

The trickling water from the underground river rolls past us on all sides, gathering in a shallow stream that runs down the centre of the cave, throwing back the pinpricks of light in soft blue waves against the creamy walls. The rippling stream leads to the centre of the dome, where it disappears again into the ground, in the shadow of a large white boulder.

Just like the one I hid behind in the Ring of Trees.

I can see a handful of tunnel mouths behind the rock, leading farther and deeper underground, and then . . . nothing but blackness.

Gathered on either side of the stream, in rank after rank between our lookout and the white rock, spreading out in dark columns as far as the eye can see, are not a few, or hundreds, but thousands of animals.

Animals I thought had been wiped from the face of this city.

There are dogs, like Dagger. Filthy and battered, short wiry dogs with legs missing and chewed ears. And ones like our neighbours had: long-haired with their collars still attached, leads trailing behind them, a couple with tiny bald dogs standing upright on their backs, trembling.

Keeping their distance from the dogs are a sprawling mass of cats like those in the flapping photos we saw on the billboard under the road, only very much alive—arching their backs and flicking their tails. There are cats with manes of fur, and some with bare patches.

On the other side of the stream there are legions of rats like my guide, crawling and tumbling on top of one another. Not just black, but brown, grey, even dirty ginger and white. They chatter and shriek at the swirls of mice around them and at the grey squirrels who skip over their backs.

The squirrels that stopped the formula train.

Look at them all, new friend, sniffs my guide. *They're so happy I'm not there with them, the wretches. But they don't know I have you!*

He twists his head up at me eagerly and I try to smile.

I follow the rat's gaze, through clouds of whining mosquitoes, to some foxes who stand in a crooked semicircle in front of the white rock, as if they're protecting it. They look skinny and hungry, their bushy tails hanging limp behind their matchstick legs. But they are not as weak as they look—every time a dog or cat tries to get nearer to the rock, one of them lunges forward with their jaws and drives the interloper back.

Stag beetles and black ants swarm over every surface, so that the crags and pointed rocks of the cave seem to glitter with their shells and armour.

And it's not just the ground that's packed. Crows and magpies flit from jagged pillars circling the cave that seem to be hewn from the centre of the earth itself. Starlings swerve to avoid a screeching flurry of bats showering down from the cave roof.

Directly below us are black spiders dangling from outcrops. These are not at all like the spider I saw at Spectrum Hall. They are bigger and more alien-looking than any spider I have ever seen, creeping over one another and shrieking in high-pitched voices.

Wasps and bluebottles dart between the spiders' shining webs, while the ground beneath pulses with slithering snakes and worms.

All of them chant so loudly it feels like they could lift the dome of the cave clean off and into the morning sky. But of Dagger, the dog that led me here, or the wolves who were chased by him—there is no sign.

Where are we? I ask the rat, who is peering over the rock with me, his nose twitching with excitement.

He turns and I can hear his tiny heart racing at an amazing speed. His eyes glitter with anticipation. *This, new friend,* he says, *is the age that began them all. The age that never ends, the age that will return to take them all. The age of nature wild and true.* He leans in close, and I shiver as he bares his yellowing fangs. *Welcome, new friend, to the Underearth of the dark wild.*

The crowd of stray dogs, missing cats, and varmints of all kinds in the cave below begins to quieten, as if they know something is going to happen. They are watching one of the foxes, who has turned from the semicircle guarding the white rock and is now climbing on top of it.

His big ears, sculpted jaw, and deep-set eyes make him look like he is wearing a mask. A mask fringed by a plump and fuzzy hood of fur. He does not look as hungry as the others. The fox scans the cave and raises a paw. Everyone falls silent—even the mosquitoes' whine fades to a low drone.

Attention, dark wild! Greet your Wildness!

The dark wild repeat his words back, crying, *Wildness! Wildness!* stamping their paws and flapping their wings, deafening us with their cheers.

Hooded Fox leaps off the rock in a bound, and scrambling up behind him, his head held high, is Dagger. For a moment he just stands there, stiff and square on his short legs, turning his head from side to side while he laps up the cheers.

The rat and I press against the outcrop, breathing in grit, trying to make ourselves invisible as we listen.

Dagger waits until every last cat has curled its tail behind itself, stray magpies have stopped flitting from rock to rock, and the spiders have scuttled round, making sure every beetle and bug are completely still.

He opens his mouth, the metal jaws squeaking. He shows the assembled crowd his pink stubby tongue, and I hear a fox-cub gasp before being nipped into silence. The dog Wildness gives a long, drawn-out breath, like air escaping from a tyre. Then he begins to speak.

The silent white dog can talk. He could talk all along.

I have taken to the white rock, so hear me! Dagger says in a high-pitched voice that is dry and cold, a voice that gets right under my skin and chills me to the bone. A voice I realize I have heard before. *After too many moons, I can now stand here and greet you once again, my dark wild of the Underearth. I have been travelling about this Island, infiltrating the human world. I searched in vain for other survivors of the plague but only found their bones.*

And I realize exactly where I have heard this voice before.

It is the voice in the Forest of the Dead that told me another wild had survived and that I would never speak for them, that they would come when I least expected it.

I didn't believe it, I thought I was imagining things, and now—

He is real. And he is lying. Because he must have seen my living wild in the same place; he must have. But he goes on.

My journey confirmed my worst fears and my greatest hopes. It reminded me that you all represent something I never forgot in my time above. Something that the enemy does not realize is happening right under his very feet!

There are furious squawks from a cluster of starlings gathered on the crumbling stone just below our hiding place. They are the noisiest birds I have ever heard. Dagger raises his paw again for silence.

I remember, he continues in his high dry voice, *when this wild was small. When we had to struggle to persuade you that our course was not only just, but the only way forward for animals in this world!*

The circle of foxes gazes up at him, expressionless. The starlings shriek louder than ever.

There were not many of us at first, because we did not know whether others existed who felt the same way. We lost so many to the plague. Then, as if our spirit had not been crushed enough, we were driven from our homes and slaughtered by the enemy.

There are angry mutterings from the dogs and cats at the front. Dagger grows fiercer.

Who was this enemy that exiled us, murdered us, and stole what was ours? He opens his jaws briefly and I catch a glimpse of his disfigured tongue. *Tell me, animals of the*

Underearth, tell me so loudly that they themselves might hear!

One word sweeps across the crowd like a fire, sparking and crackling, billowing into the air. *Humans!* they cry.

I can feel the hate bouncing off the walls in waves. I shrink back into the dark, but no creature turns around or looks up.

Don't worry, new friend, whispers the rat, seeing my face. *I still like you!*

Far away at the end of the cave, Dagger stamps his foot, his short tail wagging like crazy.

The human! he spits with venom. *Humans who burnt out my tongue and my teeth with their poison. Humans who have driven us from our homes with their glass tall-homes and firesticks. Homes that have rightfully been ours since time began!*

The dark wild cannot control themselves. They are no longer in neat, still rows but are yapping and leaping, wheeling and spinning up webs with excitement.

But what is this enemy I speak of? asks Dagger, like he knows the answer already. *A weak creature, forced to stand on two legs all the time. The only animal who kills his own for no reason. They pour poison into the earth and will not rest until they have torn out every tree and covered the land with their grey stone.*

No! roars his wild. And I start to feel angry too, but in a different way.

Then one of the starlings beneath us flies up into the air, dancing. The ripples of cave light reflected back from the stream catch its dark feathers, which shimmer with purples and greens.

Wildness, Wildness! she calls, circling above his head.

The dog glances up crossly. *What is it, bird?*

Can I just say something? Not waiting for a reply, the starling carries straight on. *I'm right with you. It's an absolute disgrace the way them humans have been carrying on, an absolute disgrace. On behalf of all the starlings, can I just say we are with you all the way on this? We're absolutely disgusted.*

The dog grunts and turns back to the crowd, while the starling dives back to her nest looking very pleased with herself. Her flock just look embarrassed with all the attention they're suddenly getting.

Well put, loyal starling. Because the humans had a choice, did they not? They could have stepped out of their glass tall-homes and seen the destruction they had brought about with their selfish blindness and greed. They could have found a cure for the berry-eye. They could have helped us, rather than drive us underground. But this is not the humans' way, and it never will be. If they cannot eat us, then they will destroy us. And we will never be allowed to return to the land that is rightfully ours!

The rat shakes his head. *Oh dearie me. No good will come of this, mark my words,* he mutters.

My blood is beginning to boil too. Not all humans are like the ones he describes. Besides, we never ate dogs—at least not on this Island. He's making stuff up.

The starling is up in the air again.

Sorry to interrupt, your most excellent Wildness, she squawks, *but you are totally right on that. I couldn't have put it better myself. It's an outrage, that's what it is, an outrage.*

The other starlings chatter noisily in agreement, and now Dagger almost lifts into the air with the excitement of his own words.

But the enemy does not know the true spirit of a wild animal! We cannot be crushed. Every one of you is fearless. What you are doing is right, not just for yourselves, but for all animals to come, and you will live on forever in their memories as eternal heroes. His voice rises higher and higher as he speaks. *We are united in the same cause, and when the time comes—when this moon has gone, casting the ancient land above into darkness—we shall rise up and wash it free of human filth. We will no longer be the dark wild!*

Yes, yes! cries the starling. *Oh, that's very good, I like that.* She turns back to the others in her nest. *Did you hear that, birds? We will no longer be the dark wild! Oh, he's good at speaking in public, isn't he? I could never do that.*

The spider cluster beneath the birds swirls with agitation as they call up. *Shussh, you sstupid bird! We are trying to leessten!*

Ignoring the bird for a moment, Dagger's beady black eyes seem to fix on me, although I know he is too far away to see us hidden here. All the same, I shrink back as he roars, *We will be the only wild on the planet!*

Then, pausing for breath, he raises his paw and calms his audience, flicking foam away from his mouth. He waits until the cave is completely quiet again and then speaks in a softer voice, meaning we all have to lean in and listen.

But we have an advantage, creatures of the Underearth. The humans are too proud and weak to realize what they have done. I have sat in their lair and studied their moving pictures on their screens. They laughed at me, but I was learning everything about the enemy, from their weapons to their feeble defences against nature herself. They are fighting among themselves right this very moment, grown humans and their children at war with one another. They do not concern themselves with what is happening right under their noses, under the earth they walk upon every day. And what is happening to that earth, my wild?

It rises, reply the animals, in voices as hushed as his.

I ask you again, calls Dagger, now raising his voice again, making it higher and more strangled, *what is happening to that earth?*

It rises! the crowd roars back, every beast and bird and bug jostling for space.

It will do more than rise! yells Dagger, now screeching, his tail ticking like crazy. A drop of drool wells up at the corner of his metal jaws and spills out onto the rock. *It will rise up and wash away the human filth as we flood forth. We will rise and swarm and scurry and crawl, invading *their homes. We will chew through the wires that bring them power. We will destroy their stores of pink food. We will bring down their machines from the sky. We will bark and buzz and caw. We will bite and sting and nip. We will chase them and tear them limb from limb!*

Now the wild under the earth are not just chanting *The earth rises.* They are echoing the dog's words. *We will bite!* say the foxes. *Wee'll trap 'em een our webss!* say the spiders. *We will tear them limb from limb!* snarl the dogs.

Then, in among the squawks and growls, I hear another voice floating above them all.

No! is what this voice says. It's quiet at first, then grows louder. *No, you can't do that!* says the voice. *It's not fair!*

I'm not the only one who can hear this voice. Other creatures stop and look around to see who is speaking.

But perhaps I am the most surprised of all to discover that it's me.

The voice is mine.

Not only am I speaking, but I'm also standing up on our cliff edge, no longer caring who sees.

Get down! Oh dearie me, do please get down, new friend! says the rat. *It'll only be me who pays the price, you know.*

But right now I don't care. I fought for every single member of my wild. I found them a cure. I can't sit here and listen to this.

First, Dagger stops screeching and chanting, fixing me with his small black eyes from his white rock. Then the foxes. Then the many eyes of the many spiders. And one by one, every single animal in the pit below twists its snout or beak or mouth around, to see what their leader is staring at.

I am a Wildness. Animals listen to me. They obey my command—that was the gift the wolf-cub told me I had. The gift that called water snakes to our aid by the whiter-force, and a mouse to stop a Kombylarbester.

I have nothing to fear from any animal. That's what he said.

Oh dearie me, new friend, gibbers the rat, darting away from me and cowering behind a rock. *Please don't get us into trouble! I don't want them to take you away!*

The cavernous hall of the Underearth stays quiet. This time, I mean completely and utterly silent, with not even the buzz of a fly's wings to be heard.

Our precipice is bathed in shadow, but I can feel thousands of pairs of nocturnal eyes trained on me, as sharp and glittering as knives. I don't sit down or move.

Instead, I try again. *No. Don't listen to this dog. He's lying to you.* Somehow my words sound weaker and wobblier than I imagined they would, echoing round the cave to total silence.

Then, after a pause that seems to last forever, as the sweat rolls down my neck . . . the dog inspects his claws. *Would you like to come here and say that, human?* he asks, back to his cold, dry voice.

If you will hear me rather than harm me, yes, I say, with no intention of leaving our cliff anytime soon.

It wasn't a question, says Dagger.

And I hear a shriek behind me. Three short, birdlike screams. But they're not made by birds. Three foxes stand at the entrance to our hiding place.

Who knows how long they have been there. I didn't hear them approach at all. It's as if they just appeared out of the dark.

Leading them is the large one who looks as if he is wearing a fur-fringed hood, the one who introduced Dagger on the white rock. His eyes are hidden and dark, but the shorter one next to him, with black-tipped ears, has eyes that are wide-open and alert. The last is a skulking fox who hangs his head so low he seems to be almost crawling along the ground.

You human louts trapped my mother in a cage and killed her, says Hooded Fox in his gruff voice.

Hee-hee! You built over my den with stone, says Eyes Wide, his eyes rolling as if there was something funny about that. *My vixen and cubs all died! Like you're going to!*

The skulker licks his lips and adds in a sneering tone, *Yeah. What they said.*

I hold my hands up. *I didn't do any of these things. I have only tried to help animals. I rescued the last wild. I am . . . a Wildness too. My father found a cure for the plague.*

The words are tumbling out so quickly and every one is true, so why do they sound like lies down here? Landing like hollow rocks in the chalk dust around me, crumbling to nothing as they fall.

You lie, human interloper, says Hooded Fox. *There are no beasts left apart from the members of our wild down here. Our Wildness has seen for himself and told us.*

But Dagger saw us in the Forest of the Dead. He saw.

The hooded leader of the foxes takes a step forward and opens his jaws. It could be a yawn or a grin or something worse. Either way, I don't like it.

I wobble on the edge of the precipice, holding my hands out to balance myself. Out of the corner of my vision, I can just see the rat covering his eyes with his paws, rocking backward and forward behind his boulder. *Oh dear, oh dearie me, I knew this would happen,* he's whimpering to himself. *You stupid, stupid rat.*

Eyes Wide steps forward, staring and blinking. If animals can look mad, this one does. *There is no cure! All the other animals are dead, dead, dead! We're the only ones left . . . and now we're just crazy about* humans. *I hear you're delicious.*

Skulker slinks along behind him. *Couldn't have put it better myself,* he says.

The three foxes are now so close I can smell their doggy breath, see their spit glisten on their teeth. They don't look so skinny or weak now.

Save yourself, new friend, save yourself now, cries the rat. *We're both doomed if you don't do what they say! Oh dear!*

We are not doomed. I am a Wildness. I can command all animals.

I raise my hands to try to calm them. *Listen, foxes. I command you to stand back. Let me help you. Let me help all of you.* I keep looking anxiously over my shoulder at the animals below, all of them twisted up and peering at me. It's like a spiky forest of fur and feathers and shells down there.

No one commands us but our Wildness, says Hooded Fox.

But I have the gift— I stammer.

Eyes Wide laughs and wheezes, more like a hyena than a fox. Skulker slyly looks up at me from below.

You know what you just said? he asks.

I nod.

I don't agree, he says. And he pounces—

The other two leap for me at the same time, thumping on my chest, punching my arms back as we roll in a ball together down the slope to the wild below. As we fall, I see the rat sticking his snout over the edge, whiskers twitching with worry.

I wish I hadn't left the others. I wish the General was still here.

Rats and mice part for us, crawling and clambering into the shadows as we land in a messy pile on a floor of twigs and dry leaves.

The foxes are snarling and biting, a whirl of ginger and white fur, tearing the skin on my knees and drawing blood, but they don't hurt me more than that. My knees are grazed and scratched, cave soot cakes my eyes, and I am too dazed to resist as they snatch at my clothes. Hooded Fox and Eyes Wide drag me through the crowd to the white boulder while Skulker follows low behind, nipping at my feet as they bounce in the dust.

They haul me to the front of the white rock and drop me like a sack of formula in front of Dagger. The dog who spoke to me in the Forest of the Dead looks down on me with his funny, tiny eyes and swollen, ragged lips.

Seeing his mouth close up again reminds me of what Littleman did to him. It's strange, but even now—the wild turned toward us, chanting and baying for my blood—I can't help feeling sorry for this strange, ugly dog.

I don't think he feels the same way.

Well done, brave fox Guardians, he says. The foxes nod stiffly and draw back, keeping their heads low, touching the ground as if Dagger was a king. No animal ever did that for the stag or for me. He gives them a sort of razor-toothed smile. *And I promise you that it doesn't matter in the least that you let a human discover our secret sanctuary. As soon as I spotted the intruder, you captured him quickly enough.* The foxes cower and whimper at this. *But now we have our first human prisoner,* announces the dog to the crowd. *Let justice be done!*

In the Underearth of the dark wild, buried miles deep beneath the city, a thousand forgotten animals fall quiet to hear my fate. I have never regretted leaving those I trust more.

In accordance with animal law, let any beast who bears a grievance against this intruder step forward, orders Dagger.

The crowd stays silent. They are unsure what to do, I can tell. I imagine this has never happened before. And I have not hurt any of them. Then murmurs and whispers begin to echo around the walls of my subterranean prison and courtroom.

I shrink back against the white rock. With the daylight now piercing bright through the domed roof above, I wipe the muck from my eyes to get a better look at the Underearth.

It is not just a cave, as I first thought, at least not one made by rocks and water alone. The wall behind the boulder is covered with paintings, not like any I have seen before. Drawn and coloured straight onto the stone, there are pictures of giant bulls, a pack of wolves, leaping deer—and splattered all over, human handprints, dripping bloodred.

These animals aren't the only creatures to have lived here.

The ragged walls are also carved, but not with pictures. Dotted lines, circles within circles, arrows, and pointed letters. Inscriptions I have seen before—at the First Fold, where the pigeons said the dream of my gift began. Beneath the pictures, crudely dug tunnels lead off to who knows where.

As the murmuring fades away, my attention returns to the mob of animals around me, but not one steps forward.

I sit up as much as I can. Perhaps this will not be so bad after all.

The dog cocks his head. *Is there not one among you bold enough to challenge a human in public?* he says. But he doesn't sound surprised or disappointed. *I understand your concern. You are right to be afraid of any human. They have ways of killing animals that are not easily discerned by the naked eye.* More lies. *Fear not—this is the perfect moment for me to call upon my New Guardians.*

And from the shadows behind the white rock, as if the cave paintings had slid down onto the ground and burst into life, Mother and her wolves appear. There is a sharp intake of breath from the assembled wild.

The foxes look at the new arrivals and back to their leader.

But begging your most wild pardon—we are your loyal Guardians, your Wildness, says Hooded Fox, while his comrades gather behind him, casting suspicious looks at the newcomers.

Dagger shakes his head. *You still are, brave fox, you still are. You are my old and loyal Guardians, the most loyal any animal has ever had. To celebrate this service, I am today announcing, before this whole and vast wild, your new role as Old Guardians. You must keep this wild safe at all costs against the enemy, as you have done tonight.*

There is not one word of protest from the crowd against the metal-toothed dog.

I don't mind as long as I still get to kill things, says Eyes Wide, his eyeballs turning somersaults in different directions, *but if we're still Guardians, what are the wolves?*

Ah, says Dagger, blinking his beady eyes. *Like I said, dear loyal fox, they are my New Guardians, expressly charged with guarding your humble Wildness—as we approach a state of war with those above. You are relieved of that most tiresome duty, effective immediately.*

The foxes start to complain, but the wolves draw in around the rock as Dagger remounts it. The foxes content themselves with fastening their jaws around my wrists and ankles, spread-eagling me flat on my back against the dirt so I cannot move. As their filthy fangs dig into my bare ankles, I feel short of breath, a nasty sick feeling in the pit of my stomach.

The dog talks from the rock above me. He begins again, as the boar did at the Ring of Trees, with the command *I have taken to the white rock, so hear me.* He turns back to Mother, who stands at the front of her line of wolves, guarding the rock like the prow of a ship. *Brave New Guardians from the north—well done for answering our call, the whispers we sent far and wide through the tunnels of this land. And well done, also, our noble battalion of squirrels who ensured your safe arrival.*

All eyes turn to the grey squirrels, who are leaping and rubbing their noses with pride. I didn't call them. But perhaps someone else—or something else—did.

The dog continues. *You are welcome to the Underearth. Do I hear that you have a charge against this human child?*

Mother's soft slanted eyes, close together above her narrow snout, are full of cleverness and hate. *Now my mate will be avenged,* she murmurs, before stepping right over me with a flick of her high-held tail to address the dark wild. I struggle and kick, getting nothing but a nip from Eyes Wide in return.

The painted cave temple is thick with anticipation, starlings swooping through the air to perch on the carvings above my head for a closer view. I scan the cliff above, but there is no sign of my ratty friend.

Mother waits for the crowd to settle before speaking in her purring, silky tones. *There were others apart from you, this is true. My pack were appointed Guardians of the last wild, the last surviving beasts aboveground. A great stag had led us to a place of safety from the plague, or so we thought, until a few moons ago the wind blew in our greatest fear.*

There is a groan from the assembled animals, and Mother's companions hang their heads.

We remained determined to protect those we served, but the stag had other ideas. Some pigeons had told him of a human boy who still had the ancient gift, and despite our entreaties that the natural order be preserved, against the wishes of the whole wild, he brought the boy into our sanctuary.

A thousand pairs of eyes are ready to pass judgment on me.

The boy tricked the stag and some others into believing his father would provide human magic for a cure.

Not true! I yell, but Eyes Wide bites harder on my ankle this time, drawing blood. I gasp at the pain.

Who would you believe, dear creatures of this wild? says Mother, in the softest tone. *Myself or this . . . animal killer?*

I have never—

The wild are in uproar, yelling at me. The noise is so great a little shower of stone dust crumbles down on me from the cracked roof, making me cough. The foxes only tighten their grip. It hurts so much, but I think of Polly and try not to show it.

*We never believed his lies about magic. My mate tried

to stop him and the stag from escaping, but they killed him. They lured our only cub to follow him out of our sanctuary, into this human land. They left promising a cure, but none came. More beasts grew sick, and more died. In desperation, we Guardians left, and in search of food found ourselves trapped on a metal machine that carried us here. After many hours travelling in the dark, we began to hear your call from the tunnels around us. We called back. Thank you, squirrels, for answering us. The grey squirrels flick their bushy tails with pride. *After the machine tumbled over, and we saw you, great Wildness, waiting for us, we knew it was our destiny.*

The wolf looks down at the stray dogs and cats, the ones with bitten ears and missing fur, some three-legged, who are staring up at her wide-eyed.

All of you, listen. We are the last of that wild and we come in peace, she says with a smile in her voice that makes my stomach curdle. *Unlike this boy, who seeks only our destruction. There is no magic; there is no cure. He has even turned my own beloved cub against me.*

The wolf is lying! I manage to get out, before being nipped by all three foxes at once, making me cry out in pain. Sparks and dots fly before my eyes and bile rises into my mouth.

Mother nods her head curtly at the ranks of beasts and withdraws back into the shade of the rock. Dagger prowls up and down above, like he's thinking. Finally he comes to a stop. *Well, my dark wild, you have heard the charges laid against our intruder: that he has lied to the last wild, murdered a Guardian, and betrayed his sacred gift—passed down through his human bloodline for generations.*

My mind is reeling, but I can't think straight—passed down through my bloodline for generations?

There is a flutter in the hazy light above.

Oh, your Wildness, your Wildness! The starling is circling above the dog's head. Mother raises her eyes in irritation. *I'm sorry to interrupt you . . .*

What is it, Starling? asks the dog, sounding short. *Have you come to add to the charges against the intruder?*

Oh no, your Wildness. I just wanted to say that I think you've orchestrated this really, really well. The whole charges thing, building up the drama, then revealing the wolf's statement, now the final judgment hanging in the air, so to speak— we in the starling nest just think it's all been so exciting to watch.

There is a pause. You could literally hear a feather drop.

Is that all, bird? snaps the dog.

That was all, says the starling, flapping back to her nest, completely oblivious of the other birds scowling at her. But it has given me my chance. I think about what Polly would do, if she were here. If only she were really here. Then she would do what she is best at—speaking out.

The cave is silent as I try to be like her. *Wait! You have to listen to me. There are good humans above, fighting your* enemies. *Humans like my father, who with his magic has found a cure for the berry-eye. You can ask any one of the animals we have saved.**

There is a buzz of excitement at my words. An excitement not shared by Dagger. *Indeed. And where are these animals this so-called cure of your father's has saved?*

Not here.

In our garden and in the Ring of Trees. If you wait here, I could go and fetch them, you could see for yourselves. The buzz turns to laughter. *I swear, you have to believe me!*

I believe we would never see you again if we did that, says Dagger, to more laughter.

But you have to let me go back. You don't understand. My friends have discovered a secret weapon they call the Iris, which will bring the earth back to what it was. We could work together, we don't need to kill each other—

Dagger peers down his nose at me. *Oh really? And what is this Iris, human? What does it do?*

The mob is waiting. Pale and frightened, I begin to reply, when I realize . . . I don't know. I know that Polly told me it was a secret weapon, that it was hope. I know that Littleman told me it was a capsule, that Aida said it could get the world back to how it was—but I still don't really know what the Iris is or does. Nothing that I can explain to this crazy dog, anyway.

The only person who might be able to tell me what the Iris does is miles away in a prison of her own.

Suddenly, like a punch in my stomach far more painful than anything these foxes or this dog can do to me, I miss Polly more than ever before. She would have known what to do now. She would know a trick with a rock or have found a special underground weed that was toxic to dogs, I know she would.

If I even knew where she was, what she was doing, that might make this feel better, make me braver about whatever comes next.

Dagger grows impatient, flicking spit from his muzzle. *I said, human, what does this Iris do?*

All I can do is shake my head.

The dog allows the gales of laughter to fall away before he speaks again. *So it is decided. Far be it from me to guide your wise judgment. I am simply your Wildness, your servant. I ask you, the wild—what sentence do you wish me to pass?*

The cry begins softly at first, right at the back of the chamber, before growing and rising to a shriek that brings more grit fizzing down from the heights. The sound is deafening, but even with thousands of different voices yelling at once, the word is unmistakable.

One word.

Death! they shout—over and over again, until it seems the earth above will fall in and cover us all. *Death to the human!*

The light from the world above shines brightly down through the holes in the roof, dazzling me. The foxes yank my wrists and ankles tight, making tears of pain stream from my eyes as they flatten me across the white stone floor, my back arching.

My nostrils seem to be full of nothing but the smell of fur and feathers, floating and filling the air like dust, making me gag. The chants, which I first heard as faint whispers in a drain, are now as loud and crashing as a thunderstorm—if you were trapped in the actual cloud, that is.

They were waiting all this time. Hundreds and thousands of creatures, driven from the city by humans and disease, waiting for revenge.

Dagger plants his stubby paws on either side of my head.

I look up, and his white head swims through my tears,

more like the ghost of a dog than an actual creature. But the hot drool that flecks my face, the clash of his steel jaws, are more than real enough. He stretches out a paw and drags his claws along the white rock behind him, making a screeching noise. The cries slowly fade away. There is a last flap of wings, and then all is silent.

Silent but for my heart, pulsing hard and thick against my chest, ringing in my ears. Dagger just stares ahead at his legions, waiting.

Child of the humans, he declares, *you, like all your ancestors, have squandered your precious gift.*

I have just enough energy to say, *What do you mean— my ancestors?*

Dagger sniffs and clears the back of his throat. *Don't pretend to me that your treacherous wild has not filled your head with lies about the dream and your so-called gift. You are just trying to delay your inevitable fate.*

And with a half squeal, half yawn, the dog leans over and stretches his jaws till they are gaping wide open directly above me. I can almost see down his pink gullet into his stomach. He tugs at my scarf, pulling it free, exposing bare skin.

I am trapped underground with thousands of animals whose only desire is to see me dead. No one knows I am here. I have never felt more alone. Perhaps Aida came looking for me. Or perhaps Dad has. But how would they find me?

I wonder if this is what Polly feels like right now.

Wait!

The dog pauses, his teeth grazing my throat. He looks up, and I raise my head as much as I can, staring down my chest at the cavern ahead.

Wait, says the voice again. It is not mine but one I recognize.

Splish-splashing down the shallow stream, caked in white chalk dust, just managing to dodge the spiders as he comes—it's the rat.

As he approaches, Dagger turns and snarls at him. *So, the traitor dares to desert his post.* He releases his paw from my neck. *Now is not a good time to beg mercy for your crimes, rat. You have already betrayed this wild by your refusal to join the war.*

A nearby cat with a chewed-up tail lashes out with a claw at my guide. *Shame on you!* she yowls, but the rat doesn't flinch. It is the first time I have seen him properly in the light. His eyes are sunken, his fur dry and patchy. *But he is my new friend* is all he says simply.

The foxes look at one another and grin.

But he is my new friend, repeats the Skulker in a baby-ish voice. The others snigger.

Do you hear this, my wild? says Dagger, not looking at the rat directly. *This traitor, who was exiled to guard this sacred place as a punishment for his crimes, now calls this enemy a friend.*

There are squeals of *Traitor! Traitor!* from the piles of rats in the far corner of the cave.

My rat just takes another shaky step forward, into the circle.

Oh dearie me . . . I know I shall regret this, but humans never hurt this rat, you see. I used to live off their food, their leavings, the precious things they threw away, and even some they didn't—they were useful to us sometimes. Rats have always lived near humans . . .

Silence! Dagger shouts him down. *I have heard enough. Guardians, take him away.*

The foxes and wolves look at one another, uncertain.

Dagger blinks. *One of you! Do I have to repeat myself, or do you want to feel these metal teeth?*

Eyes Wide leaps off my legs and pounces on the rat, grabbing him with his jaws, where he hangs unhappily, drooping out of either side.

Take him away, Dagger barks. *Throw him down the darkest and deepest hole you can find. There he can think on the damage he has already done to all animals, while he slowly starves to death. Alone.*

But I challenge you for him, the rat replies.

Dagger almost does a double take. *What did you say?* he asks, with the first thing approaching a smile I have heard in his voice.

It is the ancient animal custom, says the rat, heaving for breath. *I shall fight you for him.*

Like the stag fought for me in the Ring of Trees. And won. But that was a stag against a wolf, not a rat against a dog four times his size with metal jaws.

No, Rat, I start, but I am drowned out by a thousand animals laughing. Cackling and screeching and howling. Dagger himself is unable to speak for a moment.

Then silence. The crowd is waiting. They are looking forward to this.

Dagger gives a curt nod of his head.

I accept your challenge, traitor rat. It will be good for this wild to witness where betrayal such as yours ends. And then, briskly, to the watching creatures, *We are to fight a war; the sooner you all develop your hunger for blood, the better.*

Eyes Wide lets the rat fall to the ground. My guide turned champion picks himself up and shakes the dust off. *Oh dear,* he says to himself. *You've done it now.* Then he catches sight of me watching him and brightens. *But I do not do this for a cause, Wildness. I do it for a friend.*

Dagger snorts, and the two beasts begin to circle each other directly in front of me.

A massive, muscular lump of a dog with metal jaws. A weak and underfed rat. I can't bring myself to watch.

Dagger is still circling when the rat makes the first move. He throws himself at Dagger's muzzle, but the dog bats him aside with a paw, sending him flying on his back.

Oh dearie me, says the rat, and is still struggling to right himself when Dagger picks him up by his loose fur and shakes him in his teeth till the rat squeals so loud I wish I could block the noise from my head.

The foxes gather round to watch, as if they are drawn

by the pain. I am able to sit up, rubbing my wrists where they held me down, shuffling to the side of the white rock.

Dagger drops his foe at his feet, in front of the boulder. Dazed, the rat lifts his snout. *You silly old rat,* he murmurs to himself.

But all animal eyes are on the dog as he pads round the dusty circle, waiting for when he will deliver the final blow. He turns his back on the audience, facing the rat dead-on.

Now, traitor, prepare to face justice.

And he leaps for the rat, but as he does, the most amazing thing happens.

The rat leaps too.

He leaps high into the air, clean over the head of Dagger—who bounds straight into the rock, bashing his snout with an angry howl and collapsing in a daze.

The rat lands just on the other side of him, at the edge of a crowd. He turns to look at me. He's bloodied and torn but alive. *You see, I am a good friend,* he says. *Will you stay now?*

If I stay, I will never escape from this hole. I have to warn the others about this dog and his plans. I have to find Polly and the Iris to help us all start again—even this crazy wild.

So I don't answer. I turn away, and I run for my life.

I run and run as fast as I can, not looking back, trying not to listen anymore. I don't know where I'm going, only that I must run. Away from the animals now baying for my blood, and away from the tunnel we came in by. I have to get back to the earth above that I have left for too long, warn Dad and the wild. If they are still there, if Stone hasn't come for them already, looking for his precious Iris . . . The Iris that could somehow turn the world back to the way it was. Before there were viruses and dark wilds.

Unable to think clearly, I stumble toward one of the shadowy tunnels leading off from the painted cave behind the white rock.

One of the many, many tunnels. Some of them look freshly burrowed, soft piles of crumbling chalk gathered in drifts around their entrances. There is no time to choose. I run into the one directly ahead.

It must lead somewhere.

Anywhere would be better than the Underearth. I must be able to get back home somehow.

I run, tripping over rocks, bumping into jagged walls that twist and intrude without warning. I shine my watch as a guide, take instinctive turns at forks along the way, run flat into dead ends of boulders piled together, and retrace my steps.

Occasionally I think I can hear hungrily panting tongues echoing in the tunnels behind me, and I shiver, hurrying on even faster.

Without any other guide, I follow glimmers of light or trickles of water wherever I can spy them. I force myself through narrow holes that suddenly open into huge caves and splash around the edge of silent green underwater lakes. Shining my light up, I see that the rust-stained ceiling hangs low, with twists of slippery stone that drip onto my head as I duck past.

All the time, the only thing keeping me going, the only thing that stops me from collapsing and sobbing until I cannot move, is the thought of the wild waiting for me at home, the animals who don't want to kill me.

I had almost forgotten that animals can kill.

I mean, of course I know that animals kill other animals—that they always have done so. But what that dog was doing to that rat—

I have to blink the thoughts away, gulp down the tears.

That's not right, is it? I know animals will always kill some other animals, because they have to eat. But should any animal—including us—ever have that much power over another one?

I don't know. What I do know is that my watch light is beginning to fade. My world dwindles to a few glowing green rocks in front of me. Then from a few rocks to just my hands, and then they disappear too, till the light is barely a spark on the screen and . . .

I am in total darkness. Blackness all around, not one ray of light above, to the side, behind, or even below me. Nothing to reflect in the water or gleam off a rock. Just impenetrable dark that suddenly feels thick and foggy.

Even when the watch was working, I had tripped over enough rocks and banged my head enough times. Now, my hands outstretched, I take a step forward and then to the side, and then back. Time after time, I find nothing but damp walls. As if the Underearth is closing in on me.

I am miles underground, miles away from Dad or the stag or anyone who could help me. No one knows where I am, where I went. Far off, in the maze behind me, I can hear wolves howling, foxes barking, and the *tap-tap* scuttle of hundreds of spiders.

Other than the creatures chasing me, I am completely animal-less for the first time in so long. I attempt a Dance of Keeping One's Spirits Up While Lost Underground, but it isn't the same without the mouse.

In a way I am glad my wild aren't here, though. That they didn't see how I left that rat. Perhaps I will never see them again.

Perhaps I don't deserve to.

I'm sorry, friend, I say to the empty darkness all around. *I'm sorry.*

The only reply is water dripping somewhere.

As I lean against a wall and slowly slide down it onto the ground, a slow dread begins to creep up and twist around me, choking my thoughts like a poisonous mist.

The realization that I may never get out of here.

I left that rat on his own. I deserve to die. I didn't just leave him. I left Polly alone when she needed me the most. I could have stopped her running away, talked her round—then none of this would have happened. I left Aida at the railway. I left Dad on his own with the wild. And now where are they all? There wasn't enough formula in that train to hold Stone to ransom.

I haven't helped anyone at all. I've made things worse.

That rat should have known better than to trust me as a friend.

I'm sorry, friend! I yell out into the blackness, but it makes no difference. He isn't going to hear me. No one is ever going to hear me ever again.

Then, in the darkness, something crawls over my face. Over my face, down my neck, across my ear, and into my hair.

Goodness me, there's no need to shout! scolds an angry voice. *Where the blazes have you been, anyhow? I thought I was never going to find you.*

I have never been so happy to hear a grumpy cockroach.

General! How did you find me?

Your metal horse flung me one way and you another when it fell over. I've been searching for you down here ever since. Luckily you decided to start yelling your head off . . .

I want to tell him everything I have seen and heard, but right now—*We're lost, General. We're never going to get out of here.*

There is a very long sigh from just behind my left ear.

Enough of this "we're," if you don't mind. I am a cockroach. I was raised in what you call tunnels, trained in them, and quite frankly happiest when in them. How do you think I got into Spectrum Hall in the first place?

And how he got me out, with his cockroach army . . .

If I can't get you out of here and back to your wild in one piece, never call me General again. Now, I have heard spiders scuttling about in these tunnels—large ones—and if there's one thing a cockroach likes least in the world, it's spiders. Especially the large ones, so quick march and follow me.

Then he heads off into the black, constantly stopping and waiting for me to find my way behind. We crawl on in this way for what feels like hours, him hurrying ahead and waiting for me to catch up. He never says anything, apart from the occasional very long sigh as he waits once more for me to find my way in the dark.

Just as I begin to think he might be actually leading me in circles, I hear him scuttling over some ground that sounds different from the smooth rock slabs I have become used to. He is walking over loose stones, and then, when he speaks again, he sounds even farther away than normal.

Right, come on through here, and we're nearly there.

But do you think—

Come on. No more questions. Just get yourself through here.

It almost sounds like he is behind a wall.

I follow the voice. Or rather, I *try* to follow the voice.

I can feel fresh air on my face. I can see a distant square of light. I can hear the General. I just can't get to him.

In the darkness, I can feel that the ceiling of the passage we are in hangs very low, till it is just touching the back of my neck. I crouch down to go under it and find my way blocked by a pile of slimy boulders.

There is only a tiny gap between them.

I can't get through there!

Nonsense! Of course you can—I measured it with my antennae. A tight fit, but a fit nonetheless.

I wave my hands under the rock in front of me. There is only just enough room for them. *But—*

It is our only way out.

So I get down as low as I can, and with my hands start to haul myself into the crevice between the rock and the boulders. I am lying flat on my stomach, my head cricked at an angle, as I squeeze between two slabs of stone.

The gap is so narrow my hands are now trapped in front of my head, and it feels like it takes forever just to drag my whole body into the hole.

What are you doing? Are you trying to come out backwards?

I barely have enough breath to think, never mind reply, and I just grunt. I force myself along, using my legs as much as my hands, my mouth filling with grit and stale air.

And then, just when the General seems to sound within touching distance—I can't go any farther.

The gap has become too narrow.

I can't . . . I say to the General, and start to wriggle back. Except I can't go back either.

Enclosed in a wall of rock, the whole city above me, the Underearth beneath.

I am stuck. Completely, utterly trapped. I would rather face a whole pack of wolves than be stuck here.

All I can think, again and again, is: I deserve this. I left that rat.

So I try to move quickly, force my way forward, but that just makes things worse. I kick my legs, and my shoes get pulled off. I can feel my heart rate beginning to accelerate, and sweat pours down into my eyes, which would blind me—if I could see where I was in the first place.

And then there is a light feathery touch of antennae on my hand. My cockroach guide has returned.

Don't panic! Do you know nothing about soldiering? The first rule in a crisis is, don't panic. Now. Try not to move so fast; you're not escaping from a fire . . .

I have to focus. I have to remain calm. With my fingers

gripping wherever they can, I inch forward behind the insect.

You might need to take a deep breath here . . .

I do, and somehow—

Wriggle up to your right, on your side for this bit . . .

Painfully, crushing my insides, but slowly pressing on—

You are very nearly there . . .

Just as I think that if I have to go any farther I will need to dislocate a joint to do so, there is air above my head. Air and space. I hastily scramble forward—

But be careful not to come out all at once!

—and fall straight into a muddy pile of shingle. I have never cared less in my life about falling into a muddy pile of shingle. Gasping for air, I have never felt more alive in my life, or glad to be alive. Not just because we are through that crevice, but also because above our heads in the darkness is the one thing we have been seeking for so long.

A crack of genuine light.

PART 4

IRIS

Not a pinprick far away in a domed ceiling above, not light fringing the end of a smooth metal shaft, but an actual crack of daylight that is almost reachable if I stand on my toes.

Then the General is scampering ahead, and I'm clambering up boulders behind him, some of them slipping, hardly even noticing when they bounce against my shins or catch my feet as they fall.

I deserve to suffer. After what—

Then, where there was a crack, there is a hole, with bars across it, the cockroach easily sliding between them. Blue twilight floods through, along with warm air, which I gulp down. Then I'm banging the bars, not caring about cutting or bruising my hands or even smashing my knuckles, until, with a clang, they topple free.

I haul myself out, onto tarmac, soaking and gasping for air. Adjusting my eyes to the light, I look around—the patch of green, the red brick, the black railings—and can barely believe where we are.

Our Culdee Sack. A drain right in front of our house.

I told you a cockroach knows his tunnels, says the General.

Slowly sitting up, the first thing I do is feel the ground. It's wet. Only spotted with rain, but rain all the same.

I feel my heart lurch. Animals believe rain is the tears the sky weeps every time an animal dies.

Kester! You have to come now! hisses the cockroach.

I haul myself up and—barefoot, my soaking clothes shredded to rags—I hobble after the General toward the house.

It's very quiet. Too quiet.

I have to hope that Stone didn't return.

The front door is still smashed open, from when Aida's gang broke in. I'm surprised Dad hasn't replaced it already, or even put a temporary door across.

But it isn't only the door that is smashed.

My heart rises in my mouth as I follow the cockroach down our hallway, spattered with muddy boot-prints and scratches, tracing smears and scrapes along the walls.

There is a noise in our kitchen.

A man talking.

I slide along our scuffed walls to listen more closely.

"The Amsguard is completed," says the man.

The voice is familiar, but I can't work out where from.

"The Amsguard is completed," he says again, as if he's talking to himself.

"The Amsguard the Amsguard the Amsguard."

I walk into the room and switch off the juddering picture of Coby Cott and the giant white towers. The ultrascreen is lopsided and the projector broken, dangling from the ceiling on a single wire. Our formula bowls lie in shattered fragments all over the floor.

Dad? I say in the voice I know he can hear, but I am not surprised to get nothing in reply.

I'm too late. I never should have left them. I tread softly as I head down to the lab, just in case.

I say lab, but all I can actually see is what's left of Dad's lab. Worse than when we discovered him imprisoned inside it. Then it was just filthy, but now it has been destroyed. Every computer smashed to pieces, papers torn to shreds, chairs and desks overturned, and . . . the cure.

I run to the fridge where we kept it. Empty. The metal cabinets where we stored the ingredients, cleared out. Every last vial, every test tube gone. There is nothing left to prove to the dark wild that I am not a liar. There is also nothing left to keep the wild in our garden healthy.

And in the garden beyond, through the shattered doors dragged wide open, shards of glass lie scattered across the ground, which I gingerly step between, as fast as I can—

There is no wild either. No stag, not a single creature. They have been cleared out. The lawn is a mud bath, apple trees uprooted, bushes hacked. There is only one kind of person who would cause so much damage and destruction to get their hands on an animal.

Cullers.

The General perches on a lab step, for once stunned into silence, his antennae drooping. At least there are no bodies here. I can only hope that means they have been taken alive.

It hardly makes me feel better. Either Stone has kept his promise and taken his revenge, or Aida's deal didn't work out.

Whichever way you look at it, it's not good.

The second that helicopter left, we should have moved. We should have run somewhere. I should have made them safe. I should have paid more attention to what Polly told me about her secret, and persuaded her to tell me more. I should never have followed that crazy dog. I should have listened to what my wild said about dark calls.

I should have listened more.

General, stay here, I say. He flicks his antennae without a word, still in shock.

Tearing a strip off my shredded T-shirt and stooping as I pass back inside the glass doors, I wrap it round a dagger of glass from the floor.

As quietly as I can walk barefoot between smashed glass and piles of scattered paper, I make my way back through the house, up the stairs.

I glance into my room as I pass—totalled. Comics ripped to shreds, the stuffing pulled out of every toy from my shelf. The iris Polly left by my bed only a day ago is lying shrivelled in a pool of broken vase and water by my upturned bed. Dad's room is the same. (Although, to be fair, his room always looks like it's been turned over.)

There is a noise coming from Polly's room. Scuffling, dragging, like someone is still going through stuff. A culler they left behind.

I slide my back against the wall, glass gripped tight in my swaddled hand.

The scuffling continues.

I count to ten and leap into the room, glass held out in front of me.

But there is no culler. There is no one in the room.

Polly's window is still open, like the night she left, the billowing curtain now limp with rain. Toppled plants, pots, and soil still cover the whole windowsill. Her cupboards are like those in the other rooms, gutted, their contents spilling out in heaps over the carpet.

And underneath the bed, the mattress half slumped to one side, exposing the slatted boards, something is moving.

A bag.

Polly's battered rucksack, which she first packed when we set off from Wind's Edge. A bag that survived being nearly dragged over a freezing waterfall, and that is now moving round and round in circles under the bed.

I crouch down, reach for a strap, and drag the bag toward me. Lying on the ground, I nudge the glass inside, lifting up one side of the cloth bag to see, right at the bottom, dancing round and round like her life depended on it—the mouse.

The mouse is tired and hungry. But she is alive. I want to give her the biggest hug, only I can't do that, so instead she hurries into my hand and stands on her rear paws, shaking her front two in the air, humming. *A Dance of Close and Real Escape,* she explains.

But all I can think of is the rat. I promised to be his friend. And I let that bully dog—Without warning, I suddenly burst into tears. I'm the worst friend in the world. The room we're in just makes it worse—full of the dead plants and scattered books belonging to my only human friend.

I miss her so much.

Now what's this? says the mouse, nibbling at the palm of my hand. *This ain't right, this ain't right at all. We've all had a right horrid scare today, my lad, but you seem to have had the worst of it, and no mistake.*

I can't stop crying. It seems to come from nowhere,

making my whole body shake and shake. I'm so tired.

The mouse's paws pressed together in front of her mouth, she takes in my filthy hair, shredded clothes, and bruised, bleeding hands. Humming again, she does a light dance up and down my arm, a Dance of Mousy Concern. Her fur is warm and her touch is soft.

Slowly I begin to take deep breaths and dry my eyes. Step by step, the mouse comes to a stop again, in the palm of my hand. Catching her breath, her eyes bright, she says, *Now then. Why don't you calm yourself and tell me all about it?*

So I do. Through my tears, I tell her everything: about the mysterious secret weapon that could get the world back to the way it was, all the different human beings fighting to get it, and the animals living underground who will stop at nothing to destroy us all.

By the time I've finished, it has stopped raining outside. The air feels wet and warm, the curtain flapping damply against the glass. The mouse just sits very still in my hand, as if what I've just described has robbed her of the power of speech.

I know what that's like.

So it's true, she says at last. *The dark calls we heard. They weren't just stories.*

Yes, the stag was right, Mouse. There is another wild, and they're going to take over and destroy this city by the next moon if we don't do something.

She does half a Dance of Alarm at the Future. *Well,

*that doesn't sound very good, now does it?*_ she says.

What do you think we should do?

She chuckles. *Oh, bless my heart, I don't know, I'm sure. Don't ask me what to do. I'm not one for clever plans. Look at me—when those horrible beast-killers came, shouting and trapping everyone in nets, pulling your father along like he was one of us, I only went and hid in that blessed child's sack, which I couldn't get out of again. And full of all her strange devices. Could I have chosen a more uncomfortable place? No, don't ask me, laddie. I'm no use at all.*

I give the mouse a look.

But she has made me think of something. Placing her carefully down next to me, I empty the rest of the rucksack onto the floor. Polly wouldn't be separated from her bag before, so why did she leave it behind this time?

There's not much in it. A scattering of old leaves and a single letter tile from her word game. A tied plastic bag with a lump of disintegrated cat biscuits in it—a bag with a hole chewed in it, spilling crumbs.

I was in there for such a long time, says the mouse, doing a quick three-step Dance of Being Caught Red-Pawed. *Mice can't live on air alone, you know.*

I untie the bag and let her crawl inside to finish the rest of the biscuits, while I sift through the rest of the bag's contents. A smeared magnifying glass. A pair of binoculars with the strap missing. And—its pages curling, the spine torn and loose, but still just together—Polly's notebook.

She never went anywhere without her book. The book

of all the plants and flowers that her parents had taught her about, each one sketched and neatly labelled. I lean back against her empty bed, knees drawn up, leafing through the pictures and remembering our adventures.

Lists of the spices and powders she made the tea from that cured my fever. A cross-section diagram of the resin-filled pinecone she used to cause an explosion at Ma's farm. A drawing of the shining leaves I used to heal her sprained ankle.

And at the back, a picture I hadn't noticed before—of a flower that I recognize. The same kind as the flower lying in a pool of water by my bed, and the ones wilting in a trail of soil on the windowsill to my left.

On the last page but one of the book, Polly had made neat pencil sketches of the long stems and frilled petals, all ruled and labelled with words like "inflorescence" and "sepal."

I don't know what any of it means. It's not the flower everyone's looking for. The capsule, Littleman had said. The Iris Capsule.

I look more closely at the drawing of a bulbous pod rising up out of an iris stalk and leaves. "The iris fruit is contained in a capsule that opens up in three sections to reveal the precious seeds inside," Polly has written in her tidy handwriting.

My heart leaps. It wasn't a capsule that she was carrying with her but this drawing of an iris capsule. A drawing in a rain-soaked, blotched, and bumpy book.

And what good is that to anyone?

I fling it down on the floor in frustration. The book falls flat on its back, the iris drawing flapping in the breeze, as if it is accusing me of something. The mouse looks up at me in shock, her mouth full of old cat biscuit.

It's just a falling-apart old book, Mouse, I say. *It's not what we need. It's just a book, no use to anyone.*

The mouse gives a quick head-shake Dance of Dispute. *What nonsense,* she says, and scurries out of the biscuit bag, treading crumbs everywhere, toward the book. *You just don't look at things the right way. That there is going to make excellent bedding for one lucky mouse tonight.*

And she leaps onto the back cover and starts chewing chunks out of the pages.

No!

I yank the book away from the mouse, who tumbles off the cover with a squeal, a wad of chewed paper stuffed in her cheek pouches, no doubt storing it for later.

My hand is trembling as I hold the book in my hand.

You just don't look at things the right way, the mouse said.

She brought another voice into my head, a memory of a girl in a kitchen far away, clutching a freshly packed rucksack with everything we could possibly need on an adventure. "And a magnifying glass, in case we need to examine anything more closely."

I grab the glass off the floor and hold it above the book, moving it back and forth until I have a clear image. Looking again at the drawings of the iris capsule, looking at them in the right way.

The way that shows that it is not just a pencil sketch. I flick back through the pages and notice that every plant and flower—not just the iris—is noted and examined microscopically. Each one drawn in incredible detail, right down to the tiniest element.

Except in the iris, the tiniest elements are dots. The things you need to look so closely to see. The tiny elements that make up the bigger picture. Every line of shading, every stroke and stop of what she's drawn, is made up of thousands of dots.

Not just any dots, but the dots we were using every day in Dad's lab to store and record information on the cure.

Microdots.

Microdots. We're not short on them in this house. There are thousands of them piled up in boxes in the lab, for when Polly and I tested the animals' blood to help Dad evaluate the cure.

"Yes, they're clever things," Dad would say. "You can measure and read information, even store it on them, if you want."

Back downstairs in the lab, the mouse watching from a stack of papers on Dad's desk, I pull smashed computers and upended fridges out of the way until I find what I'm after, lying on its side in one corner.

It looks like a giant pair of binoculars attached to a white metal arm. The glass plate is smashed, but otherwise the device is all in one piece.

Dad's microscope.

I heave it onto the worktop, and the mouse peers more

closely as I slide the page of flower drawings under the light beneath the lens. I turn the dial at the side, and the drawing of the iris capsule breaks into dots, and then the dots blur and sharpen into . . . numbers.

Column after column of single-digit numbers. Millions of them, all in a seemingly random order.

More numbers than I could ever count, secretly stored in a sketchbook. Could they be the valuable prize that everyone wants? These sequences of numbers, stretching on and on into infinity—do they have the power to make everything good again?

It's not a mysterious key, an ancient curse, or an asteroid with alien powers. It's just a collection of simple numbers.

But somehow—I think this is it.

The Iris.

"The one small thing that I managed to bring from home," she said. That must be how Polly's parents gave it to her for safekeeping, concealed in what looks like just another sketch at the back of her book filled with sketches.

But I have no idea what any of it means. My shoulders sink. I'm sure I've discovered something, but it might as well be in a foreign language.

Well, don't ask me, says the mouse, as she watches me stare out of the smashed lab windows, wondering what to do next. She sighs and begins to nibble at a corner of Dad's paper pile.

I peer down through the microscope again, trying to piece everything back together in my mind. Polly, Dad, the wild—gone. Facto and the Waste Mountain Gang all after the weapon that isn't a bomb or a gun. The weapon that is, in fact, a notebook sketch only fully visible under a microscope. They've failed to get it before, but that doesn't mean they couldn't try again any minute. And right beneath our feet, an animal army hell-bent on vengeance against the lot of us.

I know these numbers are an answer to something.

But I don't know the question.

What are you doing? says a voice from the smashed lab doors.

I wish I knew, General.

I mean, what are you doing still just sitting there? You have to come with me right now—quick march!

Looking at each other, the mouse and I hurry down after him, past the few trees that still stand in our garden, past severed branches and scattered leaves, the aftermath of the helicopter's visit and the struggle that just took place there.

And past the steps where I last saw Polly. Where she first told me about the Iris.

The cockroach darts into the Garden of the Dead, the glossy bushes that protect the shady graveyard still standing in rows across the bottom corner of the garden.

Pushing through the thick leaves, the narrow space between the bushes and the wall lost in shadow, I can just make out the soft grassy humps that mark the graves of the animals we have lost.

There, says the General.

I don't understand. Crouching down in the gloom, I reach out and touch the nearest and largest hump. Perhaps he thinks their memories can somehow make me strong again, clear my head of the confusion.

But to my surprise, the mound is warm.

Not to mention furry. And it moves.

The furry mound shifts slightly, with a low groan.

My stomach leaps. I slowly follow the line of the mound along, from the rump, up a back of rough fur, feeling a shaggy neck, and then finally . . . a crown of horns jutting out of a head I know only too well.

Stag? I say, barely able to get the word out of my head.

There is a half-whispered reply, nothing I can understand. My hands now trembling, I feel along the rest of his body until I find what I was dreading. A feathered shaft, plunged deep into his side. The shaft of a culler's dart.

Without even asking, I grab the dart, pull as hard as I can, and yank it out. The stag stirs but doesn't move. His fur is matted with dried blood from where the dart entered him. Chucking it aside, I lie down on the damp ground so my head is facing his. His eyes are half-open, his breathing very faint.

Stag, I say as gently as possible, *can you hear me?*

There's a pause while he closes his eyes and takes a deep breath. Like he's summoning the energy to speak from somewhere very far away. I wait while the mouse and the

General hover behind me in silence, whiskers and antennae twitching.

His gummed-up eyes open just a crack again, and he says something I can't hear.

Words rush out of my head—

I'll go through Dad's lab, he must have a magic that counteracts those darts, we'll sort something out—

Kester. His old, deep voice never sounded so frail. Or so determined. *Listen to me. There is no poison in those flying feathers strong enough to kill me. I can feel it. I was weak after the plague and am not strong enough to fight anymore. Yet I am still here. Tired, but still here.*

The poison in the culler's dart can't be a poison after all; it must just be a tranquillizer, making him sleepy. That's not what a culler would normally do . . . I sit up, more words tumbling out of me.

What happened to you . . . ? What did they do to the others . . . ? What do you think we should do next?

Even weak and quiet, the stag has force to his words that makes me feel embarrassed.

Wildness. You have so many questions. Those flying feathers have made an old stag even more tired than he should be. He has to stop and gather more strength. *What is there to say about what has passed? While you were gone, the beast-killers came for us. Your father and I tried to resist them. They took the wild first. I tried to fight them for him at least . . .* Looking closer now, I can see that he is covered in other scratches and cuts in addition to the dart wound. *But you see what happened . . . he and the rest were taken. Well . . .* He spies the mouse and cockroach behind me. *Nearly all the rest were taken.*

I nod but don't say anything, looking down and tearing blades of grass with my fingers. My father taken prisoner again. My wild captured. The stag wounded and weak. *Enough of what we have seen,* he says. *What about you?*

I tell him everything that has happened, but when I get to my escape from the Underearth, the stag opens his eyes, fixing mine, and it looks like that alone is using every last bit of energy in his body.

You left the rat to his fate? The creature who tried to save you?

I look down at my hands, covered with shredded grass. *It was my only chance to escape . . .*

All of the animals are silent in reply. Even the General.

Why . . . is that so bad? I sound sulky. I don't want to sound sulky. *I had to get away . . . I was worried about my own wild. I didn't* ask *him to save me—*

Kester. When the stag is stern he makes me nervous, even in his weakened state. He rests up on his front legs and flicks his sharp horns toward me. *Enough of what has been. The dream foretold this would pass. Which is why I did not tell you.*

You mean it was some kind of test? I know he's been injured. I know there are drugs coursing through his system, making him tired. But this really isn't fair. How can

I make a decision about something I don't know about? *Maybe if you just told me what it said, then maybe I could do something right for once!*

The animals glance at one another in the dusk.

It is not that simple. The dream is not like one of your human stories . . . It is . . . something else.

Tell me!

The mouse is doing one of her worry dances, which mainly involve shaking her head a lot. *The dream is sacred to animals only, stag. It is the story of creation itself. We must not share it. Not even with a human with the gift.*

That would be most irregular, agrees the General.

It goes against our every animal law, but . . . who knows how many of those have been broken today in the land under our feet. Perhaps one more won't make any difference.

He takes a short breath.

This is the moment. He is going to tell me the dream, the secret animal story that has foretold everything that we've done together so far. The story that began at the First Fold, where men first kept animals for food and clothes. When men lived in painted caves like the Underearth and drew wolves on the walls in blood.

I cannot tell you the whole dream, Wildness, he begins. *We would be here a lifetime. But we shall sing you the final lines—which no animal forgets once it has heard them.*

Then, without being summoned, the mouse and cockroach gather in a circle with the stag. They begin to hum. As they hum, as if the clouds have cleared, I feel light on my face, burning with an intensity that I could not have imagined. Every cell in my body is listening and waiting as the hum turns into words that they sing together. As their words begin to cry and roar in my head, pictures seem to rise up before us in the glade. Terrible pictures.

> *Listen! For this is the end of that dream*
> *Which we have told one another since the beginning*
> *In the tongue that only animals can understand.*
> *We dreamed we saw a host of creatures*
> *Rise up out of the earth and cover it with darkness.*
> *The fiercest of all animals!*
> *Men bent down and wept for what they had done*
> *Fearful was it to behold*
> *Beasts and men tearing one another apart.*
> *Their blood ran freely.*
> *The sky turned black and wept many tears.*
> *Truly it was the storm of storms, the end of all things.*
> *The sky's tears filled the great wet*
> *And those waters spilled out over the earth*
> *Covering us all—*

Wait! I interrupt.

The sounds and pictures crumble away into blackness. Fear pulses through my body, blinding me, making me feel sick and dizzy. I don't want to know.

The stag looks at me, startled. *But we haven't finished. The final verse is—we believe it is about you.*

I stand up. *You were right not to say. I don't want to know what happens to me. Just tell me what I need to do to stop it.*

It's very simple, says the stag. *The dream says you need to bring the dark into the light.*

How?

The stag's expression softens, as if it was the most obvious thing in the world. *You need to show them that humans can be good.*

But I've told them—I told them about the cure, I told them about the Iris, it didn't make any difference—

No, he says, eyes burning bright. *I said you need to show them.*

The words and the pictures of the animals' dream burn my brain up with ideas of what I need to do. I realize I at last have a plan that might work.

I have the Iris. The one thing that Aida and Littleman say could make the world well again, take it back to how it was. If I could get them Polly's notebook, perhaps they could make sense of it. Perhaps then we could show Dagger's wild that not all humans are bad.

Before we do anything, though, the stag needs to get his strength back. The General and I leave the mouse to keep him company in the Garden of the Dead, picking mud and grass out of his fur and occasionally doing a gentle Dance of Nursing to Health (which mainly involves blowing on the deer's nose).

I return in the evening with blankets to keep him comfortable and warm. With a screwdriver I scrape lengths of bark off our old apple trees for him to feed on. The normal colour of his deep brown eyes is beginning to return, but the combination of the tranquillizer and the lingering traces of cure in his system makes him sleepier than ever.

I still don't know why the cullers only tranquillized the stag rather than shooting him or capturing him. Perhaps it was a mistake in the heat of the moment.

It is not just the stag who needs time to recover, though. I wash off all the dirt and dust of the Underearth in the shower, hearing no more whispering from the drain. The silence makes me feel even more alone in the empty house, as if the dark wild have been swallowed up by the earth completely, and I shiver as I dress myself in the mirror.

I patch my cuts and bites up as best as I can. There is a bit of formula left in the kitchen, and I make it last longer as she would have done, mixing it with berries and leaves scavenged from the garden.

It's not just me who needs patching up. I use Dad's screwdriver to replace the watch battery, and try to repair my torn scarf.

I fix the front door, not perfectly, but it shuts and locks if you give a good push. Then I tidy up Dad's lab, righting desks and straightening what few papers are left back in piles, and put all the drawers and boxes of Mum's stuff back where they belong in Polly's room.

I don't know how many days go by like this. All I know is that the clouds keep getting thicker and darker. As they grow thicker, everything feels hotter and stickier too. Even the General notices that it's getting harder to tell the difference between day and night. While he and the mouse take turns spending time with the stag as he recovers, I stare out of my window at the sky and try not to think about the storm of storms.

But what I can tell, as the clouds occasionally part, is that the moon is changing. It's getting smaller. Like the white disc is being eaten by the darkness around it, slowly shrinking, until only a thin sliver of a crescent remains.

No helicopter comes, nor can we hear any elsewhere in the city. It is as if we have been abandoned by everyone and everything—our Culdee Sack could be an island cut off from the city.

While we wait for the stag to regain his full strength, I look again and again at the Iris microdots in Polly's book under Dad's microscope. All of his computers have been smashed, their innards gutted by the cullers.

But in his room his old books remain untouched, stacked up in dusty piles by the bed. I sit cross-legged on the floor and go through each one, trying to find any clue as to what the dots mean, what the Iris could be. And very slowly, making page after page of scrawled notes, I think I begin to find one.

There are billions of dots in Polly's Iris Capsule, each dot containing vital information—the information that might show Dagger and his wild that humans can help make this earth a better place.

I know what the Iris is. It's not just one thing, it's a collection of them.

As the murky light fades for another day, I turn off the microscope, carefully close Polly's notebook, and hear a scratching at the lab windows.

The stag is standing on the steps, his fur looking golden and sleek again in the light from the house. The mouse twirls on his back in multiple Dances of Anticipation, while the General stands proud on his horns, his shell gleaming. I slide Polly's book back into her bag and pick my scarf up off the chair.

We have the most valuable data in the world, data that could reset the world. But it's next to useless without the people who collected it in the first place—Polly and her parents, locked up in the Four Towers, along with Dad and my wild.

So now I'm going to get them out—with a little help from my friends.

Sitting astride the stag, as he clip-clops his way away along the Culdee Sack, following my directions to Waste Town, I have a feeling deep inside me that I will never go back.

I don't know why. I hope so much that I will find my family of Dad, Polly, and the wild, but somehow I don't think this house can ever be our home again.

But as I turn to look at it one last time in the dusk, I see something I was not expecting.

A pair of headlights slowly sliding out of a side road after us. Headlights that belong to a bike, but not like the ones ridden by Aida's gang. In the dull orange of the street-lights, I can see a motorbike's metallic purple hood, the yellow band across the front.

A Facto bike.

They were waiting. And I realize why they left the stag

and only tranquillized him. They didn't find what they were looking for on their first visit.

Polly must have told them that the Iris was at the Culdee Sack but managed to keep exactly where a secret. Which would be typical of her. Now they've waited all this time for me to show them—but they're going to be disappointed.

Stag, I say quietly, even though I know they won't be able to hear. *I think we're being—*

I know, he says.

Of course. A great stag will always know when he's being followed; even when he's being looked at from miles away, or watched for hours on end—he always knows.

He sniffs the air and trots off the road I've been guiding him along, into a narrow alley running behind a row of houses. It is just wide enough for him to walk down without his horns scraping the sides. The alley is unlit and smells damp.

This is not the road I told you to take, Stag, I say.

Perhaps not. But it's the way to escape. You forget that's what I've been learning every day since I was born—how to avoid the human.

Behind us, the patrol bike purrs into the alley, keeping a steady distance as they edge after us. The mouse crawls into my pocket, shaking, while the General marches to the back of the stag, yelling insults at our pursuers.

The stag emerges from the alley, moving with the speed I remember from our first meeting in the Ring of Trees.

With a growl of acceleration, the bike smoothly follows, but they can't follow where the stag goes next.

He crosses the street head-on, making for a low wall ahead of us, which he leaps in a single bound. We land in a garden. In the pale light from a house, I see a sundial on a column and a pond full of weeds. Then we jump over an ivy-clad fence into another garden, the stag avoiding scattered plastic toys. And again, leaping over the covered pool running down the centre.

I am bent low over the stag to stay on with each jump, the mouse doing a Dance of Tell Me When It's All Over so close to my skin that I can feel every one of her heartbeats.

Barely drawing a breath, the stag takes us down the whole street over walls, fences, and even a washing line—a sheet flapping in my face and blinding me for a moment. Then we are scraping a holly bush that crowns a whole wall before cracking onto the pavement of the open streets again.

The stag pauses for a moment, catching his breath. And to our left two yellow bike lights slide out of the next street, searching us out.

Then we are off again, down this street, crossing that one, keeping to the darkest shadows we can find. Shadows that end in large metal rubbish bins, a pile of cardboard boxes, and a wall too high to jump. We canter round to find ourselves facing the two yellow lights.

The more I stare at them, the more they seem like eyes,

the yellow band around the purple bike like a mad, fixed smile. The bike snarls toward us.

Hold on, says the stag, and runs straight at it—

As we leap, I can hear his hoofs clip the metal of a helmet.

Now the chase is on, the stag galloping as fast as he can, the bike roaring after us—

It must be here somewhere, says the stag to himself, as if he has been here before, as if he knows the city better than I do. He is less calm and steady now, snorting, stamping his feet, frightened, his head trembling as he looks for a way out of this maze of hard streets.

There is no time to rest; the bike is nudging up behind us, letting out petrol-throated roars. I can feel the heat of it—

And we skid round a corner, finding ourselves on a wide street, with a wall of railings at the end, darkness beyond them. The stag gives a short sigh of relief and charges toward the gates.

I can't look, says the mouse, and buries her face in my scarf.

Coward! says the General, suddenly appearing on my shoulder. *Now this stag can really show us what he's made of.*

The arched gates are tied tight together with a chain and a padlock. In front of them stands a set of dusty striped hazard barriers with a sign dangling over the front.

NO ENTRY

Fuzzy clouds of something overhang the railings, push-ing spikes out between the metal. And I realize it's a place I had completely forgotten ever even existed in this city.

We're heading for the park.

The stag snorts and, taking a deep breath, gallops hard toward the arched iron gates. Behind us the Facto bike speeds up till it's running alongside.

The gates are so tall, ivy wound around the railings—

I can see two cullers on the bike, black and helmeted, reaching out toward us, trying to grab something.

Polly's bag, which dangles from my shoulder.

I snatch it away as the hands lunge again.

The stag pulls back his haunches and leaps, higher and farther than he ever has before. As the cockroach cheers, the stag clips the hazard barriers, and then we are sailing over the gates so close their spiked tips must graze his belly.

He grunts as we land on the grassy surface on the other side, and his head drops, gasping for breath.

From outside the gates, I can hear the bike skidding to a halt, the engine thrumming, while the cullers shout to each other. They are rattling the chain.

Stag, we don't have long. They'll break in soon.

I know, he says. *And then we shall see who is the mas-ter in here.*

Facto called the parks a "breeding ground for infec-tion" and cleared out the animals. Everyone thought they had been culled, but I know now where many of them went.

I remember coming to parks like this before the virus. When Mum was still alive. They were where I learned to ride a bike, racing my friends, doing wheelies . . . then eating sandwiches and drinking orange juice under the trees. Maybe in another world that's what I'd be doing with Aida and Polly, rather than persuading one to help me break the other out of prison.

Now this park is empty and silent, apart from us moving swiftly through the trees and bushes. I wonder for a moment if the Iris will bring the old park back. Or whether it will be overrun by Dagger's dark wild. But only for a moment, as behind us a pair of rusted gates clang open, a motorbike purring through, lights searching us out.

I clutch Polly's bag with the Iris book close to my chest.

Be still, orders the stag. *Learn to be still like me, and they will not see us.*

It is true. He has come to a complete stop in a cluster of trees and bushes, standing as still as one of the old park statues, every muscle as taut as a violin string beneath me. One on each shoulder, the cockroach and mouse are motionless too, antennae and whiskers tickling my neck.

It's still a dance, the mouse hisses. *The Dance of Stillness.*

Their breathing is controlled and steady. I try to copy them, but it's hard.

Close your eyes, says the stag. *Imagine you are not even here.*

I close my eyes. I try to be more like an animal. An animal hiding in the bushes in a park. How many birds, foxes, and squirrels have done exactly what I'm doing now, as walkers and their dogs went past before, none the wiser?

I can feel the soft air from the trees clustered around us, their woody smell. And I can feel the yellow light from a bike, flooding through my closed eyelids, passing across us all.

I hold my breath.

The bike hums just on the other side of the foliage, as if it is thinking. Then the machine crawls on along the path, searching other trees and bushes.

My shoulders sink as I breathe out, but the stag snaps, *Stay still! They will be back!*

And they are. They reverse with a whine, turning to face us, the yellow lights spreading full across us. They must have seen, they must have. I can hear the boots of the cullers as they dismount and what sounds like them unclipping something from the side of the bike.

Softly they tread up the slope toward us, crunching on scattered dry leaves and twigs. They part the bush branches so carefully, as if they were made of tissue and glue and could fall apart at any moment, and I see a dark figure squeeze through the gaps. I can hear his breathing; he must be able to hear mine.

Two feet planted right in front of us. A dart gun raised to a shoulder.

Now! says the stag, leaping into him, knocking him back with his hoofs, racing through the bushes, not caring how many branches whip and scratch us, as he knocks their bike over too. We're running down the hill, their shouts echoing around us.

Then the roar of the bike spreads out across the deserted park. A roar so loud and so mad I feel it will blow the cobwebs off the statues and the drift of leaves out of the dry fountain and the rust off the slowly creaking swing.

But it doesn't matter.

Because we are running faster than the wind, disappearing into the night before it even touches us.

Littleman is seated in a salvaged helicopter seat, which squeaks every time he moves, like it's in pain. The shelves on the wall behind him are stuffed with the mechanical guts of cars: the oily rib cages of half-dismembered engines, jars of cogs and gears, boxes full of circuit boards.

Even though the thick clouds gathered above the Waste Mountain are keeping everything in here at a sweltering temperature, the leader of the gang has a small gas heater, making all of us crowded into his shack drip with sweat.

The old-young man in the sun hat turns his bike horn over in his hands, thinking. Then he looks once again down into his lap, at the pages of scrawled notes I made at home before we left.

"Let me get this straight," he says. "You say some squirrels stopped the formula train, rather than you." *Parp!* He peers at me from under his drooping hat. Aida, leaning against the scaffolding pole doorway behind me, shifts from foot to foot. "You say that they were rescuing the wolves discovered in the formula train."

Parp!

The wolf-cub, lying at Littleman's feet, turns and twists his head sadly at me. I bite my lip. I have not yet told him the lies his mother told in the Underearth, what she said about her own cub. I am not sure I ever will.

"That my dog chased those same wolves into the tunnel, and that when you pursued them you found out he was in fact leading them into a secret cave miles below, full of all the disappeared animals from the city. Who are planning to take it back and kill us all."

Kind of.

"So now you have come back to us, your nonexistent tail between your legs, having run away—for what exactly?" He pulls at the metal chain chafing at the wolf-cub's neck, secured to one of the scaffolding poles. "To rescue your friend here?"

Parp!

"Then what, I wonder . . . ?"

He crouches down by the gas heater. One by one, he takes the notes and feeds them into the grill. The wolf-cub shies away in alarm, but he can't move far because of the chain.

The notes spark, flame, and crumble into ash on the filthy floor. Littleman watches them burn, the fire flickering on his sunglasses. Then he turns to face us all, his shiny face red with heat.

"I know! You want our help now, is that it? To stop my dog murdering thousands of us in our beds?"

He grins at all the children packed round the shack, and they titter back. The grin vanishes as quickly as it came.

"I mean, my dear—apart from the fact that I've never heard such a load of absolute cobblers in all my life—why should we even begin to believe you? I let you make off with my young associate here on some ill-fated caper to hold Facto to ransom. I gave you my trust. And yet all that happened was more animals kept turning up, wherever you went. Wolves that ate our formula. Then you stole my one animal and a bike. You don't return either of those, but instead reappear at my door with more illegal animals. Worst of all, there is still no sign of the Iris. Which, if I recall, was where we began."

Glaring at him, I reach into Polly's bag at my feet and pull out the battered black leather notebook.

He grasps it in his wrinkled hand. "What's this? A book?" Littleman says it like he's never seen one before, thumbing through the pages right through to the end, peering at some of Polly's drawings, flicking backwards and forwards. He turns his nose up before offering it back to me. "Very pretty, but not for me."

I try to stop my hands from trembling as I take the precious book back.

Littleman leaps up, jutting his chin in my face. "I'll tell you why that's not the Iris, my friend." He looks around the room. "The Iris is the greatest prize in the world, a thing of immense value—not a child's book of drawings. You still don't know what the Iris is, do you?"

But that is where he is wrong, so very wrong. My time in Dad's lab, and reading his books, was not wasted.

For a moment Littleman's gaze flickers, but it's only a second and then he claps his hands together, rubbing them with glee. "Well, my dear, why don't you tell us then?"

Everyone in the crowded, junk-filled shack turns to stare at me. Eric, 123, and the others. On all their faces I see the hunger to know what the Iris is. They really don't know. But Aida is the only one to speak. "You know, he right. You have a lot to answer for. I don't like it when people run away from me." She comes right up close. And I can't believe it, but are those tears in her eyes? "Do you have any idea what the Iris means? When you have only one thing to believe in, one thing that could make any of this"—she gestures to the walls groaning with rubbish—"better? So make this good, or else."

I feel my face go pale, and swallow. The meaner she is to me, the more I want to impress her.

I can't speak. I don't have pictures that can appear on an ultrascreen at the click of a finger. There isn't time to write this down. I only have the memory of a game Mum and Dad and I used to play in the winter sometimes.

So, the light from the gas fire throwing big shadows against the canvas walls of the shack, I step forward and tell them everything I know.

I draw pictures in the air, of what Littleman told me

before, and what I already knew. Polly's parents collecting bones and fossils. The bones and fossils I saw in their library, stored in dusty bottles and jars—like the one full of gear cogs on Littleman's shelf that I grab now, emptying it onto the floor.

I hold up the empty jar, and the General dives in from my shoulder to complete the illustration. The remains of insects the Goodacres saved while the virus was rampaging around them. And not just fossilized insects, but bones from animals that I point at now—like the wolf-cub.

Remains that they didn't just store, but noted and examined.

Down to the last microscopic detail.

The tiny building blocks of life itself, that made up every single creature stolen from the world by the virus and the cullers. Polly's parents must have collected their remains so carefully until they had enough. From cows to chickens, owls to otters, hawks to hedgehogs, badgers to bees.

I know exactly what the Iris is.

I made sure before I set foot in here again.

I loosen my scarf and unzip my jacket to show the T-shirt I painted myself, sitting on Polly's empty bed, using a mixture of soil and water I know she would have approved of.

Just three letters. Three letters that, like the dots in the notebook, contain everything we've lost. Everything we could have again.

DNA

I pored over Dad's books, following where he had under-lined and highlighted sections. Many of those sections had lists of numbers, like the ones in Polly's book, that looked like more codes. I discovered that the Iris numbers look like a code because they *are* a code. A genetic code—one for every animal, bird, insect, and fish that we have lost.

But perhaps if we have their DNA, we haven't lost them forever.

Perhaps we could bring them back.

The air in the shack under the rubbish dome is thick and warm. I mop my forehead and give a little bow, but no one claps.

Parp . . . Parp . . . Parp! Instead Littleman gives three short blasts of his horn and runs his finger across his top lip. "Well, I never. You quite sure of this?"

He sounds almost disappointed. When it is clearly THE MOST AMAZING THING IN THE WORLD. The old-young man laughs at my expression. "I mean, you're not as stupid as you look, boy, I'll give you that. It's just . . . not exactly what I was expecting." He rubs his hands and there is a little twinkle in his bloodshot eyes. "And you're absolutely sure there's no mention of any valuable weapon?"

Aida grabs the notebook out of my hand, glowering at him. "Don't you see? Of course a weapon. The best one against Facto there is. Bring the animals and fruit and vegetables back, they lose their power like that! Boom!"

Her boss throws his hands up in the air. "Aida, my sweet. You're a genius! If this boy is right, where would Mr. Stone and his Facto and his formula be? Gone, that's where! Banished to the back of beyond." Littleman pauses for a moment, thinking, a far-off look in his eyes. "The world would have animals again, we would have normal food once more, and perhaps"—he stands up and tightens his sun hat around his chin—"someone more responsible and caring could be put in charge this time."

Food. It always comes back to food with the grown-ups. Never just the animals.

"So can you imagine how much danger I would have placed you all in if those nice gentlemen on their bikes and helicopters had even got a whiff of what it was? I had nothing but your own safety in mind, my sweet, as ever."

He reaches out a claw to touch her shoulder, but she twists away.

"So now what?" she says, still scowling.

"A very good point, my sweet, succinctly put as usual. There's just one problem." He taps at the book with his grubby trainer. "This might be the code, if young Jaynes here is right in his deductions. But how do we actually bring the animals back? How do we realize the value?" Littleman hops over, clenching my neck, whispering stale formula breath in my ear again. "You're not that clever, though, are you, my dear?" He looks meanly at my animal friends. "And I very much doubt you know anyone who is."

Parp!

But that's where he's so very wrong.

He looks at me, a smile of realization slowly creeping over his face. "Oh, but you do, of course! How foolish of me." Littleman picks up an electric cattle prod off the floor, making it fizz and hum. He licks his finger and dabs it in between the sparks, enjoying the shock that ripples up his arm. "But that would also be extremely dangerous, would it not?"

Aida looks fearful for the first time since I've known her. "I don't get it."

I take her hands and she tries to snatch them back, but I hold them firm. I can't do this without her. Because, slowly, as her hands tighten round mine, I see she understands.

"No way—are you crazy?"

Maybe. But I also have the Iris. A code that could restart the world. A code that could show the dark wild how humans can be good. A code that only two people in the world understand.

And we're going to break them out of the Four Towers.

PART 5

THE FOUR TOWERS

Premium is so full of constant noise that it feels like the whispering from the Underearth has already erupted to the surface. But there are no foxes or rats to be seen, just people and traffic swelling onto the streets under a stormy sky.

A sky that seems to have turned the day into night, with clouds that have nearly blocked out all the light. They look more like they are made out of coal dust than raindrops.

But it frightens me more when I can't see clouds.

Because then all I can see is the tiniest thumbnail sliver of moon disappearing into darkness. I know what will happen when it vanishes completely, who will come from the ground below . . .

Which is why it's all the more important that we get the Iris to Polly and her parents as quickly as possible.

Sweat pours down our faces as we weave our way through the back streets, over the bridge, and along the far bank of the River Ams.

What the animals would call a fish-road now smells of chemicals and machines. We move along metal walkways that sway and clank underneath us, lit by swinging lamps that shouldn't need to be on at this time of the afternoon. To our right, an abandoned barge lies beached on a muddy bank, seaweed trails weeping out of its porthole eyes. Above, a rusting crane creaks in the breeze.

"I don't like this," mutters Aida. "It too quiet."

Ahead, our destination rises into view. The walkways fade away into gleaming steel fences that run right down to the waterline.

Four black chimneys that look like upside-down table legs loom high above a giant smoke-stained brick factory, built around a central glass dome. Red warning lights flicker down the sides of the towers, and bundles of razor wire cover the perimeter fences.

Behind them, and encircling the Four Towers like a moat, are parking lots floodlit by security lamps. Purple formula lorries, culler vans, and patrol bikes shine in row after neat row.

We're not attacking just yet. Littleman thought, again, that would be too dangerous. "Why do you children never consider the potential cost of these jaunts?" he muttered. Then he went into his shack on his own for a while, before coming out in a much better mood, rubbing his hands. "A compromise, my dears! Perhaps you and Aida should mount a little reconnaissance mission first? See if you can find us an affordable way into the Facto fortress. And by affordable, I mean cheap. And by cheap, I mean—don't lose any more bikes."

A wind is blowing along the river now, ruffling the water up into little quiffs. Either the banks are lower here or the river has grown deeper; it laps over the edge, splashing us. I have never known weather like this, feeling warm and cold at the same time—and I loosen the scarf drawn tight around my neck, fold it up, and pack it away in Polly's rucksack, slung over my back. As I do, I wonder for a moment whether it was wise to bring it out here with us, but there is no way I was going to leave the bag's world-changing contents anywhere within Littleman's reach.

Aida stops her bike to look out across the choppy waves. There are no more abandoned boats or cranes now, but sleek warehouses drop straight to the river's edge, and there are revolving camera eyes on every corner.

I shrink away from the cameras, but she grips my shoulder tight. "Littleman take care of all that. He playing some very different footage into those cameras, OK? Now listen. It's time I told you something you don't know about me."

She points over to the other side of the road, at a shadowy hulk of a building squatting opposite the Facto front gates—a deserted-looking block of flats with identical doors and windows running behind long balconies. "We used to live here. My mother and me. It wasn't much, but it home." She looks at the empty balcony for a moment. "Now all it good for is spying. We watch them towers from here and find a way in."

We push on toward the abandoned flats, dimming our bike lights just to be sure. The wind blowing across the water grows stronger as she carries on with her story.

"My mother and me, we make each other happy. She my friend too. My real best friend, you understand?" She turns and stares, waiting until I nod. "Mum a teacher, but also a journalist. Telling stories, she called it, only real ones. About people, the world around her, about companies."

She lets the last word hang in the air. "Not that it made her much money. I just went to school, did what I was told. Till she got a big story one day."

In front of the flats is a dead lawn, all mud and moss. We cycle carefully across it, trying not to slip. She seems to know just where she's going and doesn't even glance at the faded sign:

MAYDOOR ESTATE

"It was a real big story," she says, as we bounce our bikes up a dank stairwell. "About Facto. Said she always thought they were up to no good. They took over so much after the red-eye. Mum always checking them out, but she never got much. 'Squeaky clean,' she said."

The stairs lead to one of the long walkways, a row of silent doors and windows ahead of us. We look out at the Four Towers, the blinking red lights, the sharp fences.

Then we lay our bikes on the ground and crouch down behind the parapet.

"Things change when they took over this place," says Aida, whispering now. "Six years ago."

When I got sent to Spectrum Hall for no reason. When they locked Dad up in his basement for trying to find a cure.

"They buy up these towers and all the land next to them. Like our home, this place right here. Stone said it for the good of the country and all that, that they need privacy, security for all their 'scientific research.' Mum not having any of it. She start to dig, you understand?"

Aida's eyes are fierce and bright in the reflected warning lights across the way.

"One day she find something. She come home and tell me, excited, but real frightened too. 'The story of a lifetime,' she say. About what really happening in them Four Towers. It not just an office. It not just a formula warehouse. It something else—"

I can imagine. A prison. An animal killing ground.

She shakes her head, as if she can guess my thoughts.

"Like nothing you could ever even imagine, she say. Nothing about a virus or a cure. She say Stone building something in secret, that the world had to know about it."

The wind whips down the river.

"Then, one day—she go to work and never comes back."

I spread my arms out. And?

"And that's it. I never saw her again. They came to take me away." I wonder if she would have ended up at

Spectrum Hall if they had got her. "But I ran away on my bike. I learn to live on the streets until Littleman found me. He had computers, I had the bike, and so . . . That's how we start the gang." She gives a short sigh, like she doesn't want to let it out but keep it tight inside her. "Not all stories have a happy ending like yours, you know."

I'm not sure mine has ended. Right now it doesn't feel that happy either. But I try to give her a hug anyway. She scowls and pulls away to peer over the walkway, where we have a direct view of the Four Towers' main entrance.

With our binoculars we watch Facto vans trundle in and out of the gates, a red-and-white security barrier going up and down to let them in, up and down, up and down . . . I rub my eyes to try to stay awake.

Then the trucks stop coming and going. There is silence down on the street below. All we can hear is the wind ruffling the water, the distant hum of the city, and an occasional angry voice in my rucksack.

I say! Are we there yet? The mouse and I are allies, but I cannot guarantee how much longer that will last in these conditions.

Be patient, General, I say. *I'll let you know when it's safe to come out.*

Littleman insisted we go on our own to avoid attracting any attention, and refused to let the wolf-cub or stag come with us. But he didn't know about the two secret passengers in Polly's bag.

We huddle behind the wall a bit longer, Aida noting

down the times the trucks enter and leave, scanning the entire perimeter fence through her binoculars for any weak spot, any unlit or unwatched point we could make our target.

Then she touches my arm. "Wait—can you hear that?"

I shake my head. For once I can't hear anything.

"Listen. Like a tapping."

And then I can. A very faint *tap-tap-tapping* out in the darkness. I shrug. It's probably the wind from the river, rattling the fences.

"I think it coming from here," she says.

I listen some more. It does now seem to be coming from around here. Perhaps a loose board over a door then.

Her hand tightens around the prod dangling from her belt. "It getting closer."

She's right. It is.

A *tap-tap-tapping* across concrete.

A tapping that is coming up the stairwell, step by step.

I try not to listen to my heart beginning to pound in my chest. Aida stands up, brandishing her prod, and I grip mine as we face the stairs. The tapping stops, but whatever is making the noise is still shrouded in shadow.

"Show yourself," challenges Aida. "We not afraid of you."

There is a pause, the sound of rustling cloth, another faint *tap*.

"Oh, excusing me," says a cracked foreign voice. "But you should be afraid, girl-childrens. Very afraid indeed."

As if a cold hand has reached out from the dark and squeezed my heart tight, I realize who it is. I try to warn Aida, but it's too late.

Crook-backed, stepping out from the shadows on not one, not two, but four crutches now, like a monster spider with a white human face—

Captain Skuldiss.

Selwyn Stone's chief culler, the man I thought the stag had killed at the battle of the Culdee Sack, stands before us living and breathing.

Aida fires a fizzing electric charge from her prod, but with a flick of his crutch Skuldiss sends her weapon flying over the parapet. I hear hurried boot steps and clanking belts behind us and whirl round to see the other end of the walkway filled with masked cullers, dart guns raised.

Aida steps back toward me, reaching out for my hand.

Skuldiss leers at us. I can see now that his legs, broken after the stag flung him in the air, have been replaced by metal poles, and he still leans on his original crutches. His face is scratched and scarred but is otherwise as pale as ever.

"Hello again, boy-childrens," he says. "You like magic tricks? Oh, good. My first one, rising from the dead!" He bends what remains of his body in a stiff bow.

All I remember is the cullers dragging his limp and bloody body away after the stag tossed him in the air, then their van reversing at full speed out of the Culdee Sack . . .

"And for my next trick—" He raises his right crutch. A telescopic arm shoots out, with pincers on the end. They snap open and shut like a robotic crab. "I believe you have something for me."

"It's a trap," says Aida dully.

I raise my prod. "No!"

"Oh yes, yes, *yes*, I'm afraid!" He giggles. "I haven't been reading a good book in ages." And with a mechanical whine, the crutch arm extends until it is touching my chest. "How about . . . yes, let me see . . ." And his eyes narrow into slits. "Maybe you have one in your bags you would like to be sharing?"

His pincers grab my wrist, squeezing it tight till I drop my prod with a clatter. But he doesn't let go. "Now, boy-childrens," says Skuldiss, as he begins to twist my arm around, "give me the Iris, or I will snap your jolly arm clean out of its socket."

Aida looks at me. "Don't give it to him, Kester. It's not worth it."

"Oh really, girl-childrens?" asks Captain Skuldiss, as he twists my wrist some more, sending a wave of agony up my arm that makes me gasp for breath and my stomach heave.

I don't think I have any option. I hold up my free hand and feel the pincers soften their grip.

"What you doing?" asks Aida in disbelief. "Don't give it them. They destroyed everything. They monsters."

I know. But she has to trust me, whether she likes it or not. Not taking my eyes off her, I stretch out my free arm to put Polly's bag on the ground.

"Nice and gentles, please, little boy-childrens," warns Skuldiss, "No fun and games unless you want a broken wristy."

Slowly I pick the bag up. I didn't expect Skuldiss. But after everything I've been through to find Polly's secret, I did plan to keep it safe. *Mouse. General,* I say, trying to keep my face as blank as I can. *Are you ready?*

Oh, bless my heart! says the mouse from the rucksack. *I don't fancy our chances much.*

Nonsense! All you have to do is follow my orders exactly, chides the General.

That's just what I'm worried about, she says.

As I offer the bag to Skuldiss, I tip it up, and the cockroach and the mouse tumble out onto the ground. For a moment they freeze in the light. A wave of colour floods the Captain's pale face. It was the General's tiny jaws that helped win the battle of the Culdee Sack.

Beasties! he yells at the cullers behind us. *Get them!*

But my friends are too fast, darting between the heavy boots before the men even spot them.

Run for your lives! I shout. *Bring help as soon as you can!*

Then they are gone, disappearing into the night.

Skuldiss whacks his spare crutch on the ground in frustration. Then, composing himself, he hooks the crutch into the bag and drags it toward him along the ground.

Aida refuses to meet my gaze as he roots around in the rucksack, clawing Polly's book out and up into his hands. She's fuming. "Are you crazy? You just give him it, just like that? Have you ever fought for anything? Anything at all?"

She has to trust me. There wasn't time to explain before we left.

"The famous notebook," he says, "at last." He loosens the pincers around my wrist. It's really sore, and I rub it, but it doesn't make the redness or the pain go away.

He flicks feverishly through the pages. He flicks fast, and then he flicks slow. He holds the book upside down and peers at the cover, licks his finger and tries to separate a single page into two. Then he grips it tight with both hands and holds the open book up to our faces, screaming, "Where is it?"

And now Aida can see what I knew he would find.

Where the Iris page once was, there is only a ragged and ripped seam.

Skuldiss's face is contorted, and he jabs me in the chest with the pincers. "Where is the Iris page?" he yells.

Now Aida is actually laughing for the first time ever,

and the cullers are looking at their feet, not sure what to do.

I can't tell him. Even if I could, it wouldn't matter how many times or how hard he jabbed me in the chest. Because it's not going to bring the mouse back, with the piece of paper everyone in the world wants carefully balled up in the pouches of her cheeks.

Handcuffed, we follow Skuldiss down a long corridor with metal walls and porthole windows. We could be in a submarine. Aida skulks behind me, getting jabs in the back from a culler's dart gun when she drags her feet.

The Four Towers is full of strange noises. An elevator whizzing up and down somewhere, a humming engine far beneath our feet . . . and a cry that could be the screech of machinery or something else.

Something that I don't want to think about.

What I do want to think about, what I can't stop thinking about, is the faces we are just about to see. We might have been captured, but it's got us right where we wanted to be. I never thought I could be handcuffed, under armed guard, and so happy as I am right now. Whatever Skuldiss says or does, I'm inside the Four Towers and one step nearer to seeing the person I have looked for and missed for so long.

"What you smiling about?" says Aida suspiciously.

I shrug.

Then the Captain stops by a large metal door in the wall studded with rivets and wide enough to drive a tank through. He leers at me and then, raising a single crutch, taps out a code in the box on the wall.

I try to look like I'm not watching or listening.

With a groan, the door shudders open, revealing a large container with girders for walls and a solid iron floor. On the Captain's signal, the cullers shove Aida and me in before we can resist. I turn around just in time to see the massive door sliding shut on Skuldiss's white face.

"Don't get too comfortable, childrens," he says as the door seals us in. "We have a lot of talking to do. I am very good at making people talk."

Then we hear him *tap-tapping* away up the corridor, leaving us alone in the iron box, huddling all alone underneath one single weak bulb, the container's corners full of shadows.

At least, I think we're all alone. Every noise we make seems to echo, like we're in a big hall. It's hard to tell if everything we hear is an echo of our own sounds, or something else . . .

"Who's there?" says Aida.

And then I can hear a shuffling sound, from the shadows at the end of the room. There's someone walking toward us.

Her hair is grimy and bedraggled, her face smudged with dirt, deep rings around her eyes. But it is still *her* hair, *her* face. The face I have seen in my dreams every night since she left us. Who was never by my side but always in my mind—on the railway line, in the tunnel, underground, when I found her book, being chased through the park—

A little girl. Who happens to be my best friend in the world. And she's holding a toad in her arms.

"You took your time, Kidnapper," Polly says in a broken voice.

We look at each other for a moment.

Then the toad has jumped onto the floor, croaking and hopping like he doesn't care who hears him, and Polly and I are hugging so tight, and she's sobbing onto my shoulder, and I want to cry too, but I'm too excited.

"Whatever," says Aida, folding her arms.

Polly's words come out in a gabble. "I'm sorry I ran away, but I promised my parents to keep the Iris safe, and I just thought the best thing would be to . . ."

I know, leave it in the most obvious place and send everyone, me included, on a wild Iris chase.

"And also," she says, "I thought . . ."

"She thought getting picked up by Facto would be the easiest way to find us again," says a voice from elsewhere in the shadows that I don't recognize. "Didn't you, darling?"

I turn round to see a man and a woman whom I recognize from the photos Littleman showed us on his ultrascreen. A tall man with a long nose, his arm around a shorter woman, who has hair and eyes like Polly's. Their clothes are torn and filthy, their faces red and bruised.

"You must be Kester!" says the man, stretching out his hand. "I'm Polly's dad, Simon Goodacre . . . and as I think you've no doubt guessed, this is her mum, my wife, Jane."

"We've heard so much about you," says Polly's mum.

"I wouldn't believe it," says Aida quietly, biting her thumb.

I just look at them blankly, unable to take it all in for a moment.

"You don't mind, do you, Kidnapper?" asks Polly. "You don't mind that I went away on an adventure of my own to find them? And left you to look after the Iris?"

"Please," groans Aida, "give me a break."

"There is nothing to apologize for," booms another voice, one that I recognize very well. "Kes and I put too much pressure on you. You should never have run away, but we understand why you did, don't we, son?"

My dad looks as ruffled and rumpled as usual, probably no different from how he would be out of a prison cell, apart from the tired and drawn lines of his face. He might be tired, but it doesn't stop him from giving me the deepest and warmest hug he can.

He narrows his eyes when he sees Aida, the girl who broke into his house and zapped his hand.

It's OK, Dad, she's on our side, I say, standing protectively in front of her.

"Hmm," he says, rubbing his beard with the injured hand, which still looks puffy and sore.

"How that hand?" asks Aida, in a way that sounds half

like she's saying sorry for hurting it, half threatening to do it again.

But before Dad can reply, the rest of my wild are rushing forward to surround us, leaping into my arms. Even Aida can't resist petting the rabbits, the birds flocking about my head, Polly's toad hopping around, burping for joy—

We're back together again.

The laughter and crying do not last for long.

Instead Aida and I find ourselves doing a lot of talking and explaining. The people we came to rescue have more questions for us than we possibly could have imagined. Between us, Dad translating my replies for everyone else, we tell the story of how I eventually found the Iris and how we were captured just outside the Four Towers, the mouse escaping with the secret drawing stuffed in her cheeks. Then I explain to Dad about Dagger and his dark wild. I reassure the rest of the wild that the stag is all right, and then—

"Shut up!" says Aida. "Everyone shut up, will you?"

Slowly we turn to face her. Hands on her hips, eyes blazing, just like the night she first broke into our house. All our chatter and excitement drift away.

"It's real nice you so happy to see one another again. No, really," she says. "But there's two things that bother me."

Aida points at each of us in turn. "We been high and low for this Iris, this DNA. We bust your house, we stop a train, and now we get thrown in here by that creepy dude on sticks. Mr. Stone wants it. My boss wants it. So now we got it—or that little mouse got it—can we change the world? Can we get out of here somehow and get the world back to how it was? Bring back all them animals and stuff we lost—and blow Facto out of the picture? Because that is all I am in this for, OK?"

There's a very long pause. Dad rubs his beard again, and Mr. Goodacre strokes his long nose. Polly and her mum look a mixture of a bit guilty and like they feel sorry for Aida. The toad goes very quiet.

Now it's my turn not to understand.

Dad breaks the silence at first. "Ah, yes. A very good point, young lady. Now I've been discussing this, you know, with . . ."

But Aida waves her hands about like a windmill. "No, no, no! I don't want any young-lady stuff or discussing. Just tell me."

Polly's dad crouches down to talk to her. "So, the Iris. The thing is, I mean, what you have to understand is that . . . How can I put this? It *is* very powerful . . . I mean that it has the potential to be as powerful as you say, but . . . Oh dear, I'm not explaining this very well, am I? . . . Polly?"

Polly steps in front of Aida. They look at each other for a moment like they're going to hit each other, but luckily they don't, and Polly starts to explain.

"What they're trying to say is the Iris is a weapon against Facto. It is hope. It can be all the things you think it is. A record of everything the virus and the cullers took away. With the data Kester's mouse is keeping safe, we could change the world again. The only problem is . . ."

"You don't know how." Aida's voice is dull, like the bottom of her world just collapsed. I guess, in a way, it has. And not just hers.

"Small correction!" says Polly's mum brightly. *"Simon and I* don't know how *yet.* We were just the collectors."

"Which is why we went to Mons, to meet a scientist who could help us bring our collection back to life," adds Mr. Goodacre. "Sadly, we never got to meet him or hear his ideas."

So that's it. All of that, for some useless data.

I feel Dad's hand on my shoulder. "Don't bow your head so fast, Kes. Mr. Stone may come to regret locking us all up together. If anything, it seems typically thoughtless of him to underestimate us. I'm not the scientist the Goodacres were going to meet, but I am a, you know, scientist and . . . well, we've been having some very interesting conversations. In fact—"

Aida does a zip mime across her mouth. "OK, Professor Beardie, spare me your equations and calculations and stuff. It could still be done, right?"

Looking really offended, Dad huffs and puffs. "I've never been . . . Not in all my . . ." He looks at our waiting faces. "Yes . . . Yes, I believe we could—in time, with the right equipment—bring the Iris to life. But it's not that simple . . ."

Aida zips her mouth again. "All I need to know. Now the second thing." She points at Polly. "You had the Iris. You all knew where it was. Kester found it. Now it gone again. And all because a man on sticks was waiting for us when we came to rescue you."

She lets the meaning of her words sink in as we all watch her.

"No one else knew we even had the Iris. So how come Captain Skuldiss knew? It was a trap. Someone set us up. And it sure wasn't me."

Everyone looks at everyone else. Polly's parents draw her toward them protectively. Dad straightens his dirty tie, trying to look innocent. The toad croaks, as if to say, *Not guilty.*

And we hear, as if in reply, from beyond the iron door— the sound both Aida and I have heard many times before.

The sound of an old-fashioned bike horn.

The door to our Facto cell slides open again.

"I'm so sorry you had to find out this way, my dear, I truly am." There is Littleman, still in his sun hat and baggy shorts, standing next to Captain Skuldiss.

"No! You can't!" says Aida.

"But I can," says Littleman. "I'm afraid it was too irresistible. As soon as I learned what the Iris really was, I knew it was no use to me. I'm a commercial operator, my dear, not a scientist. We couldn't realize its value on our own . . . so I made a phone call to the only company I knew who could. You would never agree, hence your surprise encounter with the Captain here."

I knew he looked too pleased with himself when he came out of his shack and sent us off on our own.

"You double-crossing little toad!" Aida roars.

(And that's not being nice to toads.)

She runs at him, but he grabs her wrists easily in his spotted hands. "Everything for the right price, my sweet. Mr. Stone's terms were more than generous." He looks toward me. "But I hadn't counted on your young friend. The deal is not complete. Which is why we've come for a little chat."

Skuldiss bounds into our cell in a couple of crutch leaps. "You might not want to tell me or my new friend Littleman where the Iris is, boy-childrens. But perhaps you will sing a different tune when we take you to meet the big boss of this whole here caboodle."

I look around. You can see the same thing in absolutely everybody's eyes. Fear.

"Yes indeedy, Kester old chap. It's time for you to have a private little talk with Mr. Selwyn Stone."

After being marched through more portholed double doors in more submarinelike corridors, I don't know what I was expecting Selwyn Stone's office to be like—but it wasn't this.

A softly lit room, with panelled walls and paintings in soft colours. My footsteps echo across a tiled floor as the door slides shut behind me. Ahead, a circle of tall wooden stacks.

Shelves.

It must be some kind of library. I remember the one belonging to Polly's parents at Wind's Edge, full of their leaf and shell collections. Except this one has a strange smell that room didn't. A sharp chemical one.

I go up to inspect the first stack and come face-to-face with an owl, midflight, claws raised, beak open—

I stumble back, nearly falling into the stack behind—

And a fox, like the Guardians of the dark wild, cowering and snarling as if I'm attacking him.

But he makes no noise. These animals are silent, and will be forever.

They look real but they're not. Dad once showed me creatures like these in a museum. When the virus was starting, he showed me animals he thought I might never get to see alive. He showed me round room after room full of lions, tigers, and bears that were just like the ones in here—stuffed.

"Just in case," he said. He was right.

Like then, my gaze bounces off glass: a domed jar over the stuffed owl, a cabinet for the mounted fox.

I catch my breath, my heart thudding.

Going along the shelves, I can't help glancing from side to side at the exhibits around me. Two weasels, frozen in combat for eternity. A giant varnished fish in a frame. An old-fashioned birdcage with silent pigeons perched on the bars.

I duck at the sudden sight of a golden eagle above my head, wings outspread, but it's held still in the air by a dusty chain.

In between the shelves are stag horns and heads mounted on the walls. I look away. I pull open long drawers at the base of each stack and see that they are full of butterflies and beetles pinned under glass lids. And a cockroach, shiny and dead in its drawer. Farther down the corridor, a big white bear on his haunches looms up, jaws wide open with rage, paws outstretched—

"It's all right. He won't bite."

I start, but there's no one there.

"Over here!" calls the voice. It's coming from behind the bear. I would recognize that voice anywhere.

Slowly I walk past the giant animal, touching his fur as I do—it feels stiff and dry. There's bright light seeping round the corner of the final stack of shelves, making the eyes of a stuffed wolf's head glow as if they were on fire.

The chemical smell grows stronger.

I stop in between the shelves, unsure.

"Come, come!" says the voice. "I don't bite either."

I take a deep breath and step around the corner.

The man I last saw in our garden is seated at a small table on a stool, wearing a green apron this time, his sleeves rolled up. There are little beads of sweat on his shiny head.

I can't see what he's doing at first.

In a pool of light from a desk lamp, he's looking at something stretched out on a paper towel. It reminds me of the operating table in Dad's lab, only that doesn't have pots of glue, brushes, and rolls of wire.

Then I see what the something is.

Our red squirrel.

That poor frightened squirrel, who ran out from his hiding place at the wrong moment and who will never run away from anything again. He is now lying stretched out right in front of me, eyes glazed over. Without meaning to, I reach out—

"Tut-tut!" says Mr. Stone, slapping my hand away. "No touching, please, not until I ask you."

He admires the creature for a moment. "A perfect specimen, don't you think?" Seeing the look on my face, he adds, "Don't be sad. Think of it as your gift to my collection. For all the trouble you've caused me."

I want to grab the poor creature, kick the table over, and run as far away from this man as I can. But there's nowhere to run to. Skuldiss and Littleman are waiting outside.

Not waiting for any response, Stone picks up a scalpel from the table and peels the squirrel's fur off, like it was only a costume.

I turn away, bile rising in my throat.

"This is a little hobby of mine," he says as he works. "Keeps me sane from all the madness out there . . ." He points at the animal heads on the walls, and in my mind's eye I see the prisoners down below, the moonless stormy skies above, the overcrowded and hungry city all around. The dark wild deep beneath us, waiting to rise at any moment . . .

I'd rather think of them than of what lies in front of me.

Perhaps Dagger was right. Perhaps we are worse than him and his wild.

Stone prods at the body with his gloved finger. "No

marks, you see. It was a very humane death, like the other animals on display here. You saw for yourself. One single dart, as it was for all the beasts."

I must make a sound, like a gasp, because he raises an eyebrow at me. "Go on, admit it. You and your father, your friends downstairs, you all still think I'm a murderer—some kind of monster."

It's like he can read my mind.

Stone picks up a pair of scissors from the table and, peering over his glasses, does something I can't watch. When I turn back he has laid the mutilated animal back down on the table and is studying me. "You can all think of me what you like. Because I'm just the man in charge, Kester, that's all I am. The head of the company, the head of the country. Sometimes the people in charge have to make difficult decisions for the greater good."

He wipes his gloved hands with a rag.

"Contrary to what you may think, I don't dislike animals. Quite the opposite. Look at this collection!" He points to the shelves and walls behind me, the museum of dead creatures. "Of all the beasts we culled to contain the virus, I instructed my men to always save me one, the finest, if they could—for my little museum. I call it my ark. It's not just for show either." I make a mental note to ask Dad and the Goodacres whether Stone's museum could help them activate the Iris. Its owner studies me. "We're more alike than you think, Kester—we both save animals, don't you see?"

For a moment we both look at the rows of shadowy life-less shelves.

No, I don't see. I don't see at all.

Stone reaches into a box of straw beside him and pulls out a clump, which he begins to press tightly into a bundle.

"But everything I have ever done, I have done for the species I love the most. The human. I've had glass towers built so we all had somewhere to live. With the greatest reluctance I've had thousands of animals humanely culled so we didn't get their virus. The money Facto have made from Formul-A, I've spent on building the Amsguard to keep us safe from the rising seas. And, if you'd let me have that little Iris of yours, I have one final great project in mind. The most ambitious plan of them all." I wonder if that's what Aida's mum found out about. "We're the good guys, Kester! Can't you see that?"

"No," I say. I'm surprised at how loud I sound, my one word echoing off a thousand glass cabinets. But he's wrong.

"A pity," says Stone sharply, looking up for a moment. "You may believe something else, but that's what I believe." He holds up a rough cylinder of straw that he has bound together with wire. "We're really getting there, aren't we?"

Now he starts moulding a lump of blue clay into a small head. "But unfortunately the world has moved on since I made that decision. I'm afraid the planet is rather against us, it seems. Which is why I need the Iris more than ever."

If only he knew just how much the planet was against

him. I clench my fists tight behind my back, my nails digging into my palms to try to stop myself from going crazy. Every second I waste in here, listening to this lecture, the dark wild could be streaming out of the Underearth, ready to destroy everything in their path.

"The weather, then the virus—and now, would you believe it, we're even running out of the raw ingredients for Formul-A." I think the people of Waste Town would believe it all right. "The minerals, vitamins, and dried protein. There's just too many of us for this planet to cope with. . . . Now will you look at that—perfect!"

A model of a squirrel, made out of straw and clay and wire. He begins to tug the fur over it, like a hood. "Perhaps it might have been hasty to have all the animals slaughtered. But that was the decision I made, and I stand by it."

"No," I say, and fold my arms. I start to look around the room to see if there is any way out, any weapon that I could use—

"However, it has come to my attention that certain people have in their possession the scientific data that would make it possible to reverse some effects of that decision. Not only reverse that decision, but also create a whole new world."

Make a new world or bring an old world back? I hadn't thought before that Stone might want the Iris for any other reason than to destroy it.

He picks up a pair of glittering black glass eyes from a tray with his tweezers and presses them into the head of the stuffed squirrel. They seem to catch mine, dead though they are, and fill me with shame.

"Such data," says Stone, "could be extremely dangerous in the hands of the wrong people. You must understand that?"

You bet. Which is why it is in the possession of a mouse very far away.

In trying to stare him out, I accidentally find myself looking at the squirrel. Something I have been trying to avoid since I discovered Stone working on him. I no longer recognize him as a creature I knew. It looks like he once did, but it feels fake. Like an impostor.

So I just turn back to Stone to meet his gaze. I shake my head.

"That is a great pity," he says, producing a brush from his pocket and grooming the fur of the fake squirrel until it almost looks lifelike. He screws the poor thing onto a wooden base, which he swivels and turns to face me. I don't want to look at the black eyes, I can't—

"That is a great pity," he repeats, examining the squirrel, "because if I do not have that information by the end of today, I shall personally take every single one of your precious animals that we have in captivity here and . . . add them to my collection."

A tongue flickers out as he licks the sweat off his top lip. "And nothing will give me greater pleasure than to watch your face as I do."

For a moment we stay in silence.

And deep down, inside, that is the moment.

Buried deep in my brain, an electrical connection is made. I feel it. Thoughts race around my head at the speed of light, turning half thoughts into clear instructions. At least on this, I no longer feel any confusion. Like a massive weight has been lifted off my chest, I realize that no matter what else happens to me, my friends, my family, my wild, or the planet—one thing is for sure.

I will destroy this man.

Not now. But one day. Whatever the price, I will destroy this man in his shiny glasses, and everything he stands for—his empire, his big new mystery project . . . I won't rest till not one cell remains of them or of him on this earth.

For now, I simply swallow hard while Stone, his hands laid flat on the table, watches me. The lifeless squirrel watches me with dead eyes. And I begin to scope the table, trying to work out whether I can get to the scalpel or the scissors first.

He closes his eyes and sighs. "Don't even think about it," he says. "I would expect more from you."

Which is when something starts vibrating in his pocket. Stone tuts and pulls out a slim silver handset.

He places it to his ear. "What? . . . What on earth do you mean?"

I can't take my eyes off the squirrel.

"When? . . . How many?" His hands are clenching and unclenching on the table, like he's trying to control himself. "Don't do anything. I'll be there straightaway."

He snaps the phone back in his pocket and glances up at me.

"There's something happening that I think you should see."

Before I can do anything, he's standing up and removing his apron, striding out across the smooth floor toward the doors.

I'm about to hurry after him, but just before I do—something makes me pick the squirrel up off the table. Impostor or not, I can't leave him here. Hugging him close to me, I follow Selwyn Stone out of his ark and back into the maze of the Four Towers.

Selwyn Stone clips ahead in his polished black shoes through Facto's headquarters. Skuldiss is nowhere to be seen. Perhaps he got the same phone call. There doesn't seem to be anything to stop me from making a run for it, or diving into any of the several offices and labs we hurry past, but I keep following him for one simple reason.

The voices.

The voices that slide under every door like a draught, that curl through the ventilation grills in the walls like poisonous gas and even seep from the lights above our heads like leaking water.

The whispering voices only I can hear—that I hoped I had left behind far underground. The voices that can only mean one thing.

My head is so full of hissing animal cries I can hardly think, but Stone just calmly stabs at a button in the wall, and a set of doors parts for us without a sound. We step into the lift, they close again, and at a speed so fast I have to grip the handrails to stop myself from falling over, we rocket straight to the top of Tower 1. My stomach feels like it has been left behind on the ground floor.

For a moment we seem to have left the whispering far behind.

Stone stands in the middle, facing the doors, hands clasped, not even swaying as I cling to the sides.

"Our nuclear elevator, we call it," he says with a smirk. "Too fast for you?"

The lift glides to a stop, my stomach heaves again, and the doors open out onto the top of Tower 1.

I don't know what to look at first. The huge windows on every wall give a view of all Premium—the glass towers, Waste Town, the railway, the river, the park we hid in, Maydoor Estate, even our Culdee Sack—everything. And above them all, the stormiest morning sky I have ever seen.

A sky with only a slim curve of early morning moon left in it. We are running out of time. By tonight that will have vanished.

Beneath the windows are black desks, like giant dashboards. Facto officials in purple jackets are poring over the control panels and switches that cover them, talking into microphones, twisting joysticks, and snapping orders at one another.

A big digital clock on the wall counts down to the daily curfew. And in one corner, Coby Cott himself is seated under bright lights behind a desk facing a bank of cameras, while someone brushes makeup on to his face.

In the middle of it all stands Captain Skuldiss, hunched over his crutches, gazing out through the large windows. Stone strides over to join him, but I lurk a few paces behind, holding the squirrel close to my chest.

They don't say anything. They just look.

They look through the big window, at the Facto helicopter flying above the tops of the towers, just like the helicopter that landed in our garden.

A giant purple metal bird, blazing a path of light through the cloud-filled sky. It flies out from between the glass towers and across the river, back toward us.

And it's being chased.

By a tiny dot. And a very fast one at that, swooping and diving alongside the helicopter, glinting green and purple in the dawn light.

A starling.

I lean forward to try to get a closer look. I can't be sure, but it might be the bossy bird from the Underearth.

Stone turns to Skuldiss, looking down his thin nose at him. "Well? There is a bird that lives in the city. Your men still clearly have work to do. You told me on the phone just now—"

"Everything I said was being the whole truth and nothing but, Mr. Stone," says Skuldiss, gripping his crutches tight. "You must be waiting one moment more, and you will see with your own little eyes."

The bird weaves and dives so close to the helicopter's

blades that the machine has to swerve a couple of times to avoid it. Each time the helicopter swerves, there is an audible gasp in the control tower. We can see the taillights shimmering on the water below.

But as it nears Maydoor Estate, something else appears in the sky. A black shape, like a giant thundercloud, rising from behind the abandoned building. Except that thunderclouds don't rise out of nowhere behind blocks of flats. Thunderclouds don't change shape and chase helicopters.

Hundreds of starlings. A flock of speckled chests, grasping claws, and jabbing beaks that seems to envelop the helicopter like a shadowy, glittering glove.

For a moment, nothing seems to happen.

We're just watching a helicopter flying through a cloud of starlings.

Then the single bird flying ahead shoots up into the sky, and out of sight. The cloud springs apart, as if the sky has sucked the bird into itself—and seconds later it reappears as a black wave of destruction, smashing into the helicopter head-on.

Birds bomb into the windscreen, the top and rear blades, like bullets of feather and claw. They sacrifice many of themselves in the process, but the helicopter begins to shake about in the sky before suddenly dropping—clipping the side of a formula warehouse before spiralling down in a plume of smoke, flame, and feathers, into the water.

The windows of the tower shake gently as the machine explodes.

The hundreds still left in the starling flock circle above the smouldering ripples, then spread up and out across the sky before they are lost from view.

There is silence in the room. I hold the stuffed animal close to my chest. I have seen squirrels stop a train, and now starlings bring down a helicopter.

"This has happened before?" asks Stone, kneading his brow.

Skuldiss nods.

"When did it start?"

"We called you as soon as we were seeing it ourselves," says Skuldiss. "But I am afraid that is very far from being all. Very far indeed."

He points to the screens on the dashboard, and the pictures change to a building I don't recognize. A square block covered with industrial cables and pipes, like massive old-fashioned radiators.

"One of our power stations," says Skuldiss. "A little old power box doing nothing but minding its own jolly business, out by the railway line, serving lots of delicious electricity to all our good citizens, when this happens."

As we watch the recording, the deserted power station becomes less deserted. At first there are just one or two furry bodies hurrying along the ground. Then one or two turn into twenty, and then too many to count. It is like the power station is growing fur, every inch covered with a seething mass of whiskers and ears and tails.

I try in vain to see if I can pick out the one rat I am

looking for, the one I can't get out of my mind—but there are too many.

Sparks and smoke explode through the wriggling fur, and when eventually they pull back, disappearing into the shadows, the cables are ripped to shreds; the power station is as dead and useless as a lump of rock.

"And now all the peoples on the other side of this here river are in the deepest darkness," says Skuldiss, almost like he's enjoying the chaos.

"How do we still have power?" says Stone, sounding tired.

"Emergency generator, sir," says an official. "The same one keeping the Amsguard going."

"Anything else?"

Voices fire at him from all sides of the room, and freshly printed sheets of coloured paper are thrust in his face—

"A wasp swarm attacked a school playground, sir. We've got dozens in the hospital, so many that one child said they turned the sky black and yellow . . ."

"The city lost power when the station got taken out; now we're getting reports of whole tower blocks infested with snakes, crawling through the ventilation shafts . . ."

"Foxes running wild in the streets, attacking anyone they see . . ."

"Crows dive-bombing cars, smashing windscreens, causing widespread traffic disruption in the centre—"

Stone flings the pile of paper reports in the air, and they flutter softly to the ground, like leaves. A circle of officials hovers as he kneads his brow again with his fingers.

"Are you seriously telling me that the greatest corporation in the world, in the greatest city of the world, cannot get rid of a few pests?" he asks quietly. "Where are our cullers?"

"Oh, we are just raring to go, Mr. Stone, sir," says Skuldiss, hunched over his crutches. "Raring to go and out we pop."

"Then what," says Stone, grabbing one of his crutches and twisting it up between them so it faces the ceiling, "are you doing still *standing here*?"

I have never seen Captain Skuldiss hobble so quickly. He crouches over one of the desks, screeching orders into a microphone.

The circle of nervous watchers disappears back to their screens. The room hums with activity. The screens return to a live feed. I see glimpses of blacked-out towers, fires and columns of smoke, crashed and burnt cars, people running and screaming—

The old moon is about to disappear. And tonight, according to the dream, Dagger's wild will cover the earth with darkness. The storm of storms will come, the great wet—

I've failed. I haven't stopped it. I haven't stopped any of it.

I realize that Stone is standing in the middle of the room, looking at me. There is a look in his eyes I haven't seen before. A look that roots me to the spot. "You," he says. "This is all your fault, isn't it?"

I shake my head.

"Don't lie to me, child. You orchestrated this. While we were having our nice little chat upstairs, rearranging your friend"—he notices for the first time the squirrel in my arms—"you knew what was going to happen. And you didn't say a word to warn me."

He steps closer, sticking his face in mine.

I step back.

"You set your precious animals to destroy your own city. You lying, filthy little snake!"

The snakes I know aren't lying or filthy. I'm shaking my head—

"No!"

"So what I want to know is"—he yells, spitting as he picks me up by my lapels, lifting me clean off the ground—"what are you going to do to stop it?"

He's much stronger than he looks.

I glance down at the mounted squirrel, clutched tight, stuffed and dead in my arms. And a big smile begins to creep across my face.

"This isn't a laughing matter," he says, dropping me on the ground.

It's not. But that isn't why I'm smiling.

I'm smiling because, finally, I have a plan.

I look down one last time at the red squirrel.

It's your turn to be brave now, I say to him inside my head. *I hope you're ready.*

The lifeless black eyes stare back at me. I stiffen my grip on his little body.

Then I swing the squirrel up fast, clocking Stone squarely under his chin with the heavy wooden base of my stuffed dead friend.

I'm pretty sure it's what he would have wanted.

Stone reels back toward the control desks, hands held over his face.

Then, holding the squirrel tight, I run for my life.

I am shaking so much that this time I hardly notice the gravitational pull of the nuclear lift as it rockets me back down toward the bottom of the tower.

I just hit Selwyn Stone in the face in his own control room.

But when I saw what was happening outside, in the real world, it seemed the only thing to do. I have to get out there. I have to stop Dagger's wild before they destroy us, or Stone destroys them.

Somewhere, the mouse still has the Iris. We can start this world again. If I can make the dark wild believe in that—

The lift shudders to a halt, and as the doors spring apart, I carefully place the red squirrel in between, jamming them open. A whooping klaxon blares throughout the building, and red warning lights blink angrily up and down the corridor. The stuffed animal, cocked at a strange angle, stares at me blankly.

Crouching down, I stroke his head one last time. *Good-bye, friend,* I whisper. *You have been braver and helped your wild more than you will ever know.*

As I run off, I hear the doors grind and squeal as they try to shut. I don't know how much time I've bought by trapping Stone and his cronies at the top of the tower. I just have to run as fast as I can—and listen.

To the whispers and cries that only I can hear, beneath the sirens and distant human shouts.

Skidding and slipping along the smooth passages—

Almost falling down flights of stairs—

Hiding in empty rooms, pressing myself into shadowy doorways when I hear culler patrols tramping toward me—

But the cries in my head only grow louder, pulling me on.

Until, deep in the basement of the Four Towers, I find myself outside the huge ridged iron door. Sweating, not thinking straight, it takes me one, two, three, four tries to remember the code Skuldiss punched in, then on the fifth, the red light goes to green and the door groans open.

For a moment everyone just looks at me, like they can't believe what they're seeing. The alarm sounds in the background. Polly's eyes are wide. Aida steps forward.

Then they step forward together. I don't know how to explain to them what I need them to do. There's so little time, perhaps I could get Dad to translate or . . .

Then Polly puts a hand on my arm. "Your dad has told us all about the dark wild. We'll come with you if you want, but—"

"But we need to get everyone out alive," says Aida. "Me and your friend—we been talking about you since you gone. A lot."

That doesn't sound good.

"About the way you try to do everything on your own all the time." She gives me a look that says I shouldn't even begin to disagree. "So you lucky that we get on so well."

I don't believe this. Polly takes my hands. "Aida and I will help everyone escape from here. You go after the dog."

No. I just found them again. I just found her!

"Don't look at me like that," says Aida. "We can't talk to animals. But I do have a gang waiting on the other side who can help us, you understand? So go on—get out of here!"

Polly smiles. "She's right. And I've got my toad to look after me."

Then they turn and run, barking orders to the others. There isn't time for any more. I shout at the wild. *Go! Run! This is your chance!*

They need no further encouragement. Otters, rabbits, birds—they run through my legs, fly past my face, scattering into the corridor. I'm shouting at Dad too, of course. He's one of the last to leave, and he stops, placing his hands on my shoulders. *Do you know what you're doing, Kes?*

I think so . . .

He looks at me, deep into me, and nods. Like he knew I would say that.

I believe in you, Kes, he says, and gives me one last hug before following the others.

Aida is the last to leave. Just before she follows everyone else, she jabs me in the chest. "I'll get them out of here, but you better not mess this up, boy."

And then she's gone.

Following the stairs on and down, I find myself pushing at a fire escape door, which springs open, and I step out into the concrete yard of the Four Towers. It says it's alarmed, but what difference is one more alarm going to make?

I feel wetness on my face and look up, holding out a hand.

Rain. The tears the sky sheds when any animal dies.

The sky is black with clouds and flocks of screeching birds. The city on the other bank, which once hummed with a chatter of cars and sirens and radios, now shrieks with explosions, screams, and crashes. Its glass towers stand tall and dark, lit only here and there by the glow of fire, columns of smoke rising into the sky like tornadoes in between the silhouettes of buildings.

I can smell burning rubber and fuel from where the helicopter came down. More helicopters rise into the air behind me from within the Four Towers, whirring off to different areas of the city to try to contain the dark wild.

But all these sights and sounds pass around me like a dream.

Because my head is full of voices. From every corner of the crowded city, every hole in the ground, every patch of smoke-filled sky, I hear animals. The dark wild. I hear them shouting for revenge, crying attack, and cackling with victory. I shake my head, ringing with confusing calls, feeling dizzy.

I try to focus on one voice in particular that I can just make out rising above the babble.

I run past the formula delivery vans, bright lights and raindrops bouncing off them. I run till the parking lot gives way to some rough ground, circled by bristly shrubs strewn with rubbish. In the rain, the blobs of crumpled-up trash almost look like flowers.

I'm not interested in the bushes, though; I'm interested in the fence behind them—which, out of sight from Facto's spying cameras, has a large hole torn in it.

Hidden by the undergrowth and ripped by horns—a gap big enough for a stag to squeeze through, never mind a boy.

I duck down and dive through the strands of wire to the muddy riverbank below. On the shore I slide about in the brownish-red clay, in the shadow of the huge crane that Aida and I saw from the river path.

The rain is falling harder, so everything is seen through curtains of drizzle. The crane sits on a massive barge, surrounded by sacks of cement and oil drums, huge rolls of steel wire, girders piled high. A lamp hanging from the crane lurches from side to side in the wind, casting crazy shadows.

It looks more like a building site than a barge. A floating building site. *"The Amsguard is completed,"* said Coby Cott.

Still following the voice, I march up the plank leaning against the hull and onto the deck. The crane creaks above me. *Hello? Are you there? Can you hear me?*

The voice gets louder, coming from beneath me. Looking down at the deck splattered with grey mud, I see it is covered in a grid of winch lines and pipes, a single square in the middle with a ring attached.

Scrabbling over the wires and pipes, I crouch down and pull on the hatch. It is rusted, stiff, and heavy. The driving rain loosens my grip. I heave and heave until I think it will pull my arms out of their sockets—then it creaks open, revealing a ramp down into shadows.

From which a pair of horns emerges.

We are here, Wildness, the stag says, stalking forward into the flickering light from the crane lamp, his horns scratched and chipped from butting the hatch. The General sits on the stag's head, his antennae limp and exhausted. *Only just, but we are here. We fled from the children as soon as the cockroach found us. Their master has disappeared.*

Don't worry, I know all about him, I say.

The insect brought us to the stone tall-home where you were captured. Then the dark wild you told us of began to rise, so we took cover in here. But the wind blew that slab shut and closed us in.

And the mouse?

She went her own way, says the cockroach.

Another kind of alarm bell begins to sound in my head. *You don't know where she went?*

Only that she said it would be safe, he says. *That she would go where it was safe.*

I have to hope all is not lost. That she found somewhere safe. That even without the Iris actually in my hand I can persuade Dagger to change his mind.

The others nose into the light alongside the stag.

Wolf-Cub is flecked with mud and spots of dark red. There is a new light in his eyes, a deepness to his voice. Everyone, everything, changing all around me—I take a deep breath, steady myself.

Wolf, what can you tell me?

It has been hard, Wildness. I was attacked by birds. A starling! No bird has ever attacked a wolf before.

I know this. We watched from the towers. What of the white dog? Of your pack?

If Wolf still feels sad, he doesn't let it show.

The white dog and my mother have left the destruction of the city to their legions. I followed their scent farther along this fish-road before returning here . . . He hangs his head and tail. *It was too dangerous to follow any further. There were humans everywhere with firesticks. Perhaps my mother was right. Perhaps I am a coward.*

Of course not. You were very brave to follow them that far.

He grunts. *But what do we do now? We are outnumbered by humans and other beasts. This is the end of days, Wildness. The storm of storms has come, the earth has risen.*

I know, I say. *And we're going to stop it from rising any further.*

Except everything depends on me finding Dagger and his wolf Guardians. Only they can stop this.

The Ams runs on for miles. They could be anywhere.

And those waters spilled out over the earth, said the dream.

I try to think for a moment—but it is so hard to concentrate. The rain drumming on the boat and water. The helicopters whirring above our heads, now swerving and anticipating bird strikes. The starlings, still swooping in flocks, trying to bring another one down.

One bird in particular cuts through the noise in my head. The one screeching orders. I turn my head up to the rain, to the glittering creature I can just see doing loops ahead of the others.

Now come on! she is saying. *It can't be that hard to bring down another helicopter! Get your act together, starlings! For the sake of the dark wild . . . honestly . . . he never said it would be this hard, did he?*

Starling! I call up.

Wolf is nipping my hand. *Don't draw attention to us, Wildness! That's the bird that tried to attack us!* I glance at him, and he deepens his voice. *I mean . . . just let that foolish little bird come near me again and I will show her my true strength.*

Starling! I call again. *I thought I was your enemy.*

The bird is looking about her in the air.

Down here! The human enemy your Wildness seeks is down here!

Then the bird is plummeting down toward us, leaving her flock to crowd round the helicopters above. Seeing the stag and the wolf, she halts halfway to perch on the crane lamp swinging gently above our heads.

Now listen here. You can't just go shouting at me like that; I'm doing very important work for the dark wild here . . . I was specially charged by our Wildness himself, you know—

And then she sees me.

You! Why of all the nerve—you think you can order me about? I ought to peck your eyes out here and now for everything you've done. We've brought down one of your metal birds, you know. You want to watch it.

I shake my head, and can see she looks flustered.

Why waste your time with those stupid machines, Starling, when you've got the prize your Wildness wants the most right here? Think how pleased he would be if you brought him three traitors like us?

Oh, I don't know . . . He gave us very strict orders to stop the metal birds in the sky . . . It's very important for his plans, you see.

And stopping us isn't?

Well, he didn't ask me specifically to do that . . .

Just think of the praise you would receive. He might even let you speak from the white rock.

Now the starling is embarrassed, folding her wing over her face.

Me, speak from the white rock? Oh, I couldn't possibly . . . I'd hate that. She twitches on the crane lamp, hopping from foot to foot, pecking at her plumage.

We wait in silence for a moment. I try not to catch the stag's eye.

Oh well, I say, *don't worry. We'll try to find him ourselves then.* And we start to head down the gangplank.

A shimmering bullet of blue and green intercepts us, standing proudly on the shore ahead of us.

Stop! Don't go without me! She looks twitchily from side to side. *I mean, you'll never find the Great Stone Trees by yourself.*

I stop. I look down at her. I look at the building materials on our barge. And I realize: The answer was staring me in the face from the start.

Might these be nine white stone trees standing in a fishroad? I ask her.

For the first time, she looks terrified. *Never you mind. I never said that! I'll lead you there; I'll take you to the Dark Wildness. You'll never get near him alive otherwise.*

She's right. We don't have a choice.

Thank you, bird, says the stag, but he can't hide the stiffness in his voice at the idea of a Dark Wildness.

Just one thing, says the starling, still blocking our path. *When we get there—you will say that you're my prisoners, won't you?*

The stag gives a long sigh, and the bird leads us back to the river road that goes to only one place.

The Amsguard.

We follow the starling away from the barge and along the riverbank, me riding the stag, the wolf-cub padding alongside us as the rain continues to fall.

It doesn't just fall, it pours. The stag's fur is oily and drenched; I squeeze him as tight as I can with my knees to stop myself falling off. He has to watch his step as the bird guides us along a road riddled with potholes underneath the muddy puddles.

The water rolls down into our eyes too fast to wipe or blink away.

If this is the storm of storms, it doesn't stop the starling talking as she dances ahead of us in the sky, runs along the ground, or hops along a wall. The rain slicks off her glossy wings, their spotted green and purple feathers brighter than ever before.

Look over there! she squawks, as we hear a crazy barking from behind a fence. Squinting over the top through the rain, I can see houses and lawns, with cars parked in the drives.

Lawns and drives covered with the wild dogs I saw in the Underearth. They press their paws against the doors and windows, climbing over the cars. The lights in the houses have gone out, but I can see glimpses of pale faces behind the glass.

Keeping the humans trapped in their tall-homes they are! the bird chirrups. *The old moon has gone, the world is in darkness, and the storm of storms begins. Soon the great wet will flood over all things and we can start again.*

> The sky's tears filled the great wet
> And those waters spilled out over the earth . . .

How will the great wet cover all things, clever Starling? I ask her. I thought the Amsguard was meant to keep the sea out, not let it in.

That's for me to know and you to wonder. Now stop asking questions or I'll summon those dogs over here.

Let them try, growls the wolf-cub.

The starling glares at him.

I'm sure he didn't mean that, Starling, I say quickly. *We know how powerful you are.*

Ha! she says, then fluffs up her feathers and flaps off down the road, between the crumbling ramparts of an old shopping plaza.

Wildness, I do not trust this bird, grumbles the cockroach from my shoulder, the rain splashing off his armoured shell.

Don't worry about her, General, I say. *She's just a stupid bossyboots who will do whatever we say as long as we keep telling her how clever and brave she is.*

I'm not so sure. Cockroaches do not have a good history with starlings, he says. *So I disagree. I think we should go another way.*

The starling is pecking at the big cracked tiles of the plaza floor. All around us are boarded-up shop windows and shutters sprayed with graffiti.

A bench lies on its side, and soggy piles of rubbish gather in the corners and doorways of the square. For a moment I think I see another animal hurrying across the plaza, but it's just a black plastic bag blown by the wind.

Come on, come on! chides the starling. *Our Wildness won't wait, you know!*

A shiver runs down my spine at the mention of him. But it only makes me more determined. *We have to find the dog, General, and stop this. The starling is our only way.*

At first the General doesn't reply. Then, as the stag clops after the bird across the plaza and past the fountain, he blurts out—

You think you know everything, young Wildness! You are the hero now, are you? Too mighty and great to listen to your brave comrade. Have you forgotten who it was who first found you, who first rescued you from your prison? Who helped you escape from the Underearth, who summoned the rest of your wild to help you now? It wasn't that wretched bird, for sure.*

He marches down my arm to go and sit on the stag's horns, facing away from me.

General, I'm sorry if I—

No! he says. *What's done is done. No apologies required. But I shall not be responsible for the consequences.*

I don't know what to say to that, so we ride on from the plaza into an old market, one that must have been abandoned a long time before the dark wild gathered its forces. Lopsided stalls and faded trailers stand empty under a glass dome. The rain hammers down above us.

I'm worried that we're moving away from the river, where the cub last spotted the dog and his guardians.

Can you smell the dog, Wolf-Cub? Your pack?

He sniffs the ground but shakes his head.

There are no tracks that I recognize here.

Perhaps the General was right.

Starling! Where are you leading us?

I am taking you to face the Wildness of the dark wild himself, as requested. She lands on the tip of the stag's horns, making the General creep away into the safety of my pocket, and looks down her beak at me. *Would you rather I led you into the heart of the human tall-homes across the fish-road? With the foxes and the snakes and the wasps? Would you like that? I'll wait here, shall I, till you've made your mind up?*

She darts off onto a stall laden with dusty sweet jars, and

jabs her beak under her wing, plucking out stray feathers.

Through the rain cascading onto the dome above, the noise of the chaos in the city across the river can still be heard. Every other sound is a shout or a bang.

OK, Starling! I wave my hand at her. *Whichever way you want to take us—but hurry!*

The stag stops in surprise. *Did you not hear the cockroach?* he asks.

There's no time—can't you hear what I hear, Stag? If I took everyone's advice every time they gave it, we'd never go anywhere.

He doesn't reply but trudges on between the stalls.

Smart boy! says the bird, and spirals off the sweet stall, leading us out of the market square and into a narrow arcade. What daylight had been seeping in through the dome barely reaches here. I can just make out ripped sale signs on the gloomy windows, mannequins lying on their sides, the odd empty rail in the shadows behind.

Bird? I say. *Are you there?*

Her voice comes back, echoing against the shop fronts.

Yes, yes. This will be the quickest and safest way. Their walk-upons outside are blocked with destroyed machines and animals you would not like to meet.

And she flies on, just a flash of light in the shadows.

The stag takes a few steps farther, until the grey glare of the stormy afternoon outside has faded away completely. The only light comes from my watch. I shiver, thinking of my time in the Underearth. We just have to remember that we're not underground; open streets are just beyond these walls.

Then, as the stag walks on, now in virtual darkness, something brushes my face. Something grey and sticky. I flick it away, only to get more on my hands and arms, and then I can see the same stuff is plastered across the stag's horns—

The wolf growls, snapping at the thick mesh he is entangled in—

The stag stops, quivering. There is a scuttling above us, to the right of us, and on the left of us—

Noise like knitting needles moving across the floor. Down the walls.

And along the strands of the giant web we are caught in.

Starling? I say, but I know she is already long gone.

Shaking, I fumble for my watch and turn on its light. Eyes blink at me. Not just one pair of eyes, but hundreds. Glinting bunches of them, hanging from the ceiling, dangling down from every doorway, just as many of them as I saw in the Underearth.

Spiders.

I never thought I would be best friends with a cockroach. I've made friends with a rat, and I've even let myself be helped by moths and snakes.

But despite everything I now know about animals and varmints, there is one kind I still really, really don't like—even if one did speak to me at Spectrum Hall.

Spiders.

And now we are alone in the dark, surrounded by hundreds of them.

The stag makes a hoarse barking sound and tries to back up the way we came, wrapping us further in the sticky string of their web. They are already starting to climb up him with their spindly hairy legs, quicker than he can shake them off.

I have to stay calm, shining my watch into the black. *Spiders, what do you want? We are looking for your Wildness. We seek an end to all this.*

Shrieking laughter echoes back at me from the darkness.

A spider who looks more like a giant black hand without an arm attached feels his way across the floor.

I didn't know spiders like that existed. *How are you so big?*

The spider's eyes light up with excitement. *So many yearss in the dark tunnelss, waiting for our chansse. As the world above grew hotter, we grew bigger, feeding off your peenk food.*

We mean you no harm. Will you let us pass?

That traitor sstag still hass not told you, hass hee? Black Spider says in his high and screechy voice—a chirruping, wet noise that makes my head hurt. *The only posssible end to theess eess the end of your life and those of the traitorss weeth you.*

I don't understand. What has the stag not told me? *Why?*

Reevenge!

Black Spider's reply is repeated a thousand times, from a thousand different spider minds around me, clinging to the shop windows and walls, dangling from the ceiling above.

But I am different from other humans. I want to help you all. If I can speak to your Wildness—

This time there is no laughter; hate bounces back at me. Spittle-filled, web-spinning, pincer-grabbing hate. *All humanss are the ssame! You have all alwayss hated us! You squash uss, you flush uss, you sspray uss . . .*

I suppose he might have a point there. *But what about these other animals? They have done you no harm.*

There is no reply, just the skittering of jointed legs across the ground. Wolf-Cub picks up a few with his teeth and spits them out, growling, but they keep coming, clambering over his back and tail faster than he can move, spinning and wrapping him in their web all the time.

Starling! Call these creatures off! You've made your point.

If she is there, or listening, she has gone very quiet.

Now the stag is bucking and stamping to try to shake off the spiders who are nipping his shins and crawling up his fur to get to me. They drop from the ceiling straight onto his back, in my hair, spinning white silken strands around and around my head.

I jump off and into the middle of the spiders, swinging my watch light round. It is the only thing that makes them retreat for a second, although who knows how long the battery will last.

The spiders are tightening the noose around us, a noose of web that is getting stronger and thicker all the time. The wolf-cub is fierce and the stag is large, but there are so many, spinning and nipping every way we turn, when I hear a voice from my shoulder.

I did warn you, did I not? says the General. *I did tell you I would not be responsible for the consequences, did I not?*

Yes, but—

Very well then. He buzzes off my shoulder and onto

the one spare piece of ground between us and the spiders.

General, what are you doing?

But he just clicks away, antennae held high. *Showing you what sometimes has to be done, my boy.*

And he scuttles straight up to their evil-eyed leader, swaying high on his jointed legs at the front of the mob, and nips him in the stomach so that the spider squeals and draws back with rage.

What do you theenk you're doing, you sstupid leettle bug? Black Spider prods him with his legs, throat clicking. *I have never sseen one of your kind so large. A delicassy to be ssavoured.*

But rather than retreat back to us, the General rears up on his back legs, his antennae feeling the air and waving at the spiders. *Don't make me laugh, Hairy. You lot repulse me. In all my days of war, I have never met so pathetic and useless an enemy. You think that your webs and jaws frighten the General of all the cockroaches?*

The spider leaps for him with an angry shriek, but the General flutters out of the way with his wings and is clinging to the dusty glass door of an empty shop. *You're too fat to be a warrior,* he calls down.

Sseize him! shrieks the spider, and the tide of legs and hair begins to surge up the door toward him. The cockroach spreads his striped wings and soars over them to the other side of the arcade.

Idiot arachnids! he jeers. But this time he doesn't land cleanly and gets caught in a large web, shaking himself free just in time. *You'll have to do better than that,* he says to the frustrated spider, whisking higher up the wall.

As the spiders hound him farther into their midst, as he hops now from the back of one to another, the orange of his shell just visible amidst their quivering backs, he turns to us and roars—

What are you waiting for, you fools?

But, General, we can't—

I said, what are you waiting for?

Then he darts away again, just escaping the clutches of a spider spinning right down on top of him.

And I begin to understand. What he meant by consequences. The insects around us are pulling back, joining the hunt for the cockroach, squealing with fury.

We have to go, I whisper to the others, pulling as many strings of web off them as I can. *Now.*

Slowly, as quietly as we can, we begin to back out of the arcade toward the deserted market and the plaza. The General bounces and hops between the spiders, every single one of whom is determined to be the first to catch him.

Meee!

No! Let meee!

Out of my way, I ssaw heem firsst!

Our brave cockroach almost seems to be enjoying the chase. But his voice is fading. *Useless creatures . . . There we go . . . Not quite, you rascal!*

The stag and the wolf-cub are in the grey light under the dome now. *Come,* says the stag. *Don't watch.*

There is still time. They are safe now, at least. I leave them halfway out of the arcade, hovering on the edge of light and darkness, and step back in. Squinting, I can just make out a glimpse of orange shell.

The spiders have stopped chasing the General. They don't need to anymore. He has collapsed, exhausted, on the ground, not even able to crawl properly. They are closing in on him.

I feel my way toward them down the empty passage as quietly as I can . . .

The General makes one final effort, and struggles to rear up on his tiny back legs, tottering. *Goodness,* he says, sniffing the air around him, which is pulsating with quivering abdomens and oozing jaws. *There's nearly enough of you brutes to form a half-decent army. What a shame it's not going to be mine.*

And he leaps for their giant leader.

I lunge uselessly forward, a silent scream frozen in my head—

The spiders of the dark wild bury the last General of the cockroaches, piling him under blackness after blackness, until he is lost from sight.

PART 6
GOOD-BYE, PREMIUM

For a moment I stand in the empty shopping arcade, staring in disbelief and unable to move.

The spiders begin to twitch their heads toward me, and then—like a miniature orange rocket—the General is shooting up out of their scrum and toward me, yelling fit to burst. *What on earth are you waiting for, boy? RUN!*

Somehow we find ourselves outside in the shopping plaza, although I'm not sure how. Everything that happens next seems to be in phases. At first I feel nothing, as dead inside as the empty shuttered shops around us.

The General is alive, but only just, a bedraggled version of his former self. That last flight has destroyed him. He lies flat in the palm of my hand, his antennae and wings limp, while the rain keeps falling around us till the whole tiled square is one shallow pool. Yet he hardly even stirs.

Perching on the upturned bench to try to keep the cockroach dry under my jacket, I shiver and wait, the stag and wolf watching me in silence—although I can sense waves of worry bouncing off them, which I try to ignore.

Still he doesn't move.

The wolf and stag stay quiet, and suddenly I'm so angry with them. Why didn't they stop the spiders? Why didn't they help the General? Why didn't they do more to warn me about the starling?

And still the rain falls and the thunder cracks. Who knows what Dagger and his Guardians could be doing at the Amsguard by now? Perhaps we are already too late.

The wolf sits at my feet, and for the first time ever lets me stroke him. It makes me feel better, but stroking isn't going to magically make the cockroach better.

The General. The first creature I ever spoke to. He helped me escape when I thought my life couldn't get any worse. He's been by my side since then, or more usually on my shoulder, curled up in my scarf. I should have listened to him, not let him nearly die.

I think of all the cockroaches that have actually died before him. Thousands, millions—crushed, sprayed, poisoned without a second thought. Just cockroaches, everyone thought.

But this cockroach in my hand is my General.

The last of his kind, leader of a great army. There won't be another.

Then suddenly I find myself choked up, and I can't stop them—tears pouring out of me faster than the rain from the sky. *How many more?* I ask the stag, gulping through my sobs. *Rat, Squirrel, the General—how many more have to get hurt before this ends?*

He only shakes his head, as if to say, I don't know.

I stand up, showering them with raindrops spraying off my anorak, feeling shaky all over. Like I'm no longer totally in control of what I say or do.

I just don't know if I can do this anymore, I say, looking at my trainers, water seeping into them. *People against animals. People against people. Animals against animals. The whole world—it's just so broken. I can't fix it. Just because I can talk to animals, why does that mean I have to fix it?*

A shadow falls over my face.

The wolf glances up at the stag, who has lifted his head to his full height, tall above us both. Through his horns I can see the corners of old blocks of flats, bent aerials, and lightning flashing in the storm clouds behind. For a moment his eyes glaze over, like he is seeing something very far away.

I swear, I say. *I know you mean well, but if you try to tell me that I am a hero again—or any of that stuff—it isn't going to work this time. Even you've got to see, Stag, this is way bigger than all that. The world is coming to an end, and there's nothing you or I can do to stop it.*

No, I'm not, he says. *I'm not going to tell you any of that—what you call—stuff. In fact, I'm not going to say anything at all.*

And he doesn't speak. He does something I have never heard him do on his own before.

He begins to sing a call, alone, a call I have never heard before.

In a low, hoarse voice that keeps breaking.

Yet slowly, surely, the song begins to unfold around us in the grey and abandoned square, his words rising up into the muddle of my mind, as the sound drifts off over the top of the crumbling buildings and into the sky.

Words I know I will never forget, that tell me the stag's story for the first time.

A story that begins in a forest, in a drift of leaves underneath a gnarled tree. A young creature, sticky and newborn, wobbles to its feet. A baby deer, nuzzled and licked clean by his mother. He's not alone; there is another shaky and sticky deer with him.

The young fawns learn to stand and suckle milk from their mother. Then they are running and leaping in the forest, jumping over fallen trees, nudging and stroking each other.

Another figure arrives in the forest, all in black. A man with a firestick. The mother and the sister of the fawn tumble over, then he is running as fast as he can, away from the forest.

He runs through streams and tunnels, over fences and walls. As he runs, he grows. Until he reaches some mountains, where other deer graze on the grassy slopes.

The deer is older now, velvety stumps beginning to poke out of his head. Hungry and exhausted, he is allowed to join the mountain herd. He roams the mountains with them, in mist, rain, and sun.

As he grows older and stronger, he is challenged by other stags. They roar, lock horns, and fight on the lower slopes—but he always wins. Until one day he stands in a circle of all the mountain deer, who bow their heads to him in the shadows of a setting sun.

Then the eyes of the other mountain deer start to turn red, and they fall down to the ground, all around the stag.

He escapes the plague and returns to the forest where he was born. And he calls the other animals he left behind there—other deer, badgers, squirrels, birds, and butterflies— who follow him out past the mountain, to a lake at the end of the Island.

I think I know the rest.

He stops. I can barely speak. For a moment it seems the stag can't either. *Can you guess what my mother's last words to me were?* he says quietly. *"Keep walking"—that was all she said. My father I never knew. I'd lost my mother, my sister. But I had to keep walking. I walked until I found my herd on the mountains. And then, when the plague came, I walked again to the Ring of Trees. Then I walked with you to come here.* A great shiver runs from the tips of his horns to the end of his tail. *I know I will never see the mountains or the Ring of Trees again. I am too old to return now. But all I can do, all any creature can do, Wildness—is put one foot in front of another. We can keep walking.*

And as if he has been listening to the dream as well, the damp orange insect in the palm of my hand begins to stir, muttering something inaudible to himself. While the stag and the cub watch, I tuck him safely into my inside pocket, hidden from the storm. Then, frozen, soaking, and tired, without another word, we turn away from the arcade, back along the flooded river road, and march forward together.

Back on the riverbank road, the Ams seems to have grown wider, so now the towers opposite look smaller than they are, blurred and fuzzed by the streaks of rain. The river itself looks deeper too, muddy and swollen by the downpour, splashing through the railings where we walk along and try to stay out of sight as we creep through the darkened city.

Part of me wishes Polly and Aida were with me now, but I know I have to face this on my own.

The wolf hurries ahead, sniffing every building corner for traces of his pack or the dog, then disappearing into the black rain ahead. We have no guide other than the direction the starling was headed in before she tricked us.

Every now and then we hear the shrieking of bats in the sky, foxes barking in the distance, or the gritty shower of insects swarming down a pipe. The chants and cries of the dark wild cover the city, spreading confusion and chaos.

Power cables swing uselessly down, their ends gnawed to pieces. I guide the stag away from their sparking ends, like monster snakes with an electric bite.

The ground is strewn with rubbish scattered from bins or dragged from smashed doors and windows. Rats stream out of a parked car, paying little attention to us. Among them I look for a face I recognize—with no luck.

I can't see a single other person as they all hide out of sight, obeying Facto's curfew, or waiting for the storm to pass and for the animals to leave.

The paved river paths shrivel away, like the trails of forest roots, into open country of empty motorways swooping past deserted dockyards.

The wind batters road signs hanging above our heads, as we march up one potholed tarmac hill and down another. The traffic lights are all dead, but that doesn't matter because there's no traffic anymore.

Instead the roads are full of junk, hurled down the empty road by the gale—

Hazard cones, spinning single tyres, and even a stop sign, bent and twisted, come blowing our way, forcing the stag and me to stand aside and let them pass. The wolf dodges between them, trotting along as if nothing were happening, his snout bent low to the ground, determined to find a scent.

The stag and I huddle behind the shattered glass of a bus shelter and watch the lumps of plastic and metal bump past us—as if for a moment they too had come to life to destroy the city that created them—before being swept over the curve of a safety barrier onto the roofs of warehouses beneath the highway.

The stag says, *You have made this earth unrecognizable.*

But it is still our home.

One worth saving. I can't tell whether he means it as a question or a command.

I wait for the General to make a biting remark, but he doesn't because he's only barely alive. I look again at the jumble of man-made browns and greys and artificial whites stretching out before us. They blur before my eyes. And in my mind I'm not seeing them. I'm seeing the pale faces of Dad, Polly, and Aida, fleeing from their prison in the Four Towers—

But before I can reply, the wolf is hurtling back toward us out of the dark, his eyes shining through the wet. *Listen!*

I listen, but all I can hear is the wind and the rain, the explosions and animal cries—

Not those sounds, Wildness. Listen again.

I strain, cupping my ears with my hands. The stag is stock-still, not moving a muscle.

And then I begin to hear it.

So faintly, floating out across the city—the animal call any human can hear.

That any wolf can hear from a very great distance. The howl of another.

It is my mother, he declares. *We can find them now. My mother and her pack were here. This is the trail.*

The cub leads us down one last dip of abandoned motorway and off onto a muddy side road, past a sign.

FACTO CONSTRUCTION ZONE
UNAUTHORIZED ENTRY FORBIDDEN

Beyond a security pole swinging loose in the wind is a sentry cabin with smashed windows. There is no sign of the Facto guards who must have been here, but I can guess—if Dagger and his New Guardians were here—what has happened to them.

I push the barrier open and we stumble along ridges of mud made by heavy trucks that now run deep with water, but that doesn't stop the wolf-cub finding paw-prints that I would never have seen.

The track only seems to get deeper and muddier. The river beyond the barbed-wire fence is rising. The mud is covering and coating our feet so the stag and wolf are more clay than fur as we force our way past the wind that tears into us, along canyons between scaffolding towers and stacks of metal containers.

I feel like an insect among these metal rocks, says the wolf.

I don't want to think about insects. Despite the mud forming around my shoe, the rain beating into our faces, all I want to think about are those we left behind in the Four

Towers. If I turn around, I can almost see the red lights twinkling in the murk.

Then, just when I'm not sure I will be able to take another step, we emerge onto a concrete plain.

We stop dead in our tracks, facing the river.

I guessed right.

There they are, shining in the first glimmers of morning light.

Nine colossal stone towers, rising out of the surging waves like mountains, spanning the whole width of the Ams. The concrete mountains are connected by white metal gates the height of whole houses, which scoop down into the water. Flood barriers with hydraulic hinges the size of oil pipes, with suspension-bridge cables holding them tight.

Nine stone trees. The Amsguard.

The man-made structure standing between us and the rising seas of the world. The river laps hungrily at this side of the gates, while spray is already washing over the tops of the gantries from the other side.

It is not yet, however, strong enough to wash away the silhouetted line of figures dotted across the central tower.

The unmistakable ears and tails of a pack of wolves—

And standing on his hind legs, almost more human than beast, leaning against the railings, facing away from us out to sea—

A white dog.

Standing in the deserted building site at the base of the Amsguard, I look around for a way up to the dog and the wolves parading along the top. It's nighttime now, but the gloomy morning sky doesn't shed much light on the situation.

I can see a lift tower dead ahead, the gates chained and padlocked. Bundles of razor wire cover the fences between here and the shore—and besides, even if I could get over, even if I was crazy enough to swim in the freezing, frothing water, the first tower is too far out to reach.

But it is connected to the unfinished concrete floor we stand on by a tree-sized cable, punched with rivets, raindrops rolling off the fresh white paint. Raindrops and—just very faintly—the smeared splodges of muddy paw-prints.

While I study the cable, the stag comes up behind me,

sniffing it suspiciously. *Even if I could,* he says, *I am too old for such adventures now.*

I stroke his damp flank softly and notice for the first time that there are grey hairs around his muzzle. *No,* I say, shivering like crazy, *but you are not too old to wait here, and if I am not back by dawn, you must return to the Four Towers, and somehow—find Dad . . .*

What do you mean, if I am not back? says the wolf-cub. *You are not planning to climb this fallen white tree alone, are you, Wildness?*

I look at the slippery cable stretching away and up to the nearest gantry, suspended high in the air above first rock-hard concrete and then thrashing river. Then I look back at the wolf-cub.

I'm not sure I could climb that, Cub.

It is just like walking across a fallen tree in a ravine, at which I am the . . . He falters and corrects his voice. *Which is nothing for a near-grown wolf like me.*

Would you like to put that to the test, cubling? says a gruff voice. Hooded Fox steps out from the shadows of the lift tower, his ruff beaded with rain but no less thick and handsome than before.

The wolf's tail is straight up, tip pointed, and he is completely silent—which he always is at his most dangerous.

Hee-hee! Looks like you upset him! says another fox voice, its owner dropping lightly onto the ground behind us from the top of a steel container. Eyes Wide looks even madder than before, the fur on his head stirred up by the wind into a crazy quiff.

What they said, adds Skulker, detaching himself from one of the sheaves of rusting wire and slouching toward the stag, who grunts and lowers his horns.

Foxes, I say, *you know the dream as well as all creatures. Whatever that dog is planning, if he goes ahead, it will be the end of us all.*

The end of us all! echoes Skulker.

We're all going to die! shrieks Eyes Wide with delight.

These are just more of your human lies, says Hooded Fox stiffly. *But even if that is the case, all the more reason to take our revenge first.*

You had your chance in the cave— I begin, but he pushes me aside with a wave of his bushy tail.

Not you, he sighs. *I mean this excuse for an animal.*

He squares up to the wolf-cub. *Your mother and her pack took our positions as Guardians,* he spits. *Now we are left behind to guard against children such as yourselves, while the heroes' honour is claimed by them.*

That has nothing to do with him, Fox, I say. *Why not join us against those who took your place?*

He rounds on me, eyes blazing, his black lips pulled right back over his jaws as he flashes his teeth.

Of course! How the humans respond to everything—"Not my fault, it's his fault, it's their fault." Hooded Fox looks around at the plain of concrete and steel, the swirling clouds and the foaming river. *Well, look where we are. Is all this no one's fault? Someone made our world like this, and, forgive me, but I don't think it was us.*

Yeah! You lot! I mean, you really . . . you know . . . I think you're . . . doing all that stuff and things, says Skulker. There's an awkward pause while we all try not to look at him. *I mean . . . what he said basically,* he finishes lamely.

Hooded Fox ignores him.

All humans must pay the price for the actions of their brothers and sisters. Starting with you and your treacherous allies.

The three foxes circle the cub hungrily, as the animals try to out-growl and out-snarl one another. The stag told me once that animals prefer to scare another beast off with sounds and threats, that they prefer not to fight unless they absolutely have to. I can only hope he's right.

Wolf-Cub glances at me in surprise. *Why are you still here? Go!*

I feel like he is suddenly at the end of a long tunnel, falling away from me. *No, Wolf-Cub, please. Not you as well.*

Eyes Wide springs at him, but the cub bats him away. The crazed fox picks himself up, unbothered, as Skulker starts to pull and tug at the wolf's tail. Hooded Fox is doing a dance with the stag's horns, but the stag is not as fast as he once was.

Go! he too says to me, not taking his eyes off the ruffed fox. *Have faith in us.*

He doesn't add *for once,* but he could have.

The only thing that human should have faith in is his own destruction, which will come all the quicker if he makes it as far as those wolves, says Hooded Fox.

I turn to my wolf. *Please! If you hurry, they will not be able to follow us up there . . .*

Go! he says. And this time there is no childish crack or squeak to his voice. It is a voice deep and gruff enough to match Hooded Fox's, but steady too. *Go, Wildness. Let us decide this the animal way. But don't look back.*

Perhaps the wolf-cub is growing into a wolf at last. Our eyes meet one final time, as Eyes Wide snaps at his flank.

Don't look back, the wolf says again.

And I don't. The General is tucked safely away in my pocket; the wolf and stag have gotten out of worse situations before.

It's my turn to be brave now.

I try to stand on the white cable, but it is too slippery, the wind too strong. I will fall over or get blown clean off. So instead I straddle it, pulling myself along with my arms and legs.

I have only the steadiness of the wolf's voice to hold on to.

Steady and calm, unlike me.

I think of the voice of the wolf as an invisible rope, as the ground falls away beneath me and the cable begins to sway in the high winds.

I try not to hear that same voice rise and fall, in snarls and cries of pain. The howling and barking comes from all sides, the cable itself whining and shaking as tussling bodies are slammed against its base.

I think of the stag, just putting one foot in front of another, as I haul myself along, squeezing with my knees as hard as I can. I can't bear to listen to the sound of his horns clanging and scraping across concrete.

I will not look back.

But I daren't look to the side either. Not at the containers piled up below me on one side, the jetsam of empty plastic sacks and forgotten tools that have gathered on their flat roofs so small and far away now that they look like toys. Nor at the razor-wire fence and slopping river on the other side.

I shut out the cries and noise from below.

I pretend that the wind isn't whipping the skin from my face and lips, that my hands aren't being torn to shreds—

And I pull and crawl until I am nearly three-quarters of the way there, the railings of the Amsguard walkway within sight—

Until I—

Slip.

My stomach lurches, as out of nowhere I topple over to one side—a bad move, a gust of wind, who knows?—and now I hang upside down.

Wind blows my scarf into my mouth, rain in my eyes.

As I kick to swing myself back up onto the top of the cable, a soggy trainer falls off, spiralling down beneath me, swallowed up in a single tiny splash far below.

I take deep breaths, my hands now beginning to slide on the slippery metal. There is nothing to hold on to, just rivets and ridges no deeper than my fingers, which feel like every muscle in them is about to spasm as they grip.

Freezing spray kisses my neck.

My eyes open. Upside down, behind me, I see the city I was born in blooming out from the river, like a stain of steel and glass upon the earth. Four towers, red lights twinkling, stare at me from across the way, like they're watching me and don't care one way or another if I fall.

I don't know if the stag's right. I don't know anymore if all that is worth fighting for. All the people, all the mess we've made of everything—perhaps the world has just had enough of human beings. Human beings like Stone or Littleman. Even humans like me, who abandon their friends to their fate. Perhaps we need to let go.

Yes, that's it. Just let go.

It suddenly seems so easy, so obvious.

Why didn't I think of it before?

My fingers begin to loosen around the cable.

A huge feeling of relief slowly sweeps over me. I didn't realize letting go would feel so good. I let my head hang back, eyes open, for one last glimpse of the city upside down from a giant white cable, the strangest thing I ever saw.

It looks like the towers of glass and red lights now make the sky, hanging down from the ground above a sea of storm clouds.

Then, perhaps I'm delirious with fever or pain, but it

looks like there is something else in the sky. Something that wasn't there a moment ago.

Something flying toward me.

Dots at first, but definitely flying toward me. Not helicopters or starlings.

At first I can't be sure what they are—some grey dots, one white. Getting closer now, without doubt . . . they are what I think they are.

I can't believe it.

Isn't it funny how when you think it might all be over—

That it's the smallest things—the things you never thought would make the grade, the things so easy to ignore because they were there every day, all around us and forgettable—that make your fingers tighten once again around the rope?

It's the last of the birds we used to see every day and everywhere—

Flying toward me now, crying out my name—

No grabbing with beaks and claws required this time.

As I haul myself back onto the cable, they flurry around me, showering me with their feathery warmth, pecking and cheering me on.

My pigeons are back.

As I struggle onto the walkway of the Amsguard, collapsing facedown in a puddle, the birds flock down, fluttering over my head and pecking softly at me.

We completed your mission, Wildness! the ninety-nine grey pigeons chorus in their singsong voices as they crowd around me. A few frayed purple ribbons hang around their necks—ribbons that were carrying precious gel batons packed with Laura II. *We delivered your father's cure to the Ring of Trees.* Then their voices quiet. I can feel my chest tighten, fearing the worst. *Unfortunately some of our wild were no more . . . but we left behind many more who will live on.*

The white pigeon lands square in front of me, peering over the other side of the walkway, where the sea throws up salty wave after wave onto us. A splash sends him staggering back to me, his pink eyes swivelling from side to side. *Yes, unfortunately, some of our wild will live* *on,** he whispers to me, as if it were the worst news in the world.

I can't hide my smile. Not because the white pigeon still hasn't learned to speak any better, but because they might just be able to persuade the dark wild that Mother Wolf is wrong—some humans have helped animals. *Are* helping animals.

*How did you find me?** I ask the birds.

*Pigeons always return home,** they say simply.

I gesture to the water-lashed walkway, the concrete and cables stretching away beneath us. *This isn't your home.**

*No, but you are,** they say.

I stand up and grab the railings to stop the wind and sea washing me straight over the other side. I have never seen the sea so angry before. The sea that spread and covered so many other lands, sending their people hurrying to our shores, looks ready now to cover us too.

A surging plane of water, lightning strikes flashing across it, rolls and boils, hurling white-crested waves at the man-made gate we stand on. It may well already be lapping at cliffs across the coast, but if the sea is let into the rain-swollen Ams behind me, the whole city will go under.

When I peer over the edge, like the white pigeon, the drop makes me feel dizzy. I turn away, and with the pigeons hopping on railings and bouncing behind me—a few daring to let themselves be carried in the air by the gale around us—I edge along the thin walkway that connects the nine pillars and barriers, my scarf blowing in the wind.

Ahead, through the swirling grey wet, I can see a structure on top of the third pillar: a cabin with wide windows, perched like the bridge of a ship, with aerials and satellite dishes stiffly rotating on the roof, warning lights flashing.

As we near it, hurrying across the top of the second pillar, I can see shadowy figures through the windows. A door at its base stands busted open, chains and locks sheared in half. Only one animal in the world has teeth that can do that.

Telling the birds to stay where they are, I peer around the doorway and up a spiral staircase to the bridge of the Amsguard.

I can hear a human voice coming out of a speaker. "Hello? Amsguard, this is Tower 1. Please update your status, over. We've had reports of power outages on the north bank—"

And there, beneath the speaker, are the grey squirrels that stopped a train, busy yanking wires out of a box on the wall. As they do, the voice asking questions from Tower 1 goes silent.

A flock of starlings swoops in the clouds outside, pinpricks against the bruise-coloured sky—their brightly feathered leader darting in and out of the cabin below.

I can see rats chattering—but not the one I left behind.

There are swishing tails of wolves across the floor—

And a white dog. He staggers up onto his hind legs, front paws resting on a large wheel jutting up from the deck. Dagger coughs and taps his paws against the wheel.

The squirrels pause in their work, and the roomful of beasts turn their heads toward him.

Brave wild, he announces, *this is the moment we have been waiting for. The old moon has gone. Under the new moon's cover, we have risen up and forced the humans to live—like we have for so long—in darkness. And now, as the old dream tells us, so shall the great wet cover them all.*

The rats shudder with excitement.

That old fool who tortured me—he laughed when he saw me watching their moving pictures on their giant screen.

I move in a bit closer, crouching out of sight at the foot of the stairs.

But I didn't care. I was watching, listening, and learning how humans planned to stop the great wet from devouring them. I watched as this wall across the fish-road was built, and a plan began to form in my mind.

It's not too late to change your mind, though.

This time I know better. I'm not going to let him rouse his followers into a frenzy like before. My voice is as hard as I can make it. I walk up the spiral staircase toward him in slow, steady steps, my frozen hands clinging to the railings. The pigeons hover anxiously at the doorway.

Dagger hates being interrupted, I can tell. But he doesn't even look at me. *Starling,* he says to the purple and green bird flitting around his head, *I thought you had dealt with the human.*

Oh, I had, she replies. *I did my bit, Wildness, you can be sure of that. I'm not one to shirk her responsibilities. It'll be those spiders who didn't finish the job properly.*

You shouldn't have trusted those useless foxes either, mutters Mother.

Silence! roars Dagger. *What is this squabbling?*

Your wild aren't even united anymore, dog, and they never will be. Because you're wrong.

He glares at me and leaps down from the wheel to face me, the wolves clearing space for us in the middle of the cabin. *Not united? Just one word from me, and these wolves will tear you to shreds in an instant.*

His New Guardians growl, lowering their heads, ready to pounce.

But I don't flinch. I can't. There is no one else left to hide behind.

Like you did to that rat? I say.

What rat? says Dagger, with a smile in his voice. He can't have forgotten already.

The rat who was brave enough to alert me to your plans, who challenged you for my life . . .

Oh! says Dagger, with a note of triumph. *You mean this rat?* He turns to the cluster of animals behind him and barks, *Slave!*

Yes, master! comes a weak voice from the back of the crowd. *Coming now, master.*

Silently the animals part, and they all look down their noses at the creature hobbling through their ranks. He is ragged and torn, limping badly—but he is alive. Rat looks down when he sees me, and won't meet my eye.

It is I who should feel ashamed. I want to speak, I want to say something, to touch him—but I know that no words can make up for the fate I left him to. I don't look away. That is all.

I have an itch on my back, slave, would you mind? says Dagger, never looking at the rat, never taking his eyes off me once.

Yes, master, says the rat, and hobbling over to the dog, begins to rake through his fur with his claws.

That's better, says Dagger, stretching as the rat combs his flank. *You see, human, when you fled our lair, we chased after you, and so this traitor was spared my final sentence. But as you see, perhaps death might have been preferable . . .*

He moves to make himself more comfortable, half squashing the poor rat against the deck, but he doesn't seem to notice and the rat stays trapped where he is, cowering and combing.

Suddenly I don't care how cruel Littleman was to this dog, or how many animals Stone's cullers have killed—I could take him right now and . . .

Oh, do be careful, Kester, coo the pigeons outside the door.

Trying not to look at the rat trembling with cold as he scratches the dog's back, or at Dagger's gleaming razor teeth, I hold the dog firmly in the eye. *You can't do this, dog. All of you, listen to me. What he and the wolves told you—it's wrong. I did help save the animals from the Ring of Trees. Not all humans are against you.*

Dagger sighs.

We have already heard enough of your lies—

It's true! I call out to the pigeons. *Birds, tell him.*

And the pigeons, circling around my head, tell them everything. How they found me in Spectrum Hall and rescued me, how they brought me to the Ring of Trees, about our journey to Premium, and their return with the cure.

The dog is silent at first, thinking. Then, chewing slowly, like he is actually eating my words, he replies, *This doesn't change anything. Do you think I would believe some foolish birds over my own Guardians?*

Mother Wolf tosses her head, standing proud on her colossal paws, her pack lined up behind her.

But how about the child of those Guardians?

The voice is ragged and hoarse, from the bottom of the stairwell. We all turn and stare as my wolf-cub limps up the steps—soaking, torn, and bloodied. Even his mother's eyes soften as she sees her own cub.

His tongue lolls out of his mouth, and he is short of breath. *The old dreams are true. The pigeons do not lie. This human saved the animals of the last wild from the plague.*

Now his mother sharpens her tongue on him, her eyes flashing. *Do you dare to contradict your own mother, child? A traitor still?*

Tired, with red scratches ripped through his fur by the foxes, he turns to face her. There is no mistaking his voice either. It is not high and squeaky but strong and steady—like the waters beneath us.

Yes, Mother, I do. I am no longer a child, and I am no traitor.

But this human killed your father, Cub—

The stag killed my father. They were fighting, in the animal way, and my father lost. He takes a deep breath. *And I am no longer just a cub. I am a full grown wolf.*

The female wolf bares her teeth, as if she would fight her own son. The rest of her pack shows their fangs alongside her, crouching low.

But the wolf-cub—now truly the wolf—doesn't flinch. *So you will attack your own son. Will that bring my father back?*

It will teach you your place.

My wolf growls. *And what is my place? Is it with you? Lying to other beasts, attacking those who would help us?*

She does not reply but circles him, her pack watching warily. Her tail is down, though, and she is not growling. She is thinking.

He stands his ground. *You would reject your own son because he dares tell the truth to this wild—is that it? Has that not always been the true role of a Guardian?*

For a moment, between the crashing waves, the cabin of the Amsguard is so quiet you could hear a spider spin its thread. His mother no longer threatening, Wolf dares to take a step closer. *Do you admit that I might tell the truth? That perhaps our wild was saved despite you abandoning them, rather than because of it?*

I see real doubt pass across Mother's eyes as her son

stands up to her for the first time. But she doesn't get a chance to reply. Dagger stands on his hind legs at the instrument deck and thumps a paw down, setting a sequence of buttons alight, as if they were flashing with worry at his strength and anger.

Enough of this squabbling! Can't you see it makes no difference? His bulging, beady eyes gaze round at us all. *So what if this human did help save your wild? Perhaps he did. Perhaps these treacherous pigeons and wolf-cub are telling the truth. It makes no difference.*

He turns to look out through the foggy windows at the city laid out before us. The sky is thick with black clouds and flames, flames that continue to burn despite the rain.

Just one human, who stands before us now. One human among millions. He will go, and then there will be others. One human after another, breeding and filling every available inch of earth for their towers and their roads, taking every last drop of water, every last gulp of air for themselves. They will not stop breeding till they have covered what remains of the earth.

What's so wrong with that, master? asks one of the rats from the crowd. *We would too.*

The dog turns his withering stare upon him. *But, you fool, no rat in the history of creatures has ever built a city as vast and alien to nature as the one before us now. Or built a flying bird to poison the air, or slaughtered thousands of other creatures with a click of its paws. Enough is enough. What do a few fine words or noble deeds matter? The humans will *never give us any quarter—their own interests will always trump ours. We have sacrificed enough for them. What have humans sacrificed for us? Nothing. So now it is time.**

He bounds off the desk up to me, his mouth half-open with excitement, his stub of a tongue visible, his tail wagging.

*Come, human,** he says, rearing up on his back legs and tapping my thighs lightly with his paws. *Why not say good-bye to your city before we tear you to pieces?**

Then he stands down and barks at the squirrels. *Let the great wet in!**

And with a furious chattering the grey squirrels scramble onto the console behind him, gripping the wheel with their paws. It's stiff, but, straining with the effort, they begin to turn it.

With a grinding, roaring sound, the white gates of the Amsguard slowly shudder open beneath us—and the sea that will wipe away the last great city on earth floods hungrily through them.

So this is how it all ends.

Not with a bang, not with a whimper, but with a roaring wave that slowly surges down the river, already flooding the construction site below, with containers and diggers bobbing about on the surface.

There is no sign of the stag or the foxes.

But I'm still here.

No, I say to the dog. *This is not how it ends.*

It is, human, and for all your kind. Your time on earth has passed.

But what about your own animals—the ones you left behind to crash our helicopters and attack people on the streets—won't they drown too?

The dog snorts. *Our tunnels are deep and dry enough. We have waited this long to reclaim the earth—what difference will retreating for a few more moons make? The sun will come again. Soon the earth will be dry once more—and ours!*

Through the windows of the cabin, we can all see a rolling wave, getting higher all the time, pushing down toward the glass towers of the city. The Amsguard itself shudders and groans under our feet with the pressure of the sea pouring through it.

I look at the rat stroking the dog's back. He won't look at me, instead humming to himself, very quietly, *I'm just a lonely rat, as lonely as can be . . .*

The dog's words run through my mind.

We have sacrificed enough. What have you sacrificed?

And, as if the Amsguard had collapsed into the torrent beneath us, dragging us down in an avalanche of shattered steel and concrete, it hits me. My stomach lurches, and I have to lean against the wall for a moment to catch my breath.

What have you sacrificed?

The red squirrel took Stone's poison dart. Polly let herself be captured to keep the Iris safe. Rat challenged Dagger for me in the Underearth. The General is only just alive in my pocket. Mouse risked her life so Skuldiss couldn't get what he wanted. Wolf-Cub and the stag prepared to face the foxes so I could escape up here.

What have I done?

I ran away—from home, from the Waste Mountain, from the train wreck. I ran away from the Underearth, I ran away from the Four Towers, from the spiders in the arcade, from the foxes down below . . .

I ran away from the wounded rat now picking through

his master's fur. He still won't look at me, as if I no longer exist. I remember what he said in the cave. *I do not do this for a cause. I do it for a friend.*

Perhaps that's it. I can't sacrifice anything for people I don't know. I know there are plenty of humans back there who probably aren't worth saving. I can't pretend that the animals are wrong about much of what we've done.

But I can do it for a friend. For Rat, and for all my other friends who have helped me.

I can do it for them. For Polly and Aida. For the brave mouse hiding the information that could change the world back to how it was.

Unless this dog changes it first.

Dagger has his paws up on the deck again, his gaze fixed on the waves spreading out toward the city. I tap him on the back, but if he notices, he doesn't show it.

I challenge you, I say.

I'm sorry? says Dagger, still staring straight ahead, paws up on the smashed control deck, looking greedily at the floodwater piling up toward the bridges of the city centre.

I said, I challenge you. For the lives of my kind and the future of our world. We have made mistakes, but we have the right to live here too.

He turns to look at me, his head cocked. *Humans are famous for having a strange sense of humour, but you are exceptional.* He bares his massive metal teeth. *That old *man thought it was funny to give me these. Perhaps it would amuse you to be torn apart by them.*

Nothing frightens me more, but it didn't stop the rat. Being outnumbered by the spiders didn't stop the General risking his life for us. The wolf and the stag didn't run away when they saw the foxes.

I have been running away from the moment the helicopter arrived in our garden, from the moment I first saw this dog staring at me through our window. Pretending that this moment would never come, that somehow we would find another way. But we haven't.

That was why Dad and the stag didn't want to tell me the dream. Because they knew it would come to this.

I have only one way left to make a difference to this planet.

And I'm not frightened of it anymore.

The dog shakes his head, like I am a young pup who is not learning as quickly as he should. He leaps down from the desk with a thump. *I gave you the chance to delay your death, to see your land one last time before it was destroyed—a chance so many of those we lost never had. But if you wish to die sooner, far be it from me to stand in your way.*

So you accept my challenge?

Readily.

I turn to Mother Wolf. *And if I defeat your Wildness, will the rest of you submit? Will you stop this madness?*

She glances at her son. For the first time, she begins to

look at him like a mother again. *If you defeat our Wildness, of course we will abide by the animal laws.*

Very well then.

Finally I crouch down to talk to the pigeons who are shivering with worry around my feet. *If I don't win, don't let him lie about what happened here today. Tell the others the truth. I don't want this to be totally forgotten.*

Oh yes, says the white pigeon. *I won't let the others tell the truth. You will be completely forgotten, don't worry.*

I ruffle his tiny head and turn back to the dog, a barrel of pure muscle behind a set of razor-sharp metal teeth. His eyes narrow. *Wait—you have no concealed human magic or weapon?*

I stretch out my arms and open my palms to show him. I come just as I am.

Very well, says the dog, twitching with excitement.

I look out the window and take one last look at the blurred skyline of our city before closing my eyes.

There is a hushed silence.

Then it happens, quicker than I am expecting, the heft of muscle slamming into me.

Dagger pauses, surprised to meet no resistance, then attacks again. We tumble down the spiral staircase, my head cracking against the steel banisters and steps—

And fall through the door and onto the walkway, pigeons exploding out of our way, the rain driving down—

As he sinks his artificial teeth into my arm—

I scream with pain. Unimaginable pain.

I am going to enjoy this, he says fiercely, toying with me.

Why? I am just able to gasp.

Because every human I have ever known has inflicted intolerable pain on me. I shall do the same.

It doesn't have to be this way . . .

But he just sinks his teeth deeper into me.

I'm on my back, the dog's teeth clamped around my arm as he drags me toward the edge of the walkway. It feels like he will pull the arm clean off—

I'm barely aware of the other animals filing out of the cabin, their shadows crowding round as we struggle. With my one free hand I try to grab the dog, but it's useless, I can't even begin to get a grip on the tight folds of smooth muscle. Shaking and worrying at my arm, the dog nudges me closer to the edge so my head and neck hang over, the foam from the torrent below enveloping me . . .

My thoughts start to swirl like the clouds of mist in my eyes. I feel like I'm floating away, my mind leaving my body.

But I don't feel frightened. I don't feel alone. I feel the stag by my side, as warm and strong as if he were right here. He whispers to me once more what he said in the Garden of the Dead.

To bring the dark into the light, you need to show them, the stag said.

Light.

I need to show him the light. I only have one light.

On my watch.

Dagger shrank from light in the Waste Mountain, on the railway track.

With my one free hand, I am just able to reach it on my trapped arm, directly under the dog's gaze, and hope there is enough battery as I press it.

It shines one last time, directly into Dagger's eyes, dazzling him.

He recoils back, releasing my arm. Thrown off balance, he skids on the wet walkway, clipping his head on the railings and sliding off the edge between them with a high-pitched squeal. The sturdy metal of the Amsguard has done what I could not: dislodged, his metal teeth tumble out as he cries, disappearing into the foam and spray below.

I'm lunging after him with my good arm—

Grabbing a paw—

He twists his bull-like head up at me, his black eyes softening, about to fall into the floods of his own making. His mouth, half-open, is raw and damaged inside.

Let me go, he grunts. *It's what you want, isn't it?*

I'm holding him by a single white leg, the wet fur sliding in my hands. I'm trying to grip . . .

No, come on, I can pull you up!

But the dog, all muscle, is so heavy. I'm so weak. It's like my own muscles have stopped working.

I can't pull him on my own.

No, he says in a flat tone. *This is unnatural. This can

*never be. Beasts are beasts. Men are men. You will always win.**

I'm trying and pulling with all my might, but he's too heavy, the winds are so strong. His eyes close, and there's the trace of a doglike smile on his jaws as his leg starts to slither down through my grip—

It's not what I want. It's what he wants. To become a martyr and famous for all the wrong reasons.

Let me go, he whines, wheedling at me.

And then, just as I think I can't hold on any longer—

Something starts to tug at my scarf, jerking me back.

I twist my neck around and see—my wolf-cub. Pulling at my scarf with his teeth. Behind him, his mother, her teeth firmly around his tail. Behind her, her pack, all gripping one another.

The wind is swinging Dagger about beneath me as I try to grab his other paw—

The wolves begin to drag me back from the edge, the dog still in my grip.

Pull harder!

Now the birds join too, the pigeons and the starlings, pecking at the scarf and pulling as hard as they can. The squirrels, grabbing my jacket all together and finally ... Rat too, nipping at my collar, ready to save his tyrant master.

Working together, we heave Dagger back onto the edge of the platform, where his legs collapse beneath him as he chokes and splutters water from his toothless gums, all his power gone.

But, his huge head bowed, he is not spluttering enough to hide his words, which sound like they are being dragged out of him.

You gave yourself to me, he mutters. *You, a human, you let me attack you. You were ready to die. And then you saved me.* His tiny black eyes are full of confusion for the first time since I saw him staring through our kitchen window. *I don't understand.*

Perhaps that's how we're different, I say. *But you don't need to understand. You need to concede. Do you?*

Dagger looks at the wolves, who turn away. At the starlings, flying high in the sky and pretending not to see him. At the squirrels, gathered together behind my legs. He gives a sigh as long and as drawn out as that of the Amsguard gates opening. And the Wildness of the dark wild bows his huge head, conceding defeat.

I don't know whether to feel happy or sad. In fact, all I
feel like doing is sitting down, so I do—with a thump.

Drifting away from the white dog, Dagger's wild gather
round me in a circle. The wolves are staring at me with a
new expression. It's not the suspicion or anger of before.
It's something else.

Concern.

Mother's eyes are suddenly soft as she stares at me. *I
never believed I would see the day a human gave himself to an
animal like that . . . We were wrong to doubt you, Wildness.
I'm sorry.*

She bows her head, as do all her pack.

Wildness. She called me Wildness.

She turns away from me and nuzzles the young wolf
next to her. *I can see now how you have taught my cub to
be a brave wolf, a son his father would have been proud of.*

The wolf's eyes light up, and he looks like he wants to say something but then thinks better of it.

A flash of green and purple swoops past my face. *Oh, I must say, I thought you handled that really well, Wildness. Letting yourself be attacked, then the thing with the light, then saving the dog . . . We're all really impressed, aren't we, birds?*

The starling stops in front of her flock, spread out like a fan of iridescent feathers across the walkway. They stare down their sharp beaks at her with a stony expression.

Birds? We're all in this together, aren't we? she says, a bit less cocky than before. There is no reply. *Birds . . . ?* she says again.

Then, with a great chatter, the starlings form another fist in the air, but this time one that envelops their bossy leader, pecking and batting her with their wings, until she cries out feebly from beneath them—

What? What do you want?

And for the first time I hear all the other starlings speak—as one, as they swirl and dive around her. *Will. You. Stop. Speaking for us. When you don't!*

Yes! Yes! she sobs. *Anything! Just stop pecking me, please . . .*

The starlings pull away and the bird that brought down a helicopter, her glossy plumage ripped and ruffled, creeps to the back of her flock to nurse her wounds.

I want to say something to her, something about the

General, but for some reason I can't form the sentence clearly in my head.

The pigeons line up along the railings behind me and are silent too. I don't know why everyone is so quiet. We should be happy.

The wolf-cub is suddenly on me, licking my face. His weight on my body hurts for some reason, and I try to push him off.

You must stay awake, Wildness, is all he says.

That's not important. *The mouse . . . the Iris . . .* It's very annoying how I can't form a proper sentence. Like the words won't add up in my head. They keep disappearing like clouds every time I try to get a grip on one. *And the gates . . . the floods . . .*

I'm sure it will improve as soon as I get my breath back.

But my breath isn't coming back.

Don't worry, says my wolf. *The squirrels are turning the wheel the other way now.* As he says it, I feel the walkway beneath us shudder and groan once more, as the huge gates of the Amsguard slam shut against the world's water.

How did you . . . ? I mean, the foxes . . .

Them? Oh, the stag and I, well, let's just say we convinced the foxes that their cause was lost. You don't need to worry about him either. He's gone to find your father and your friends.

I'm . . . not . . . worried, I say.

Yes, you have no need to be worried, dear friend! says

a voice from my lap. And I look down. There is the rat, giving me a ratty grin, curled up on my legs, eyes closed tight. *I knew you would; I always knew you would. You said you would never leave me, and you haven't. You came back! So now I will never, ever leave you.*

Then softly he begins to sing a familiar song to himself. The tune is the same, but the words have changed.

*I'm a happy rat, as happy as can be.
Old but alive, don't mind me!
Don't worry yourself, don't say another word.
Why should I go? That would be absurd!
I'm a happy rat, as happy as can be . . .*

I want to say something, but all I can seem to do is let my head fall back and stare at the sky.

Which is when I realize the clouds above are finally parting, and the rain is easing. The storm of storms is fading away. Instead of damp grey air, there is bright sun beginning to break through, making the puddles on the walkway glimmer with life, trembling as the mighty barriers beneath our feet once again take the full strain of the surging sea behind us.

Then my head flops forward of its own accord, which feels weird, and I see myself in the puddle between my feet.

Only it doesn't look like me.

Half of me looks like me—the side with the arm I pulled Dagger up with.

But the other half—the side with the arm Dagger attacked—doesn't look like me at all. For a start, the arm seems to be at a funny angle, like it's only just attached to my body. Staring at the puddle, I tentatively raise my good arm to touch it, and find warm, sticky blood, spongy flesh—

Now I know I'm not going to sleep.

The dog ripped one side of me to shreds. I'm bleeding badly.

Everything starts to happen at once—the pain, my heartbeat racing, my mind too. I'm stuck miles above the river on a metal walkway with some animals; they can't patch me up. I try to stand up but can't, and my hands are pale and clammy.

No, I mutter. This isn't fair. I'm not meant to die.

But the birds, pigeons and starlings alike, start to crowd round me, saying nothing, just blocking the sky with their wings, light shining through feather, skin, and bone, as they fix their beaks and claws around me.

No, I try to protest. *I'm not ...*

Yes, yes, you are, says the white pigeon, suddenly very close to my ear.

The Four Towers, I say, then I can't speak another word.

As the walkway falls away beneath me, all I can see is the bright white light, shining through their wings, filling me and lifting me up—with the rat in my good arm—through the rain clouds, above the water, above the towers, up into the sky, where everything is very quiet and still.

When I wake up, everything is still white and bright, blinding me at first. Sunlight streams in through a window. A window I don't recognize. A window in a small room, with lots of people and animals in it.

I can hear them, smell them.

Beyond the light there are faces, blurring and swimming into view. Faces all seated on chairs around my bed.

As my eyes begin to focus, I can see we're in someone's front room. Someone who hasn't decorated in a while. A sofa, old-fashioned TV, and little table, all covered in dust. Peeling wallpaper with faded curtains round the window. I'm not in a bed, just a mattress on the floor.

A hand dips a cloth in a bucket of water, wrings it out, and presses it to my brow. It's a nice feeling. "You OK now," says Aida with a smile. "This my old home. Remember the estate we got nicked in?"

I nod. The abandoned Maydoor Estate, opposite the

Four Towers. We must be behind one of the identical-looking doors and windows. Where I last saw the General and the mouse . . .

The mouse.

I try to sit up, but I can't. My arm is wrapped tightly in bandages, too stiff to move. There is a rat, though, curled up on top of the sheets, snoring happily to himself.

"Don't worry, you safe now," says Aida. "For a while at least. Facto don't know where we are."

"Your friend led us out here after you helped us escape from the Four Towers," says Polly, sounding just a bit disappointed that she hadn't had the idea. "She was very brave—leading us all through the different doors and corridors, with cullers everywhere," she adds quickly.

"Hmm. Your friend not as goody-goody as she looks either," Aida says, also sounding a bit disappointed.

"We waited and waited. We saw the water coming toward us . . ."

"Many parts of the city are still flooded," says Aida with a gleam in her eye. "It could take months to get back to normal."

"Then the waters, you know . . . receded. But still no sign of . . . We were so relieved when we saw the birds in the sky," says Dad, standing above them. "I called out to them, and they brought you down. I very nearly thought that . . ."

His voice chokes, then turns to the animal voice we share in our head together, holding my good hand tight in his. *I'm sorry, Kes. I'm sorry I didn't tell you, well, you know . . . what my father told me, and what his father and so on. . . . *

What?

That we were the last, as it were, family to have a gift all humans . . . you know.

The humans who lived at the First Fold?

Indeed. But that animals believed one day there would be a—what d'you call it . . . reckoning between us . . . that mankind would be forced to make a, you know, choice. That a Jaynes would have to make it. And if we made the wrong choice . . . I couldn't bear to think . . .

He looks away, rubbing his eyes.

"The Professor thought you were going to die," says Polly in a matter-of-fact way. "And he didn't have his medical equipment with him," she adds.

"He not even a doctor either, just a vet," says Aida, sounding unimpressed.

"I did the best I could in the circumstances," Dad says huffily.

I look down at my bandage, made out of torn strips of bedsheet. My precious scarf has been turned into a sling. I don't even want to know what he sewed my wounds together with.

His big hand messes my hair. "But there is one piece of, ah, good news."

My heart misses a beat. Perhaps the mouse . . .

He spreads his arms wide with an old Dad grin. "Tomorrow is your . . . birthday!"

I fall back against the pillows in a slump. I'd completely forgotten. Thirteen tomorrow. If that is the only good news there is . . .

But Dad just pats me on the head. "Quite right. You rest, Kes . . . You need to get your, you know. . . . fully back before we, ah . . . make our next move."

I don't understand.

Aida explains. "Things are changing, see. Real fast. Faster than we can control. Since those animals went crazy, seems like people have begun to lose faith in Facto. They don't believe them anymore."

"Helped by Aida's friends and their computers," says Polly.

"When the power went, the Facto newscasts on the ultrascreens went down," Aida continues. "Eric and 123 took the chance, started broadcasting some facts of their own on everyone's ultrascreens. What you tell us—about the virus, the cure, and the Iris."

I almost feel sorry for Coby Cott, trapped in the control room of Tower 1, unable for the first time to be everywhere at once.

"Don't get too excited," she says. "Facto are back, broadcasting their lies again. But there's no sign of anyone getting out anytime soon. Not Stone, not Littleman, not the dude with the sticks. You'll see."

"Thanks to you," says Polly, patting my hand. She exchanges a smile with Aida like they know something I don't.

Dad furrows his brow. "He's still too . . . He can't go anywhere with that wound. I don't want to, you know, shock . . ."

What is it, Dad? Tell me.

Just speaking to him in my head hurts. My whole body feels like it is stuck together with sticky tape and paper clips. Dad can sense the pain in my voice.

I don't want any sudden moves now . . .

Then my stag is behind him, only just able to stand upright in the tiny flat, the General fast asleep in his horns.

I took the liberty, Wildness—in your absence—of giving your new wild some orders of my own.

New wild? What is he talking about?

Aida claps with excitement. "We have to show him. Please, Prof, you have to let us show him."

Dad scratches his beard for a moment, thinking. Polly and Aida look poised for action, hands raised, just waiting for the word from him. After what seems like an age, he sighs and nods.

Then Polly and Aida are lifting me up, off the mattress, putting my arms around their shoulders—

Dad shouts after them—"But please be careful—he hasn't had his stitches out yet!"

And they're carrying me, quickly but carefully, to an old armchair in a sagging flowery cover with a flat cushion.

Gently they lower me down.

The armchair faces a window, one of many identical

windows in this block of flats. Every single one facing the Four Towers.

I put a hand—my good hand—to my mouth.

The last time we were here, it was dark night. There were storm clouds in the sky. Ahead were the four black chimneys of the old power station, blinking red lights, fleets of shining vehicles parked all around them behind razor-wire fences.

Now the sun is shining in an almost cloudless sky.

That much I have seen before.

But the Four Towers themselves—

Have changed.

I don't know if they are still black and blinking with red lights underneath, because they are covered, each and every one, from the very top right down to the bottom— with birds and insects.

Birds of every kind and every colour perching on and around their tops. From the crows and starlings of the Underearth, the eagles and seagulls from the Ring of Trees, the pigeons, shrikes, yellowhammers, and redpolls from my wild. Bees, dragonflies, and butterflies cover the industrial brick and steel in great clouds, so all you can see are glittering colours and fluttering wings.

If the vans and bikes are still there, around the base of the towers, they are nowhere to be seen. Either they were taken out to try to contain the rising, or they have been covered too by the sea of wildlife now circling the Facto HQ.

Leaning forward, wincing—and making Dad give a small cry of concern behind me—I try to make them out.

Aida lends me her binoculars.

There they all are. Mother and her wolves. Hooded Fox and his foxes. All the stray dogs, cats, grey squirrels, rats from the caves below. There are hordes of deer and badgers from the Ring of Trees. The only animal I can't see is the toothless white dog we left behind on the Amsguard.

"Like I said," said Aida. "The Facto crew ain't going anyplace anytime soon."

Your new wild, says the stag behind my ear. *You brought animals back together. Stronger than ever before.*

My new wild. An army of animals, besieging Stone in his lair.

"Are you proud, Kes?" says Dad, crouching next to the chair, squinting in the bright sun.

I don't know.

I think of Dagger, the dog humans were so cruel to that he didn't want to live in the same world as them—even when I tried to save him. He let me win that battle but I don't know if I won the argument. Who knows where he is now? But my eyes well up thinking of those other animals who aren't here—like the red squirrel, and those who died in the battle of the Culdee Sack. The chaos and fires and floods we didn't stop.

Perhaps I have brought some animals back together, shown some of them that not all humans are bad. But there is so much still to be done. Stone might be trapped by my wild for now, but for how long? Will other people ever trust animals again after what happened these past few days? Will we find the mouse and the Iris and bring back those we have lost?

I don't know the answer to these questions yet. But that's not what Dad asked me.

He said, "Are you proud?"

I sit up as much as I can in the chair.

Tomorrow I will be thirteen. Together, with the best friends in the world, we have fought and made peace with those who wanted to destroy us. Wounded, crowded into a tiny flat, so much yet to do, so much to be sad about, but—

"Yes," I say to him and them all in the second word of my new speaking. My throat feels rough and sore, but I say it one more time all the same. "Yes." Yes, I am.

Because we're still here. Because the sun is shining bright in the clear sky. Because there are birds on the towers and deer on the street. Because I know in my heart that somewhere—in some dry corner of this huge flooded city—the bravest mouse that ever lived is waiting to be found. And when we find her, we're going to start this world again.

Me and my whole new wild.

PIERS TORDAY was born in Northumberland, which is possibly the one part of England where more animals live than people.

After working as a producer and writer in theatre, live comedy, and TV, Piers now lives in London—where there are more animals than you might think. Now that he has written *The Last Wild* and *The Dark Wild*, he is working on the third and final part of Kester's story.

Visit his website at www.pierstorday.co.uk.